They waited, like children standing at the door of a dark upstairs room after father's best ghost story, certain that something was about to leap from the shadows...

Madame Miranda was slumped in a chair in the middle of the stage; she was deep in trance. A filmy white substance flowed from her, pulsing outward, luminescent.

The silence was punctuated by gasps and pounding hearts. The ectoplasm began to take shape like a developing photograph. It formed the face of a pretty young girl. Unmistakable hurt and pain showed in her eyes.

A scream like that of a mortally wounded animal sounded in the front row. A man lurched out of his chair and flailed his way through the aisle. He reached the canvas tent and hammered furiously on the fabric, searching for the exit, demanding that it release him. Then he fell dead.

The girl smiled.

HEX

ROBERT CURRY FORD

PLAYBOY PRESS
PAPERBACKS

*For Bonnie
and to the memory
of Alvin Napack
I. C. D. B.*

i

A shiver ran through Duff Reeson's naked body, though he was not cold. The small, sparsely furnished apartment was heavy with the fetid smell of unwashed clothes and spoiling food. The room was dark save for a single candle on the bare oak floor. Several wooden chairs, a table, and a badly sagging couch appeared as dark silhouettes against the crusty brown walls.

Reeson's knees buckled as he stepped for the last time into the center of the strange symbol chalked on the wooden floor. It was a five-pointed star surrounded by two crudely drawn circles. They told him it was called a pentagram—a sanctuary, a haven from evil that was as old as time itself.

Long, unkempt hair fell forward, covering his face, as he knelt to kiss the Cross of Lorraine affixed to the small altar alongside the pentagram. The act was repugnant to him, but there was no alternative. He could feel the pain driving down from the top of his stomach into his testicles. Nausea gripped him constantly now, and the fear pervading his inner being was registered in the tears of self-pity that flowed down his unshaven cheeks.

He had suffered through three days of incantations and grisly sacrifices performed with small animals. At times he had been confused, disoriented. He had fallen into semiconsciousness and had visions of reaching out to his mother only to have her spit contemptuously and turn her back on him. During the second day, he lost perception of time. And because he had hung shroud-

7

like drapes over the windows, it was impossible to distinguish night from day.

From the outset, he had known it might be like this. But time was growing short. In desperation, he turned to this ancient ritual, forcing himself to repeat childlike rhythms which, in truth, he did not understand.

A large black rat eyed him apprehensively from the confines of its narrow cage. Reeson stared back with a look of virulent loathing that one reserves for the bitterest of enemies. The candlelight caught the long silver blade in Reeson's right hand as he removed a knife from its sheath. With his left hand he drew the cage into the circle with studied deliberateness.

The rat's long incisors struck out at the bars, hoping to nip a careless finger. It seemed to sense what was coming.

Reeson laid his knife atop the cage as if to taunt the rodent with the specter of its death. Then he carefully picked up the candle and dipped the flame into a tortoise shell that cradled a pungent blue liquid. Instantly, it gave birth to a dancing orange flame that hissed and crackled. Reeson winced and drew back as the noxious stench curled up toward the ceiling.

Again, he picked up the knife and brought it into position. Removing the bolt that secured the door of the cage, he flung it open. The rat, oblivious to everything but the opportunity for freedom, dashed toward the opening. Down came the knife. Reeson was a second too slow. The blade caught the animal in the hind quarters. It let out a piercing screech and turned, biting Reeson squarely on the meaty part of his hand.

Reeson screamed and tried to shake it off, but the rat's jaws clamped deeper, drawing blood. He batted at it desperately, cursing and crying. Pain shot up his arm and with it the horror of infectious diseases he could not name. The orange flames grew higher as man and rat did a gruesome dance about the pentagram.

The knife dislodged and fell to the floor. Reeson

grabbed for it with his free hand and drove it into the rat's soft underbelly. The rat screamed again and fell, its body twitching in death throes. Quickly, Reeson made a lateral cutting motion, exposing the bloody pink entrails. Then he took the flaming blue liquid and poured it into the bowels of the rat. One last spasm and the rat was dead. The sacrifice had been made.

Reeson stared at the gory mess in front of him, panting, waiting for he knew not what. Bile raced up into his throat, burning. He clutched at his wound, drew the hand into his belly, and bent over trying to seal off the pain with the pressure of his body.

At first, it was almost imperceptible. A slight stirring of the air. Reeson welcomed it as a momentary respite from the oppressive heat. Another rush of air, this time strong enough to carry away some of the acrid odor that assailed his nostrils. Surprised, he looked up searching for the source of the draft, but the windows were closed and the heavy drapes hung unmoved.

The candle flickered and shadows swayed on the walls, dancing to a night-so-silent tune. A low hum filled the room. He cocked his head slightly and listened intently.

It was an atonal piping, much like the sound of wind passing over large hollow reeds. Maybe this is it, he thought. It had never been made clear to him what to expect.

The winds struck with cyclonic fury. Suddenly, he was pummeled by a gale force. The candle snuffed out and the room came alive with objects flinging themselves against the walls. Reeson tried to stand, but the whirling wind drove him across the room, tumbling him over the pentagram; it slammed him against the floor and pinned him there.

The temperature plummeted, freezing the sweat on his body. The room yawned and groaned under the strain of the unleashed force. His breath came in short gasps; his heart pounded. I'm going to die, his mind screamed. I'm going to die! He felt his bowels let go and a warm stream of liquid sprayed his naked thighs. His thoughts were impaled on a stake of fear, leaving only his most basic reflexes to cope with the maelstrom.

Soon it was over. The wind stopped as quickly as it had begun. The cold silent room became warm again, stifling, suffocating. A spark appeared on the wick of the candle. For a moment it glowed . . . then sputtered, and finally a flame appeared.

Reeson half crawled, half dragged himself across the room to the window and ripped off the black drape. The room exploded with the brightness of the morning sun. The hot, piercing sting of light clamped his eyes shut and he buried his face in the dark folds of the drape. After a moment, he opened his eyes to a squint.

The scene that greeted him sent a shudder through his battered body. Debris was scattered everywhere. The wooden chairs had been smashed and reduced to kindling. The covering on the couch had been peeled back like the skin of a grape. A metal lamp had been twisted and bowed. The walls were splattered and discolored with the bloody entrails, and the floors were slick with a repugnant blue slime. The severed head of the rat, its long incisors strangely luminous in the sunlight, lay at the base of the Cross of Lorraine.

Reeson grimaced and leaned back against the wall below the window. There had been no change. He had failed to break free. All the pain, the nausea, the heavy cramps in his chest were still there, more intense than before. And now there was the deep, throbbing gash in his hand. Slowly, blood trickled down his fingers and dripped on the floor.

With great effort, he pulled himself up and staggered into the small alcove kitchen where he poured half a bottle of gin over the wound. He gritted his teeth and fought back the tears. He wrapped a dirty dish towel around his hand and then sank slowly to the floor, his face flushed, his eyes glassy.

"Why me?" he moaned, drawing his knees up to his chest and rocking back and forth. "Why me?" he cried as though expecting a response. But none was needed. He knew the answer.

Reeson was vaguely aware of the heavy rain shower that passed through in the late afternoon. As dusk settled outside his window, he mustered the strength to stand up, brace himself against the wall, and stagger down a short hall to his bedroom. With painful deliberateness he pulled on a pair of blue jeans, then tugged a dark-blue sweatshirt over his head. Slowly, gingerly he pushed his injured hand through the sleeve. He shoved his sockless feet into a pair of worn sneakers but made no effort to tie the laces. Then, as though ignited by some desperate urge, he bolted for the front door and lurched into the dimly lit hallway of his apartment house.

Reeson lived in an older, seedier section of the small city of Hammin. The buildings, mostly apartments and multifamily houses, looked tired and showed the burden of time. As he stepped into the street, he paused and glanced around, momentarily disoriented. His eye caught the flicker of a neon sign on a small restaurant and bar halfway up the block. He lowered his head, folded his injured hand under his left armpit, and walked tiredly toward it.

As he approached the bar, he saw an old woman standing in the darkened recess of a nearby alley. Slowly, she inched her way out to the sidewalk and into a pool of light cast by the streetlight overhead. A black short-sleeved dress hung limply on her small frame. Despite her petite stature, sinewy muscles showed in her forearms and legs. White hair was pulled back in a bun and her face was deeply lined. Her hooked nose and tight-lipped expression made her appear curiously predatory. In her hand she clutched a sheaf of papers.

When he was about to pass, she stepped directly in front of him with a catlike quickness uncharacteristic in a woman her age. A piece of paper was thrust in his face.

"Here!" she said with a low, guttural intensity.

Reeson flinched and jerked his head back. "What the fuck . . . !" he blurted out and started to sidestep the woman. Immediately, she moved to block his way and again shoved the piece of paper into his face, this time so that he could not avoid looking at it.

"Read it!" she commanded.

It was a handbill in yellow, blue, and red, advertising a local carnival. The face of a pudgy middle-aged woman, slit-eyed and smiling enigmatically, stared back at him. Her picture was surrounded by a bold pentagram. Directly beneath it was the caption: "Madame Miranda shares the gift of inner sight . . . nightly through June 10th."

He had forgotten about her. Forgotten that she was coming. He stared hypnotically at the picture as the old woman spoke in a low, cold, matter-of-fact tone.

"Miranda is waiting. She understands and she can help. You must go to her tonight. At the carnival." She pressed the paper into his unresisting hand and scurried away quickly, losing herself in the shadows of the alley.

Reeson did not attempt to follow or call after her. There was no protest, no attempt to reject the command. He simply crumpled the paper and stuffed it into his pants pocket.

Duff Reeson knew he had no alternative.

ii

The city of Hammin—population 16,500—was just one of the many stops for the Apollo Carnival. For two weeks they had held forth on the old fairgrounds on the outskirts of town. This was their last night and had they drawn the expected crowd, the receipts would have been among the best of any night during the stand. As it turned out, they would not break even.

Curtains of rain had swept down about four in the afternoon. At seven, when it stopped, the midway was a morass of mud. The sun managed to make one last brief appearance through a sliver of sky opened by the receding clouds. The early evening light was strangely cold and foreign for June.

By seven thirty, roustabouts had laid long planks between the booths and the rides. But these wood causeways sagged under even the lightest steps, letting the mud ooze up over the sides. Either the men had little hope of the carnival's drawing the usual crowd or they had very few planks.

By any standard, this was an unimpressive-looking affair. The wood frame booths with their frayed canvas tops, the faded tents, and the paint-worn rides all showed the effects of too many seasons, too many set-ups and tear-downs. The midway consisted of a Ferris wheel, a merry-go-round, and a Tilt-a-Whirl, which looked like a wire-mesh cake pan as it spun around holding its riders firmly against the sides by centrifugal force. Between the rides, little white trucks with serving windows in the sides dispensed hot dogs and cotton candy and syrup over ice. Everything was either over-cooked or overpriced.

Flanking the midway were two rows of brightly lit booths with their games of chance and their offer to "win a watch and satisfy the competitive spirit. Only a quarter."

The most impressive feature was a large orange-and-white-striped tent at the far end. It was a show tent capable of seating several hundred people. There, Madame Miranda held forth nightly: seeing, reading, predicting the most extraordinary things about people that, presumably, she had never met or seen before. She was the draw. And the people of Hammin, as expected, had responded. They came in droves, willing to be awed, prepared to believe.

Dr. Dan Frederickson stood beside the white ticket booth just outside the midway entrance. The small, pretty woman next to him linked her arm in his and pulled close as though to find refuge from the chilly evening air. A small ticket line had formed and several of the people smiled at the couple and nodded a "good evening" as they passed by.

Dan Frederickson looked the part of a doctor. He was just over six feet tall, lean, with a flat, hard stomach and an athletic confidence in his body. His light brown hair framed a ruddy complexion. His deep blue eyes projected a sense of calm and understanding that served him well with his patients. And his hands—long, firm—seemed capable of healing all by themselves.

Dan tugged at his tie and unbuttoned his brown sport coat as an unconscious response to his growing impatience. He glanced down at Carole Peters—her light blue scooped-neck dress revealed a discreet amount of breast—and thought how much he'd rather be home making love than slogging around the wet fair grounds.

"I don't think they're coming," he said without conviction, scanning the half empty parking lot opposite the midway.

"Of course they're coming," Carole replied.

"Do you think they'd be upset if I had a sudden call from the hospital and had to miss all this?"

Carole laughed, her eyes crinkling. "Oh, no. You can't get out now—you promised!"

There was something about Carole Peters that Dan found incongruous against the background of Hammin. There was a European look about her. Maybe it was her large hazel eyes and the upturned nose which, by itself, seemed a trifle too long. Or the slightly protruding mouth. Or the casual elegance of her short brown hair that varied with her moods. Hers was a unique face, hinting that behind the opalescent glow there was something reserved . . . something private that might never be known.

Dan's attraction to her had by no means been immediate. At first she was just his nurse and the daughter of the man the town had called "Doc" for more than forty years. Carole was working in a hospital in Chicago when her mother died. Six months later, her father took ill and she came home to be with him. Within two months, old Doc Peters was gone, too. Carole had planned to stay in Hammin only long enough to settle family affairs and sell the house. Then Dan arrived and she changed her mind. From the outset it was obvious to everyone that she had fallen in love with him. And though Dan gave no indication of wanting to develop anything beyond a working relationship, the townspeople assumed they would fall in love, marry, raise children, and Dan would look after the sick just as Carole's father had done.

But the expected never materialized. Inexplicably and without warning, Carole rented her house to a couple of school teachers and left Hammin. In a curious way, many people felt threatened. But this feeling passed, and Dan became "Doc" in his own right. Then, after an absence of a year, Carole came back. Within a month she was working for him again. In those first few weeks after her return, Dan caught himself exploring her face, finding things he hadn't seen before, discovering subtleties that fired his interest. Then one evening he took her home and their clothes fell away as if the moment had been ordained. Their passion unleashed a hunger that found them ardently tasting each other's bodies and making impassioned love until just before dawn, when they fell asleep. From that moment on, it seemed as if they had always been together.

"Here they come," Carole said, nodding toward a spotless silver Jaguar XJ-12. The impressive car bypassed a lineup of other cars waiting for entry into the parking lot and headed straight for the entrance.

One of Hammin's policemen, sweating profusely under his yellow slicker, stepped into the glare of the headlights and held up his hand. The Jaguar came to a stop and the window on the driver's side opened with electrical efficiency.

The policeman reflexively touched his cap. "Good evening, Mr. North . . . Mrs. North."

"We won't be staying long, my good man," Anderson North said. He sounded like Cary Grant delivering the line to a parking lot attendant. Since Anderson was tall, distinguished, with salt-and-pepper gray hair and a profile not unlike Cary Grant's, people often commented on the similarity—which only fueled his ego.

The policeman understood Anderson's not so subtle remark and knew what he was expected to reply.

"Why don't you just pull up over there?" He gestured in the general direction of the area in which he'd parked his patrol car. "I'll keep an eye on it for you."

"You're a good fellow." Anderson smiled and hit the window button, bringing an end to the conversation. As the car pulled forward, the left rear tire dropped sharply into a pothole, sending a small wave of water onto the policeman's leg. It soaked through his sock and trickled down inside his shoe.

"Bastard!" The policeman spat out the word under his breath and then quickly looked around to be sure no one had heard him.

Dan smiled at the scene. He had known Anderson North for over three years. They had never been close, although Anderson thought they were. But then, Anderson never really made friends, he simply adopted people. As president of Hammin's largest bank, as owner of different businesses and stores and several tracts of undeveloped land, Anderson was the town's unofficial patriarch. From that lofty position, he found it possible to limit access to himself and in so doing became highly selective of those he favored with his friendship.

Dan had been a resident intern in a New York City hospital when a mutual friend introduced them. Anderson was on a shopping trip looking for a doctor to adorn the new wing he had donated to Hammin's hospital and to fill the void left by the death of Carole's father.

At another time, the thought of picking up and moving to some forlorn little town so far from either coast would have been unthinkable to Dan. But it was February and there was a garbage strike in New York, and it was bitter cold . . . and the girl he lived with had decided to live somewhere else.

Anderson had an innate sense for saying all the right things. With an incredible adroitness, he probed for Dan's vulnerabilities and then wooed him with such subtlety that it was several months before Dan came truly to appreciate Anderson's skill.

Anderson closed the car door behind him and walked toward Dan and Carole, gingerly stepping around the puddles. His dark blue Yves St. Laurent blazer, open blue sport shirt, and white pants and shoes gave him the appearance of someone who had just stepped off his yacht. His wife, Rita, trailed behind, inappropriately wearing high-heeled shoes. She was exceedingly slender, a condition which she monitored with daily dedication. Her frosted blond hair was swept back from her face, culminating in a mass of short curls. Her designer clothes and lavish use of make-up did little to conceal her forty-nine years. But people nodded and smiled privately when she professed to being only forty-two.

"Jesus, Dan, how'd we let ourselves get talked into this?" Anderson asked. "I don't know why we couldn't have stayed home and played a few hands of bridge."

"Hey, you two, come on." Rita had grabbed Carole and pulled her toward the entrance gate. "If we don't hurry, we'll miss the whole show."

"That'd break my heart," Anderson said sarcastically.

The two men dutifully followed after the women, Dan bringing up the rear. As they filed along the planks, Dan saw Anderson's foot slip off the board into the muck.

"I hope this is worth a sixty-five-dollar pair of shoes," Anderson groused as he tried to scrape the mud off the bottom of his soles.

"Well, watch where you're stepping," Rita snapped and walked on.

"All I can say is, I hope like hell I don't break out with a laughing fit in the middle of this thing."

"If you do . . . !" Rita threatened.

"Bonnie Cagwin has been to see her three times," Carole offered. "She's supposed to be absolutely amazing."

"And Hilda just insisted that we go," Rita added. "She says the woman is fabulous. I know I'm just going to hate myself for having come only this once."

Anderson jumped on the line. "I'll probably hate myself for coming this once, too. What is she supposed to be, a mind reader?"

"A psychic," Carole answered. The two women

glanced pleadingly at Dan as though looking to enlist his support. But he remained noncommittal.

"Knock the milk bottles off the stand! Come on over and limber up the ol' pitching arm. Knock 'em off and pick any prize."

The voice came from one of the game booths on the opposite side of the midway. Dan recognized Crawford Spencer, preparing to try and regain the pitching form he'd lost some twenty years previous in high school. Crawford undid the button on his gray sport jacket, exposing a white polo shirt that bulged slightly around the belt line. Except for his waistline, Crawford looked very fit for his forty years. His curly black hair showed no signs of gray and his high cheek bones and prominent jaw were firm and tight. As he loosened up his throwing arm with a windmill-like motion, a voluptuous redhead that Dan had never seen before egged Crawford on.

Anderson had seen her, too, and he stopped. He lowered his voice so that only Dan could hear. "I see our local stud has found himself another bitch." Anderson's tone underscored his evident dislike for Crawford. "I think he'd fuck a snake."

The girl at Crawford's side, wearing too little to be warm in the cool evening air, rubbed her arms and pressed her body into his. "Go on, try it again." The girl patted his stomach as a suggestive gesture of encouragement.

Crawford pulled away and looked across the midway, his glance locking onto Rita North. Her eyes narrowed momentarily, then she turned away and urged Carole to hurry on. Crawford grinned knowingly at Rita's discomfort as he spun around and whipped a ball toward the bottles.

Zaaap! It slammed into the canvas behind the target.

"No hit Spencer!" The girl laughed.

Crawford's jaw tightened and his dark eyes flashed

in preparation for a stinging reply. But considering the evening's ultimate objective, he turned instead and patted her on the fanny.

"Don't worry, I'll score," he said.

The girl smiled. She was counting on it.

The foursome continued down the midway to the orange-and-white-striped tent where a three-foot-high sign proclaimed: "Madame Miranda, here . . . tonight." Ropes zigzagged back and forth in front of the entrance, forcing ticket purchasers to snake their way to the ticket booth.

Anderson stopped short of the ropes, looking for some way to reach the ticket booth directly. Rita headed for the entrance, her arm locked in Carole's, and called back to Anderson, "Come on, I already have the tickets."

"Damn," he said. "I was hoping they'd be sold out."

As Dan followed the others into the tent, he quickly surveyed the interior. The lights were low, making it appropriately dark and murky. Wooden folding chairs were set up to accommodate an expected crowd of about two hundred people. But the rain had reduced the turnout to about a third of that. Anderson motioned to an empty row of seats near the front and Dan sat down next to Carole. He turned his attention to Madame Miranda, who was already well into her performance.

She was on a large, raised platform, dramatically pacing back and forth in front of a brilliant blue curtain. Dan was unable to restrain a short laugh when he noticed that the blue backdrop bore an assortment of different sized stars and cometlike silver arcs.

He whispered to Carole, "I think their scenic designer thought she was an astrologist."

Carole smiled and nodded her agreement. But she didn't take her eyes off Madame Miranda.

Dan contented himself with looking at Carole's profile and then dropped his eyes to her well proportioned legs. He wondered again how he might gracefully bring the evening to an early close so that he and Carole could be alone. From her expression he could tell that he'd lost her momentarily to the psychic. Both she and Rita were hanging on every word. Dan tilted back and looked down the row to Anderson, who folded his arms and grunted to summarize his disdain for the whole affair.

Dan did not dispute the idea of psychic or telepathic power. In years past, he had witnessed what he considered to be some remarkable and mind-expanding demonstrations. However, he was fully aware that some practitioners were simply clever showmen or downright frauds. For that reason, he looked upon Madame Miranda with a good deal of skepticism.

He guessed her to be about five-foot-one or -two, possibly about forty-five years old. She wasn't fat, but at the same time she didn't appear to have any discernible figure other than a cylindrical shape made more so by a red floor-length gown. He watched intently as she read different people in the audience. There was nothing particularly profound in what she said, but it was obvious her readings were hitting the mark with a high degree of accuracy. She was good, he'd give her that.

"And I believe that after a most difficult period of financial hardship, you and your wife have been able to completely turn the situation around." The psychic paused and closed her eyes to focus her concentration. "In fact, things have become so much better as of late that within the next two months you plan to take a long vacation. It's not only long in time, it's long in distance. Let me see . . . you're going over water . . . of course, the British Isles. You're going to vacation in the British Isles. Am I correct?" She looked directly at the man standing in the fourth row.

His open-mouthed expression was ample confirmation. "Right again," he said, shaking his head in admiration and wonder.

"What's more, you've already made the plane and hotel arrangements."

The man indicated it was so.

"And ladies and gentlemen, I swear to you that I am not his travel agent."

The audience broke into laughter and applauded appreciatively.

Dan noticed Crawford Spencer and the redhead making their entrance. They sat in the back of the tent surrounded only by empty chairs. Crawford eased himself into the chair next to the girl and dropped his left hand onto her knee, mechanically sliding up her leg, pushing her dress back until his fingers came to rest on her warm inner thigh. Crawford kneaded the ample flesh with casual indifference, never taking his eyes off the medium who paced back and forth across the platform.

The girl placed her hands on his—not to remove it, only to cover it from anyone who might be looking their way. She shifted her weight suggestively and then pressed toward Crawford murmuring a breathy, "Hon-neee!"

In return, he offered only his profile, making no attempt to hide the smile of smug confidence. It was his way of testing to see if the promise of bed still held more interest for her than the medium. It did. He took his hand away. She'd have to wait. Crawford could not remember a time when he had not had his way with women. Of course, this girl hardly offered much challenge.

The psychic buried her face in her hands. After a moment, she dropped them to her sides and looked up at the top of the tent as though searching for some sign.

"I'm getting . . . I'm getting letters. Initials, I believe. Would the woman with the initials J . . . D . . . and S please, please stand up. J.D.S.," she repeated.

A woman in her early forties answered the summons. Her bleached blond hair was pulled back tight in a bun revealing the dark roots on her forehead. Sharp, angular features gave her a hard look which softened considerably when she smiled. Dan recognized her as the cocktail waitress from the Hammin Inn. Judy something—he'd never heard anyone use her last name.

"That's got to be me," she answered in a husky voice.

The man with her—partially obscured from Dan's view by a woman's hat—made some crack which only she could hear. She replied with a playful swat that missed its mark.

"May I have your full name?"

"Judy——" She corrected herself. "Judith Diane Simpson."

"J.D.S.," the medium reaffirmed. "Have you ever seen me before? Have we ever had any previous contact to your knowledge?"

Judy shook her head no to both questions. Again, the man at her side made some remark and it was all she could do to hold back a giggle. It's Skeet Fischer, Dan said to himself, recognizing the bartender from the Hammin Inn.

The psychic was totally oblivious to the exchange. "This is a special day for you, Judy . . . well, of course, Happy Birthday."

Judy's face brightened with surprise. "That's right."

The audience automatically applauded.

Anderson leaned over to the others. "If she asks us to sing Happy Birthday, I'm leaving. Jesus!" he added to punctuate his disgust.

"You'll do nothing of the kind," Rita hissed.

The applause died out.

"Okay. Now tell us how old she is," the man with Judy shouted.

The woman broke into a large grin. "In deference to Miss Simpson and in the belief that women are entitled to some secrets—even from a psychic—I draw a complete blank when it comes to a woman's age."

The women in the audience greeted the announcement with a round of concurring applause.

Once again, Anderson turned to his companions. "There's got to be some trick to it. I remember a movie I saw once——"

He did not finish. Rita cut him off sharply: "Shhh!"

Dan watched as Anderson rocked back in his chair, trying to find a maximum comfort spot so that he could endure the rest of the performance. For a fleeting moment, Dan wondered how Anderson would react if she called on him. That might make the whole evening, he thought laughingly.

The psychic stared at Judy for a long while as though she had locked onto some telepathic wave length that was transporting all manner of information. It appeared to Dan as if Judy had found herself strangely unable to pull away from the hypnotic gaze.

It was only when Skeet loudly suggested that Madame Miranda was trying to count up how old she was that Judy managed to break the hold.

"Am I through?" she asked.

The psychic broke her concentration. "Forgive me, Judy. I find that I'm getting terribly strong and vivid images. Let's try something. Think about your home. In your mind, just walk around the living room. Look at things . . . notice the color . . . pick up objects." She closed her eyes and her right hand seemed to float up to her chin.

"It's an apartment . . . on the third floor and it overlooks a street . . . Taylor Street. As you enter, there's a red sofa on the right side . . . with a mirror over it. The mirror is trimmed with a blond walnut frame. To the right of the sofa, there's a cherry end table with a copy of an old Tiffany lamp on it. Next to the lamp, a large picture in a gold frame. Your mother, I believe. Stop me if I'm wrong about something."

"You're exactly right. And I just bought that frame for my mother's picture yesterday."

The woman continued to describe the living room in great detail. Judy kept saying, "Incredible . . . I don't believe it." The more the psychic talked, the faster the images seemed to come. The mention of another picture set off a series of comments on Judy's past.

"Admit it, Anderson, she's phenomenal," Rita whispered.

Anderson only grunted and nodded a partial agreement. Dan studied Judy Simpson's face and concluded that the sustained look of astonishment was genuine.

"What do you think, Dan?" Rita asked.

Carole volunteered his answer. "He thinks she's just fabulous." She gave his arm a squeeze to punctuate the comment.

"I've got to admit, she's very good." But Dan wasn't ready to accept it all at face value yet.

"I get the impression, Judy, that you have a rather peculiar combination of talents." The psychic had become more reflective. "On the one hand, I see you as a. . . ." She paused. "Music . . . people . . ah, a hostess in a restaurant or cocktail lounge of some sort."

"Yes, the Hammin Inn," Judy responded. She turned to the audience and added, "And they won't give me a nickel extra for the plug, will they, Skeet?" She glanced down at him.

Her comment was greeted with scattered laughter.

"But I also have the image of you in some medical work. Not recently. Actually, this must have been some years ago."

Dan shifted his gaze from the psychic to Judy. He

was mildly surprised to see her smile fade. There was just the slightest hint of panic in her eyes.

The woman continued, "A nurse. It seems foggy now. Could you have worked as a nurse or a nurse's aide at some time?"

"No—no." Her reply was clipped and short. "I've always been a waitress." Judy turned to pick up her raincoat off the chair so that she could sit down.

"You've never been a nurse? Or even some kind of a volunteer in a hospital?" There was a note of challenge in her voice.

"No, never!" Judy curled her lower lip and bit down hard. She was refusing to give the woman any more eye contact.

What's that all about, Dan wondered.

Madame Miranda continued to focus on her. "I must be getting some interference. But I think we did pretty well." She looked out to the audience for confirmation. They clapped enthusiastically.

Carole laid her hand on Dan's arm. "I wish she'd read you."

He chuckled lightly. "I'm a blank page."

"I sense we have an unbeliever here tonight." She was pacing again on the platform. "A Doubting Thomas whose name isn't Thomas at all."

"No, his name is Anderson," Rita said loud enough for Dan and Carole to hear.

Dan grinned and looked over at Anderson. Anderson didn't think it was funny.

"His name is. . . ." She stopped on the far side of the platform and pointed to a bearded man with long hair. "Will you tell us your name, sir?" Dan craned his neck and saw the man, in his early thirties probably, slouched in his chair and looking to either side hoping that she was indicating someone else. It was obvious she wasn't. The man tried to ignore her, but she wouldn't let him go.

"I sense you believe that all this has been some sort of put-on. Isn't that right, Mr. . . . . Mr. . . . ." She waited.

The man straightened up in his chair, glanced up at the woman, turned away again, and mumbled, "Reeson."

"Reeson," she repeated so that everyone could hear. "And your first name?"

"Duff," he answered quickly as if that would somehow bring her attention on him to an end sooner.

"Mr. Duff Reeson, let me see if I can make a believer out of you."

Reeson mumbled something unintelligible and squirmed in his seat. The psychic stood motionless, watching . . . staring him into submission.

"Mr. Reeson, you've been worried as of late." Her voice was low; it carried a touch of sympathy. "Worried about your health, I believe."

Even from where he was sitting, Dan could tell the man was not well: wan complexion, hollow eyes festooned with dark bags, nervous gestures, tightness in the neck muscles, loose-fitting clothes that suggested a loss of weight.

Dan also noticed that for the first time in the evening, the audience was becoming slightly uneasy. The fun of it was slipping away. Madame Miranda sensed it, too, and moved quickly to restore the previous mood.

"With this weather, maybe we should all be a little concerned about our health. Perfect conditions for the summer cold."

The audience nodded their agreement.

"I also get something else, Mr. Reeson. Maybe this will be a happier thought. It's a name. It's coming through very strong. It's a name that you've thought about a lot lately." She paused. "Catherine . . . somebody named Catherine. That name has some deep personal meaning for you, doesn't it?"

Reeson straightened up as though hit with an electric

shock. Beads of perspiration broke out on his forehead. "No . . . no . . . not at all," he protested. "Never
heard of her."

The woman seemed taken aback. "Are you sure? The
name Catherine comes through very, very clearly, Mr.
Reeson," she said with insistence.

"I don't care what's coming through!" He was angry
now. "I never heard of her!"

Dan would not have been at all surprised to see
Reeson stand up and walk out. He didn't. He seemed
unable to.

Without taking her eyes off Reeson, Carole whispered to Dan and Rita, "He knows who she is . . .
look at him."

"The other woman," Dan replied, making a weak
attempt at being funny.

"God, look at that freak, will ya?" Anderson in-
jected. "I'd like to take some sheep shears to him.
What's he doing here anyway?"

"Now, Anderson," Rita said, patting his leg, "we
must learn to be more tolerant."

"I'll give him a 'tolerant' kick in the ass," he retorted
contemptuously and turned away. Looking back at
Rita, he said, "Say, haven't we had enough of this?"

She ignored him.

The psychic backed away from Reeson. The look
on her face told the audience she was not interested in
provoking him further. Her gaze still fixed on Reeson,
she signaled to a man standing off the platform to her
right. "Homer, shall we move on?"

Dan watched as her assistant stepped up on stage.
He was a thin, elderly man with little hair and a bul-
bous nose. He wore a black suit with thin lapels and
a narrow bow tie that was cocked at an angle in front
of his stiff white collar. She sure did a great casting job
with him, Dan thought. His mannerisms and general
stiffness tended to give him the countenance of a man-
servant. He was very proper and exact in his move-

ments. He placed a chair in the middle of the platform
and dutifully stood by it until Madame Miranda came
over and sat down. He lifted his hands as some kind
of signal to the men in the back working the lights.
The spots dimmed and changed color, leaving the
psychic bathed in an amber pool.

Homer took his place on the edge of the light so
that only his face was illuminated. Amber is not your
color, my friend, Dan thought. He felt a smile take
over the sides of his mouth as he watched Homer stare
blankly out over the heads of the audience. There was
a long period of silence which Dan recognized as a
calculated and probably much practiced attention-get-
ting device. It worked; the audience was primed.

"Ladies and gentlemen," Homer began in slow,
measured tones. Great voice, for this kind of thing,
Dan mused. "Because you were kind enough to brave
this frightful weather and come out this evening . . .
and because this is our last performance in your fair
community, we have decided to attempt a special
psychic experiment."

Dan studied the people around him. He could literally feel the tremor of expectation as it blanketed the
audience.

"Up until now, you have witnessed only the most
elementary of Madame Miranda's powers. She is, ladies
and gentlemen, a sensitive with an extraordinary God-
given gift."

Homer eased sideways, a step at a time, until the
light fell off, leaving him as nothing more than a silhouette. The woman was in the process of putting herself in a trance. She rolled her head gently from side
to side, accompanied by a breathy humming sound that
came from deep inside.

Dan glanced at Carole and then Rita. Both women
had edged forward on their chairs, waiting. Even Anderson had let himself be drawn into the drama of the
moment.

"If we are fortunate—and I hedge a little because we can never guarantee success—but if conditions are right, you will witness an event that will take its place among the most memorable experiences of your life. Now, I must ask for your complete cooperation. We will need total silence. If anyone would like to leave, please do so at this time."

Dan looked around. No one was leaving. He glanced over at Reeson, thinking that he might take the opportunity to go, but he seemed locked to his chair and in a slight daze.

Homer was gone from the platform. The sound coming from the psychic was louder, more pronounced. Her head rolled slower and slower, back and forth. Then it stopped and dropped to her chest. She was slumped in the chair, arms dangling at her sides, breathing deep and slow.

A draft. Dan's first thought was that someone had opened a flap on the tent. They were all closed. He was not the only one who felt it. People reflexively pulled coats and sweaters tighter. In the back, the redhead shivered and tried to snuggle closer to Crawford Spencer.

From somewhere overhead, Dan heard music. No, it was not music, rather the sound of wind blowing across the mouth of hollow reeds. Multiple pitches, minor keys—it flowed down over their heads, lingering, surrounding.

"Christ!" Anderson muttered, "they can turn that off." Rita jerked her head toward him with the coldest look she'd given him in all their twenty-six years of marriage. She was not about to let him take this moment from her.

Carole tightened her grip on Dan's hand. Her knuckles turned white.

They waited like children standing at the door of a dark upstairs room after father's best ghost story, certain that someone or something was about to leap out of the shadows.

The flow was first perceptible behind and to the left of the psychic. As it moved slowly forward and to the right, it seemed to draw some of its luminescence from the amber light. It gained substance, pushing out . . . growing . . . a phantasmagoric specter.

Sound. Distant. A woman weeping.

All around him, Dan could hear the shortness of breath.

His heart pounded. His whole being was focused on the apparition taking shape before him.

An incredible performance, his rational mind said. He wanted to test his will against that which was happening in front of him. I'll turn away, he thought to himself. But it was impossible.

Seconds. Minutes. There was no way to measure time.

The form took shape like some 3-D photograph in a phosphorescent developing bath.

Blond hair . . . petite features. Young, no more than twenty-two or twenty-three. Tear-streaked face. There was hurt and pain in her eyes. Unmistakable.

"I know her!" Dan's whisper was forced and intense. "I know that girl!"

A hospital room. Flowers on the nightstand provided by the women's auxiliary. Sunlight, cut into long, thin slats by the venetian blinds, falls across the floor, climbs the side of the bed, and stops. She has put on lipstick today for the first time since she has come out of shock. A nurse has helped fix her hair. She is pink and gold against starch-white pillows. She is dew coming alive to the morning sun. The doctor enters. She is a little bit in love. It is not unexpected.

She looked at no one, seeing without seeing. Her voice floated, "I trusted you." Only the people in the very front could make out what she said. Judy Simpson's hands were clammy cold. The tightness in her throat caused her to gasp for air. A woman in the row behind her fainted.

"I trusted you." Louder this time and everyone heard.

Like the cry from the bowels of a mortally wounded animal, Duff Reeson's scream was a crescendo of pain that froze everyone in open-mouthed horror. The spasm that sent his body lurching from his chair propeled him into the darkness. He flailed his way into the aisle and sprawled into a section of empty seats, collapsing them like dominoes with a hardwood clatter.

Crawling, stumbling, beating his way through the terror that gripped him, Reeson reached the back of the tent. But he could not find the exit, and he hammered with unrestrained fury on the canvas, demanding it release him.

"Son of a bitch!" someone said in awe.

The girl and the light were gone. The medium had slipped to the floor and her body writhed with epileptic contortions.

The lights came up full. Homer rushed to her side.

"I'm sorry, ladies and gentlemen," he shouted. "I'm sorry! Please forgive us!" Two other men joined him, gently lifted her into their arms, and carried her off through the blue curtains.

Some of the people stood up. Anderson was among them, looking for the most immediate exit. Others remained fixed in their chairs waiting for someone to tell them what to do. Dan noticed that many of the older women and a few of the men were on their knees, heads bowed in prayer. For them it had been the deepest kind of religious experience.

"Oh my God, oh my God! I've never . . . I've never. . . ." The girl with Crawford Spencer babbled incoherently as he pushed his way out of the tent. "What was it? What was it?"

Crawford, his face ashen, said nothing.

"Dan!" Rita said, her voice trembling a little. "Did I hear you say that you knew the girl?"

Dan turned to her and noticed Carole groping for a tissue in her handbag. He touched her shoulder. "You okay?"

She nodded and wiped her eyes.

Rita persisted. "Dan, what did you say about that girl? Who was she?"

"Her name was—" he groped, "—*is* Cathy Parks. At least I think it was her."

"Come on, let's get out of here," Anderson demanded.

"But who was she?" Rita pressed.

Dan never had an opportunity to answer. From the other side of the tent a panicked voice shouted his name. It was followed by a chorus of high-pitched female screams and a clot of confused shouts.

"Doc Frederickson! Quick! Over here!"

Dan craned his neck to locate the source of the shouts. He saw a group of people huddled around something on the far side of the tent. Quickly, he stepped out in the aisle and slipped through the crowd.

"I think he's had a heart attack," a man offered as Dan approached.

"He just keeled over," another said. "Is he dead?"

Dan pushed into the group clustered around a fallen figure. One person had covered the man with a rain coat. Another had placed a rolled-up jacket under his head.

"Here let me," Dan said as he knelt down. He reached for the man's wrist and felt for the pulse. Weak, but still there. Almost in the same motion he rolled the man over on his back.

It was Duff Reeson.

This seems ample opportunity to consider conflicts.

iii

U.S. 81 stretches long and flat across the farmland outside Hammin, then brakes to 30 mph as it enters the city limits, passing sections of chain-link fence that stand between the highway and the low structures that house Hammin's light industry. It rolls past used-car lots, a lumber yard, a golf-driving range, empty building lots zoned for industry as per the billboards which broadly proclaim—to devoutly desired developers—this or that lot's availability. Past eating places and discount shoe stores and filling stations and signs—many signs—making their singular contribution to the preservation of visual pollution. Over the rail crossing, past the turn-of-the-century railway station, atrophied now that passenger trains don't pass that way anymore.

From there the highway becomes a street and seems to lose purpose. It meanders through a forgettable residential area. After a while it begins to hint that U.S. 81 might be headed somewhere after all—the business center that dutifully surrounds the American Gothic courthouse.

At this point, all traffic becomes one way to the right around the court house square. Along with its nineteenth-century centerpiece, the square boasts Anderson North's bank, several office buildings—the highest of which can muster but six stories—department stores, appliance outlets, dress shops, and the like.

Carefully programmed stoplights demand that even the most disinterested traveler stop at least three times. This assures ample opportunity to consider contribut-

ing to the Hammin economy with the purchase of
lunch, sundries, auto services, or anything else that
might come to mind.

Once out of the square, 81 is bisected by state road
421. To the left, the hospital. To the right, about a
mile farther on, the municipal ball fields and fairgrounds. Crossing over 421 the grade ascends through
a long ceremonial arch created by stately broadleaf
sycamores. This is the section of Hammin known as
"The Hill." Here, lush green lawns sprouting white
iron furniture surround the large Victorian homes of
Hammin's better families. At the summit are three
churches, a park equipped with mute cannons, and the
cemetery. From there the street descends past a small
tract development and becomes a highway once again,
curving north across more fields until it is obscured
from view.

Hammin was not a place to visit. People lived there
or they passed through there. In years past, much of
the adult citizenry spent hot summer evenings sitting
peacefully on the endless front porches that lined U.S.
81—grandstands at a parade. Life passed by on rubber
wheels at 30 mph.

Then one summer it all but stopped. The Interstate
was opened by the governor. From that time on, life
passed by at more than twice the speed—twenty miles
west of town.

Toby Mitchell had been Chief of Police for fifteen
years. There were those who said he'd added an inch
to his waistline for every year. Though it was not quite
true, his short stature and pendulous stomach gave
him a distinct profile that was clearly identifiable even
at a distance. His hairline had receded to the very top
of his head, which he tried to hide by combing his
hair straight forward creating uneven bangs. His eyebrows were heavy under deep-set brown eyes and he

continually pulled and fingered a full mustache which he claimed had a kind of dandruff all its own.

Toby had lived in Hammin all his life. That, he regarded as his most grievous mistake. Several times during his late teens and early twenties his older brother had come home for a visit. Each time he offered Toby the opportunity to leave with him, once to sign on board a tramp steamer . . . once to go wildcatting in Venezuela . . . once to immigrate to Australia. But each time Toby was in love—twice with the same girl—and thinking of marriage, so he refused. Now, twenty years later, he was no longer married, no longer in love, and there were no offers to refuse any more.

The call about Duff Reeson reached him at the police station, which was located in the basement of the courthouse. The policeman on duty at the carnival —blue light flashing, siren full out—had driven Dan Frederickson and Reeson to the emergency entrance of the hospital. Normally, Toby wouldn't have given the incident a second thought, but the affairs of this particular man were of some interest to him.

Toby parked his blue-and-white patrol car in front of the new three-story wing of the hospital. Without question, it was the most modern edifice in Hammin, and yet the red brick exterior and functional design gave it a decidedly institutional look. Over the main entrance, a sandstone block had been set into the facade. On it was inscribed, "The North Wing," in honor of Anderson North who, alone, had funded the construction. Toby found it humorous; there would come a day when people would think the name referred to the direction rather than the man.

The elevator took him to the third floor. The doors parted revealing an attractive young nurse.

Haven't seen you before, he said to himself as he nodded a greeting.

"Good evening," she smiled. "I'm afraid visiting hours are over." Until a person met Toby or had him pointed out, there was no way to know who he was. He steadfastly refused to wear a uniform—he was partial to brown suits with patches on the elbows. "My face and my badge are all the identification I need," he had told the town fathers.

"It's okay, honey," the night nurse called to the girl. "That's Chief Mitchell."

"Oh! Nice to meet you," the girl said, disappearing in the elevator.

"How's it going, Gloria?" Toby approached the night desk.

"Can't complain," said the squat, graying nurse.

"Where's Dan?"

Before Gloria had a chance to answer, the double doors down the hallway leading to the operating room swung out. Dan appeared and untied a white surgical gown that had been hastily put on.

"Rotten hours you keep," Toby said, walking toward him.

"Toby!" Dan was mildly surprised. "What are you doing here?"

"Just thought I'd find out what's with that long-haired freak you brought in. I've been keeping my eye on him for a month or so now. Something in my gut tells me he's the source of the hashish we've been picking up around town."

"If he was, he won't be anymore."

"Dead?" Toby's slack-jawed expression indicated he hadn't expected that.

"Just a few minutes ago. Cardiac arrest is all I can tell you without an autopsy." Dan motioned toward his office and opened the door for Toby. It was a plain room with white walls, green tile floor, a metal desk, and several chairs.

"Well," Toby said as he found the nearest chair, "with the way that guy lived, I'm not surprised." Toby chewed for a moment on his left index fingernail. "You think he OD'd or something?"

Dan tossed his gown into a clothes hamper and sat down behind the desk. "No, no chance of that; though he might have been a user." He paused to consider the possibilities. "Reeson wasn't well, I can tell you that. He might have had some heart problems—maybe an aneurysm—could have had it all his life. Then something like tonight just set it off and . . . !" he snapped his fingers.

"Like tonight?" Toby raised his eyebrows.

"They had a seance out at the carnival and Reeson went out of control right in the middle of Madame Miranda's act."

"Madame Miranda," Toby repeated with unmistakable distaste.

"Have you been out to see her, too?"

Toby pulled at his mustache and rocked back on two legs of his chair. "If I had been to see her, it would have been to see her out of town."

Dan was unable to suppress a laugh. "I should have known better than to ask. You want me to go on?"

"By all means," Toby invited in his droll, cynical manner.

"Well, there was a seance and—" Dan hesitated "—a girl materialized."

"Materialized? My ass!" Toby slapped his leg in protest and stood up. "Right out of The Occult Handbook to Mind-Bending Illusions—Chapter Six, page fourteen."

"Call it what you like. It certainly set Reeson off. He thought it was real and so did just about everybody else who was there."

Toby plainly was irritated. He started to pace. "Of course they thought it was real! Because they wanted to! I'll bet they sucked up every bit of it. They always do!" Toby paused by Dan's desk, picked up a glass paperweight, and bounced it in his hand. It seemed to compose him a bit. "You know, the day a guy figures out how to put all that spook stuff in a box, he'll make a fortune in this town. An honest-to-God-damned fortune. And a lot of it's the women. It really is. If their bodies were as fertile as their imaginations, we'd have one hell of a population explosion. Jesus!" He sat down again.

"Toby, you don't have to tell me about what the people in this town are ready to believe. I know. And I'd be the first one to second your doubts about the validity of the seance . . . and maybe I do anyway. But there's just one thing—I knew the girl."

"You *knew* her?" The admission confused Toby.

"She was an ex-patient of mine."

Toby started to grin. He couldn't resist: "They all come back to haunt you, don't they, Dan boy?"

The motel manager looks at the young doctor blankly and asks, "What phone call? What girl?" He points to the parking lot. There are but two cars, one is his and the other belongs to a couple loading their luggage. Everyone has checked out. No one ever stays much past ten. What for?

Dan suggests that maybe the girl was left behind. The manager asks one of the room maids if she's seen or heard anything of an injured girl. She shakes her head, no, but says that she's not made up all the units yet.

Dan insists they look in the rooms the maid has not been in. One by one the manager opens the doors with his passkey. He's perturbed and mutters something about other things to do. Dan convinces him it's best to play safe, check all the rooms.

Room 28 . . . empty. Room 29 . . . somebody had a hell of a party. Beer spills hardening on the dresser top. Damn, the manager says. Room 30 . . . somebody has taken the pillows and the towels. The manager makes note of it. Room 31 . . . blood. Sheets awash in it. A young blond woman is sprawled on her back bleeding from her vaginal area. Dan grabs for her pulse

*with one hand and reaches for the phone with the
other. Pulse weak. He tells the hospital to be ready.*

*"Jesus, God! Jesus, God!" the motel manager
screeches. "This will fucking ruin me! Shit . . . I never
checked her in! Honest to God, I never seen her before in my life. Is she dead? There's blood all over the
goddamn room! Look at my carpet. Not even a year
old and it's ruined. Is she dead?"*

*Dan shouts at the manager to get hold of himself and
to bring his car up to the door. The manager dashes out
of the room to get the car. Dan rips a blanket from the
other bed, wraps her up, and then carries her out into
the parking lot. Must hurry. No time. So light she
seems to float. His shirt grows warm and sticky. He
has to stop the bleeding. The manager brings the car
up and jumps out to open the rear door. Her life is
running down Dan's fingers in little rivulets of red. For
a moment she seems to flutter to the edge of consciousness, only to sink comatose in his arms. "Hang
on," he whispers with commanding intensity. "You're
going to be all right." The words have come from his
own mouth, but he does not believe them.*

Toby stepped into the empty corridor as Dan closed
his office door. "You can say what you like, but I was
there and it was absolutely incredible. If it had been
anybody but Cathy Parks. . . ." He gave up trying to
figure it out.

"When was the last time you saw her?" Toby could
not resist another gibe. "In the flesh?"

Dan took it without flinching. "Three years ago.
She was in the hospital for almost a month. After she
was released, I saw quite a bit of her."

"Professionally?"

"Partly. Then one day, she was gone." Dan prodded
his memory to recall the exact sequence of events.
"That was the last I saw of her before tonight."

"Well, now you know what happened. She ran off and joined the carnival."

Toby had pushed Dan about as far as he was willing to go. "She wasn't the type," Dan said, looking straight ahead. His voice was low, but intense.

Toby got the message, but at the same time made a mental note to run a check on this Cathy Parks and her Madame Miranda. He hated loose ends.

"Well, I think I'll go on home," Toby said. "Can I give you a lift?"

"Do you mind dropping me off at Anderson North's? Carole is waiting for me there. Maybe we can get him to break out some of his good scotch."

Toby followed him down the hall toward the nurses' station and the elevators. "Maybe he'll break out the good scotch for *you*. The only time *I* ever got a decent drink at North's house was the Fourth of July party last year, when I brought my own."

"Dr. Frederickson," Gloria called as he approached. She picked up a box off her desk. It was about two feet long, ten inches wide, eight inches deep, and gift-wrapped in bright red paper.

"Look at this," the nurse said, holding it out for Dan's inspection. "It's for Duff Reeson." She pointed to a small white card with Reeson's name neatly typed.

Toby shook his head. "I was in this hospital for eight days and didn't even get a card. This guy is in here for half an hour and gets packages."

Dan stared curiously at the box and scanned the card for some clue. "Gloria, who brought this?"

"I don't know. It was on my desk when I got back from answering a room call. Nobody was on the floor, so it must have been dropped off while I was gone." Gloria paused and looked at the package, then back at Dan. "Well, are you going to open it? Or are we just going to stand here in suspense?"

"As Chief of Police," Toby said with feigned pomposity, "I hereby authorize you to open it."

Dan pulled the ribbon and the bow came neatly undone. He carefully removed the wrapping paper and lifted the lid. Mounds of white tissue concealed the contents. Gloria reached in to pull it away.

Her scream was short, shrill, and quickly captured in her hand.

There, nestled among the tissue, was a doll with long hair, a beard, and tattered clothing. It was unmistakably meant to be Duff Reeson.

Thrust deep into its chest . . . a dozen long silver needles.

Toby led the way across the lobby, out to the patrol car. The box, roughly rewrapped, was firmly under Dan's arm.

"All I've got to say is that some asshole really has a perverted sense of humor." Toby slid in behind the wheel and reached over to unlock the other door for Dan.

Dan got in and put the box between them on the seat. Toby glanced at it apprehensively as he fumbled for the ignition keyhole. "Is that thing supposed to be what I think it's supposed to be?"

"Possibly." Dan's tone was noncommittal.

"Judas Priest!" Toby shook his head as the engine turned over and he pulled out of the parking lot. That seemed to sum things up for the moment.

Toby was quiet and Dan appreciated the chance to think. First Cathy and now this. His hand came to rest on the box. Suddenly a heavy lump of despair welled up in his stomach. Cathy. Dear Cathy. He had not thought about her in over a year. Was it really you on the stage tonight? Has it come to that? What kind of charade are you involved in? He stopped. But I'm not absolutely sure it was you, am I?

Dan looked down at the box, took the doll out, and examined it as best he could in the dim interior light. The head was made of wood. The beard and hair felt real, and Dan guessed that it was in fact human hair. The features bore a remarkable likeness to Duff Reeson. The mouth was open wide as though gasping for air. The nostrils on the delicately carved nose were splayed. The eyes had been painted with the skill of a miniaturist, capturing the deepest sense of fear and horror. It was almost as if the doll had been animate at the moment it felt the penetration of the silver needles into its abdomen.

The body was soft—stuffed. And the clothing, like the face, reflected a dedication to detail. The shirt and pants were worn and stained, similar to those Reeson had been wearing. There was even a slight fetid smell rising from the garments. Like a messenger from the past, the doll's presence rekindled the old fascination which had once consumed Dan. The use of human hair, very possibly that of Reeson himself; the soiled clothing stained with what could well have been Reeson's own sweat—it all called up distant memories. Dan felt a twinge of dread settle deep into his stomach.

Toby slowed down for a red light and light from the street lamp overhead flooded in through the front window. Dan slowly turned Reeson's doll over in his hand and heard again the deadly *basiko* and *dayama* incantations. He saw the human effigy, the baptismal, the entire litany of events that could kill a man with the same finality as the poison on a native dart.

Years ago, he had let himself be pressed into a detailed account of what he'd witnessed by a lady friend with whom he was enthusiastically cultivating an intimate relationship. But she found the description so personally threatening and emotionally disturbing that it served to signal the end of their relationship. Dan had resolved never to bring it up again. There, in the police car with Toby, was not the place to break that resolve. Yet, as Dan gingerly placed the doll back in the box, he found himself voicing the one question that mattered.

"I wonder if Reeson thought he'd been hexed?"

"Oh, Christ!" Toby shot back. "I've got enough problems. Let's not lose our heads." Toby gestured toward the box. "Hey, do me a favor, will you? Get rid of that thing before word gets around town and they decide to display it in a store window. That's all we'd need, voodoo on top of a seance." His tone was acid with disgust. "Everybody and their mother would be on the phone to me."

"If you're suggesting we keep this quiet, I think we're a little late."

"How come?"

"The nurse, Gloria. We should have said something to her. By now, most of the hospital knows, and I'll bet she was on the phone the minute we walked out of there."

Toby pounded the steering wheel. "Shit!"

The patrol car turned onto U.S. 81 and started up toward The Hill district and Anderson's stately Victorian house. They stopped at the bottom of the North's circular drive. Dan moved to get out and take the box with him.

"No," said Toby loudly, "what the hell, leave it. There's no point in getting rid of it now. Especially if it's evidence."

"Evidence of what?" asked Dan.

Toby grinned, "Witch doctors, of course." And he sped away, leaving Dan to stare at disappearing taillights.

Crawford Spencer rolled over and turned the electric clock so that he could read it. Three thirty a.m. As far as he could tell, he hadn't been asleep. He heard the girl next to him murmur something in her sleep. A quick calculation told him that he'd known her for less than twelve hours, yet here she was in bed with him. Not a record, he thought, but close. Around four that afternoon, Crawford had dropped into the Hammin

Inn for a drink. There he'd been introduced to Natalie Tate. It was only a matter of seconds before Crawford determined that Natalie was an easy make. He ordered two drinks and the preliminaries began.

Natalie was not one of the more attractive girls Crawford had met over the years. But she did possess two large, round breasts that seemed to float well above her low neckline. The lavender and white dress clung suggestively to her buttocks and she positioned herself on the bar stool so as to provide Crawford with an unrestricted view of her long attractive legs. Her red hair fell straight to her shoulders where it flipped up into a small, tight curl. With all that her body offered, Crawford was prepared to overlook her face, which was slightly pocked by what had obviously been a bad case of teenage acne. Her eyes seemed much too close together and her nose about a size too large. She had full lips which she moistened constantly with her tongue. That act alone sent Crawford's fantasies flying.

"Say, why don't we go on out to my place? We'll put on some steaks, have some wine. . . ." Crawford made the offer while automatically reaching for the bar check.

"Hey, I'd love to, I really would," she cooed, "but . . ." She paused as though somewhat perplexed.

"You got something else on?" Crawford asked, sounding a bit incredulous that she'd refuse his offer.

"Not really, except that I really wanted to see the psychic they have out at the carnival. This is the last night, and I just don't want to miss her." Natalie looked at him, her eyes full of promise. "I know, why don't you come with me and then we can go to your place afterward."

Crawford turned away from the clock on his nightstand and looked at the head on the pillow next to him. He hadn't noticed it before, but Natalie slept with her mouth open. The pillow was wet with her saliva. God, she was unattractive asleep.

He'd made love to her earlier, but not very well and with little enthusiasm. Much to his distress, she'd been indelicate enough to comment that his performance was something less than she'd expected. At the moment, her assessment didn't bother him. His stomach was bloated and he felt an acid burning sensation creep up into his throat.

Might as well get it over with, he thought. Crawford got out of bed, went into the bathroom, and turned on the light. He stood over the toilet for a moment, dreading the thought, then quickly stuck his finger down his throat to induce vomiting.

He gagged. His stomach convulsed. Nothing came up but bile. He tried again. Dry heaves. He felt even worse than before. The door opened behind him. Natalie was wearing only her bikini underpants. She covered her eyes to protect them from the light.

"You all right, handsome?" she asked sleepily.

Crawford looked at his reflection in the mirror. He didn't feel handsome. "Yeah, I'm fine. It was something I ate. Go back to sleep."

"Ummmm." Natalie accepted his explanation and closed the door.

Crawford opened the medicine chest and rummaged through the bottles looking for something to settle his stomach. He found a bottle of Bromo Seltzer, took it out, unscrewed the cap, and looked inside. Empty.

"Shit!" Feeling very nauseous and a little sorry for himself, he sat down on the toilet and wondered if maybe he had an ulcer.

A week had passed since the night of the carnival. The seance, Reeson's death, and the arrival of the doll had been the number-one subject of conversation in Hammin. But Anderson North was much too busy to give it his full attention. It was after ten p.m. when Anderson North returned home from the zoning commission meeting.

He parked his car in the garage and walked to the house. Like the other homes on The Hill, it was a huge, white frame structure rising dramatically for three floors. The front was accented with a semicircular tower that rose up the face of the house and seemed to break free at the roofline, ending in a picturesque cupola. The tower stood watch over the expanse of yard and thick-trunked oaks and sycamores.

The night was clear and the full moon wrapped everything in a silver veil. A light breeze sprang up, catching the leaves and causing their moon-backed shadows to play across the side of the house and over the freshly cut lawn in patterns of black and silver.

Rita had gone to bed early, so Anderson undressed in his bathroom, then made his way across the darkened room to the king-sized bed they shared. He didn't try to sleep; the zoning board meeting was on his mind. I'd like to bang their smug heads together, he thought. Don't want them cutting up that fair grounds—at least not until I can get that Transteck deal worked out. Wish I held deed on that land, especially last month. Never would have let that broken-down carnival in there. Jesus, that was an awful night. Damn, all I'd need right now is to be compromised. Well, it's been almost two weeks and nothing so far. Just goes to show what can come of sharing a taxi. Where was I that day? Oh, yeah—trying to talk that paper company into locating one of their plants here. Almost had 'em. And that was the trip I met Dan for the first time. Haven't been to New York in a long while . . . ought to plan a trip soon. Maybe get away with Rita for a while . . . could use a rest. . . .

The sound was so low that at first he thought he only imagined it. But as he raised up on his left elbow, he was sure that he heard the sound of wind blowing over hollow reeds—the same as that night at the carnival. The music seemed to fade now and then into the strong rustle of the wind-swept leaves.

He sat up, swung his legs over the side of the bed, and stepped to the window. Below him, as the wind blew, the shadows created by the leaves tossed back and forth on the ground. The contrast between the light and dark was the most pronounced' that Anderson could ever remember seeing. Again and again the wind-driven shadows crept forward only to be pulled back. Then the wind changed. What had been an orderly to and fro became a swirling tribal dance.

Anderson found himself mesmerized by the rhythmic motion. Back and forth, around and around the swirling movement continued. He caught just a glimpse of something. Or thought he did. Something dark was moving through the shadows. He shook himself to break the hypnoticlike daze he'd drifted into and made a quick visual search of the yard.

Nothing. If there had been something, it was gone. Or so he thought.

Kin said, pointing

iv

Nearly a year ago, when their monthly food bills had suddenly altered, Anderson North had accused his housekeeper of petty thievery. She had vehemently denied the charge, pointing to her ten years of loyal service as sufficient grounds upon which to base her plea of innocence. But the evidence was conclusive and Anderson refused to believe her.

A week later Hilda Nesbit, a lean, energetic woman in her late fifties, was hired by Rita as a replacement. Hilda had come to the Norths highly recommended and she proved to be a good cook, highly efficient and organized. Unfortunately, she lacked the geniality and gracious warmth of her predecessor, and Rita missed what had been an almost maternal relationship. But the new woman seemed tacitly to insist on remaining properly subordinate and apart.

This morning, Rita thought it strange—from the moment she tied the drawstring around her yellow silk dressing gown and started downstairs—that she did not smell or at least hear any of Hilda's usual breakfast preparations. When she pushed through the door into the kitchen, she discovered why.

Her urgent calls brought Anderson, still in his white pajamas and brown robe, quickly downstairs. A shocked Hilda, hands clutching her print apron, was standing in the center of the large kitchen. She was staring at an 8-by-10 glossy photograph which had been taped to the outside of the bay window.

"What's going on?"

"Look!" Rita said, pointing.

51

"What is it?" Anderson snapped, clearly annoyed at being disturbed. "What in hell is that supposed to be?"

Hilda's face was chalk white, her eyes big, unflinching. "It's a sign, Mr. North . . . a sign," she said in awe.

"A what?" He looked closely at the window. There was a photograph of a male doll dressed in a business suit. On the left breast pocket, in fine detail, were the initials "A. N." Driven through the initials and into the heart, a long silver pin. Anderson's eyes focused on the face and an electric shock of recognition stiffened his body. The face on the doll was his—an exact replica. But the expression! It looked as if the face had been frozen at the moment the needle went into the doll's heart. The mouth was open in agony, the face muscles contorted and the eyes squeezed shut in pain.

"Someone is trying to kill you," Hilda said in a grave tone.

Anderson whirled around. His jaw dropped. "What are you talking about?"

"It's the same kind of doll that poor Reeson fellow got the night he died." She waited to see if more explanation was needed. The consternation in his face said there was. "He was hexed, Mr. North."

His scoff was loud, too loud really, and laced with unsuppressed anger. "That's the most ridiculous thing I've ever heard. You've been watching too much television. You know what that is? It's some idiot's idea of a joke!" He was vehement in his conviction.

Rita's voice trembled. "I'm scared, Anderson, I really am. What if it's some kind of threat?"

"Rita, the only threat that concerns me is the threat of your imagination going on overtime. Look at both of you! Standing here shaking in your shoes over a goddamned photograph. And that's all it is . . . a photograph!" He looked directly at Hilda, but she was not about to be badgered into recanting.

"I just don't understand who would do such a thing," Rita said.

"Well, *I* understand. It was some malcontent bastard who hasn't got the guts to face me so he resorts to this . . . for what purpose I don't know!"

"Do you think there's some connection between this and what happened to Duff Reeson?" Even had Anderson been inclined to answer, Rita didn't give him a chance, but went right on. "Maybe we'd better call the police. This could be much more serious than you think."

"Oh, for God's sake, get off it!" He turned and hurried toward the back door.

"Where are you going?"

"To get that thing off the window."

Anderson pushed his way through the juniper under the kitchen window and ripped off the picture. As he did, he could see Hilda in animated conversation with Rita. There was only one subject they could be talking about. Suddenly, he found Hilda extremely undesirable. Got to get rid of that skinny old bitch, he thought.

"Now look," Anderson said, entering the kitchen, "no more talk about this, understand? It all stops right now. The last thing I want to do is give whoever did this—" he shook the picture emphatically,"—the idea that they've succeeded in upsetting us, even for a moment. I'm sure they want us to call the police and make fools of ourselves. We're going to do the opposite, we're going to ignore it—starting now!" He paused and looked at both women to make sure he'd made his point. "I'm going to get the paper." With pointed sarcasm he said to Hilda, "If it's not too much trouble, maybe we can have some breakfast."

As Anderson walked through the center hall toward the front door, the adrenaline generated during the last few minutes began to ebb. Methodically, he drew up a list of possible enemies who might resort to such an outrageous tactic. Who might represent an actual physical threat?

Crawford Spencer. He's got to be number one. I'm

sure he's capable of doing something like this. A lot of people heard him swear he'd get even. I'll break that son of a bitch in half! Another name popped into his head. What about that guy, Engles or Eagles, whatever his name was. I had to foreclose on his factory. Might be him. Or Tarus Duncan—bastard, thought I owed him a living. No, he's crazy enough, but this is not his style.

As Anderson opened the large oak door to pick up the paper, he resolved not to think about it until later. It did no good. Rita's sullen mood, Hilda's furtive glances, and his snappish remarks during breakfast served only to strengthen the uncertainty and feed the pall that was ever-so-slowly enveloping the house.

Crawford Spencer got up off the well-worn couch and crossed the brightly lit waiting room with its Danish-modern furniture, its stacks of old magazines, and reprints of uninspired art on the walls. Dan, wearing a knee-length white cotton coat, held open the door to the examining room as he greeted Crawford with a smile.

Dan told Crawford to strip to his shorts and get up on the black-vinyl-covered examining table. As Dan made his routine check, he rattled off a series of questions.

"The bile regurgitation, have you noticed that it comes more often at any particular time of day?"

"No, I don't think there's a pattern to it," Crawford answered.

"What about after eating? Do you notice any pain, bloating?"

"Sometimes. I guess it depends on what I've been eating."

"What about alcohol?"

"What about it?"

"Any unusual reactions?"

"Well, the other day I was with one of the guys I

give lessons to and we stopped in at the club house for a couple of pops before going on to the tenth. He had some new scotch he wanted me to try. Two belts of that and I thought I was going to explode. To tell you the truth, I've been manufacturing so much stomach gas lately that I could win a farting contest hands down."

"Is that so?" Dan replied in a droll tone. He picked up his patient's chart and scribbled some notes. Dan's peripheral vision picked up Crawford examining his expression for some clue. Dan revealed none. He had mastered the noncommittal medical mask.

The door to the examining room swung open. Dan looked up and Carole stuck her head in. "Excuse me, I have the bandages off Mrs. McDonald. Do you want to look at her before I apply new dressings?"

"Yes, I guess I'd better." He turned to Crawford, "Give me two minutes. I'll be right back."

"Take your time, I'm in no hurry." Crawford was happy for the opportunity to get off the table. He paced around the room, stopped at the window, then pulled up the venetian blind and looked out.

Dan's office was on the third floor of a semiprofessional building facing the courthouse. Crawford watched the people on the street below. Two women were arguing over a parking place. His gaze wandered across the square to Anderson's bank, then immediately flashed to the sporting goods store. "North Sports." Just over a year ago the sign had read "The Hammin Pro Shop." Crawford had owned 49 percent and the other 51 percent was held by Anderson North.

The decision to open a store had been Anderson's, but the dream was Crawford's. Two summers earlier, Crawford had come back to Hammin the winner of a minor PGA tournament. But with the coverage given it in the Hammin paper, people came to regard the victory as something akin to winning the Masters.

In those days, Crawford's expertise on the golf

course qualified him as a member of Anderson's inner circle of friends. As tribute to Crawford's accomplishment, Anderson hosted a dinner at the country club in his honor. That evening, while both men lavished one another with effusive compliments, Crawford let it be known that his ultimate goal was to open a first-class sports store in Hammin.

"Hell of an idea," Anderson said, slapping Crawford on the back. "Why don't we go in on it together?"

"Jesus, I'd love to, but I haven't got that kind of cash."

"Ah, shit, Crawford," Anderson grinned, "money's no problem. I got a bank full of it."

"What are you saying, that you'd own it and I'd run it?" Crawford didn't wait for Anderson to answer. "I wouldn't be interested in that."

"Hell, I wouldn't either, because that's not what I'm proposing. Look, let's work up the figures on what it would cost to lease a store, fix it up, and buy the inventory. Then you put down as much as you can, and the bank will loan you the remainder of your share. I'll bankroll the rest. Just give me 51 percent so that the bank can have controlling interest. I gotta board of directors to answer to, if you know what I mean." Anderson threw his left arm around Crawford's shoulder and held out his right hand. "We got a deal?" he asked with a grin that made it a *fait accompli*.

Crawford's face exploded with delight. "You bet your sweet ass we do."

The deal was made. The store opened and turned a profit by the third month.

Then, a year later, without warning, the bottom fell out. Crawford, just returned from a short vacation, got word that while he was gone the store had gone into receivership. At first, Crawford refused to believe it. He hurried down to the store and found it padlocked. For a few moments, Crawford could only stare in stunned silence at the locked door. Then the reality of it fired his anger and he sprinted over to the bank, hurdled the low railing outside Anderson's office, and slammed through the door.

"What the hell's going on? We're not bankrupt! The store's making money. I saw the books myself not three weeks ago. I don't understand. How could this happen?"

Anderson maintained a calculated coolness in the face of Crawford's string of frantic questions. "I'm afraid the figures you saw weren't all that accurate." Anderson picked up a folder and tossed it across his desk. "You'll find it's all pretty well spelled out in there."

Crawford picked up the folder and tried to understand the numbers, but was immediately subdued by their complexity. He shook his head in frustration and dropped the folder in front of Anderson. "Fuck, I'm no good with numbers. I can't even understand what all that means."

"Sorry, Crawford, but you were out of town and I felt I had to file for bankruptcy to protect the bank's interest. Unfortunately, there was not much I could do to help you. I'm afraid you've lost everything."

The weight of Anderson's statement struck Crawford like a blow in the head. He blanched. The strength seemed to flow out of his body. Without a word, he turned toward the door.

Anderson waited until Crawford had crossed the room before he spoke. "I'll have my lawyer work up your share of the debts."

"Debts?" Crawford asked incredulously. "But I thought in a bankruptcy . . . ?"

Anderson shook his head. "There are debts. We'll talk about it. I'm sure we can work something out." With that, he let a thin smile cross his lips and swung around in his chair to signal the end of the conversation.

Distraught, angered, and totally confused by the turn

of events, Crawford considered leaving Hammin. But his job at the country club presented the only viable means of paying off his share of the debts which, like the bankruptcy itself, seemed to materialize out of the endless columns of numbers and ponderous paragraphs of legalese. He'd been had. He was sure of it.

From that time on, there were no more invitations to Anderson's home. No more requests for pointers on Anderson's swing or long bull sessions over drinks at the club. The final proof came when, two months later, the store reopened as "North Sports."

As he stared at the store from Dan's office window, Crawford's stomach knotted. He no longer wondered why Anderson had done it. It was an act of retribution. Somehow, Anderson had discovered that Crawford was giving Rita North a lot more than golf lessons. It had been something less than a torrid affair. They'd been to bed only three or four times and it seemed to Crawford that each time Rita's climaxes brought on instant remorse. But how had Anderson found out? Maybe Rita had let something slip . . . or possibly she'd used the information to spite Anderson. He had no way of knowing.

No, the *why* was no longer on Crawford's mind, but something else was.

"I'll have my day." He savored the thought of revenge until he heard the door open behind him.

"Okay, back on the table," Dan said. Crawford sat on the edge of the table while Dan wrote more on the chart.

"When are you going to let me work on your golf game?" Crawford asked.

"Just as soon as I can put four open hours back to back."

"Doc, you've got to make some time. I mean, it's great to be dedicated, but a man has to have diversions."

Dan gestured for him to lie back on the table. "We'll

get to my problems later. When was your last nausea attack?"

"I don't know—yesterday sometime. That and the acid burning sensation just seem to come and go."

"And you've never had any history of intestinal disorders, colon problems, ulcers . . . ?"

"No."

Dan made some additional notes. Then he checked Crawford with a stethoscope, took some blood for a SMA 12 test series, and performed a brief rectal exam.

"How's the old prostate?" Crawford asked.

"Well, it's still there." Dan took off the rubber glove and stepped over to the sink to wash his hands. "You can put your clothes back on."

"What do you think?"

"So far I can't find anything wrong—at least not from what we've done here. Of course, I've never been able to figure what keeps you going anyway. With the amount of alcohol and women you consume, you should weigh about seventy-five pounds and be eighty-six years old."

Crawford took the analysis as a compliment and smiled. "Doc, you're dealing with a medical mystery."

Dan dried his hands and sat down behind his desk. "Ummm, maybe, but it could be catching up to you."

"If you tell me to give up booze and broads, then don't send me a bill. Just call in the undertaker."

Dan laughed. "Abstinence? No. Moderation? It couldn't hurt. Tell you what I'd like to do. Let's set up an appointment for you at the hospital. I'd like to run some barium through your intestinal tract and take some pictures. Stop by Carole's desk on your way out and she'll arrange a time. We'll need a couple of hours." Dan made some additional notes while Crawford finished dressing.

"Dan, what was your reading of the doll that guy Reeson got?"

"You heard about that, huh?"

"Listen, that's the most excitement this town has had since they caught Reverend Kraft out in the graveyard with the organist."

"Well, next week they'll be onto something else."

"But why would somebody do a thing like that?"

"Why do people do half the things they do?" Dan came back. "I think Toby has written it off as a sick joke, and I guess I go along with that. Why do you ask?"

Crawford turned away to take his coat off the back of a chair. "Because I got one, too."

"A doll?"

"No, just a picture of one. But it was made up to look like me. Even had a golf club in its hands."

"Pins, too?" Dan probed.

"Pins, too," he nodded. "One in the stomach and the other . . . right smack in the balls."

Dan couldn't resist, "Well, that's getting you where you live."

"Nice guy you are," Crawford said, feigning hurt.

"When did this happen?"

"Oh . . . two weeks ago."

"Was it delivered to you?"

"No, I found it. Somebody had taped it inside my locker at the club. Can't figure out how they opened it; the lock wasn't broken."

"And you say, that was two weeks ago?"

"Right. It was on a Friday."

"Which means that you got the picture before——"

Crawford finished the thought. "Exactly. Before Reeson died. If it were afterward, you'd assume that one of my buddies was just picking up on it. Now, understand, I'm not superstitious. I put things like that in the same category as boogeyman stories. But what bothers me is the idea that some weirdo gets off sticking pins in a guy's balls. And if thinking about it's not bad enough, the bastard has to call and describe it to me."

"What?" Dan was taken aback. "You were called?"

"Yeah. Right after Reeson died . . . I think it was the night after. I get this call and a voice starts to recite some crappy poem. I don't remember the words exactly, something like: "Stick a pin, Stick a pin deep in your loins. . . ." Anyway, the gist of it was they were putting more pins in the doll. Now, that's pretty fucking weird," he said with emphasis.

"Was it a male or female voice?"

"Funny you should ask. It was hard to say. Sounded kind of falsetto and distorted. Obviously they were trying to disguise it. But I got the feeling it was a man." Crawford lifted his foot up on the chair to tie his shoelace. "I just had a thought. What if this guy gets tired of sticking pins in dolls and decides he wants to work on the real thing?" Crawford laughed, but it was forced.

Dan smiled in response. "At six-foot-three and two hundred and ten pounds, I don't think you have much to worry about."

Crawford nodded his agreement and turned to the mirror and put on his tie. Dan stared at the chart, but his eyes saw nothing. His mind had spun back ten years to the hot, steaming jungle where he had first learned to recognize the signs. First, the victim exhibits an inordinate awareness of his bodily functions. Every visceral pain, every minute variance in the skin and eyes and hair is examined in obsessive detail. Given enough time and concentrated worry, even imagined problems can become very real.

Dan's attention jumped back to the chart and Crawford. "Who else knows about your getting the doll?"

"Nobody really, except you and . . . well, Natalie, of course. She knows."

"Natalie? Is she the girl I saw with you at the carnival the other night?"

"Yeah."

"You're sure you've told nobody else?"

Crawford nodded. "This is not the kind of thing you

run out and announce to the world, you know. Why do you ask?"

"No reason, really. Just wondered," Dan said lamely.

A frown crossed Crawford's face. "Say," he demanded, a little bit afraid, "what was it that really killed Reeson?"

Dan gave Crawford a straight answer. "Simple cardiac arrest. It happens all the time."

Crawford seemed a little skeptical. "A guy's heart stops just like that, huh?"

"No, not just like that. There's always some root cause." Dan glanced up from his file to see if Crawford would probe deeper, but the answer seemed to satisfy him.

"That was weird, wasn't it? The psychic thing, I mean." The edge in Crawford's voice suggested he was leading up to something.

Dan reached for his pad, nodding his head in agreement. He wrote out a prescription to help neutralize Crawford's acidity.

"And that materialization," Crawford said, continuing, "I'll tell you the truth, I just about pissed in my pants."

The thought of Crawford sitting in the tent wetting his pants brought a thin smile to Dan's face. "It shook a lot of people up," Dan replied.

"Yeah, except in my case it was different."

"How so?"

"I knew the girl."

In the soft evening light, a breeze blows the sheer curtains away from the window and they billow into the room like fluffy white clouds. The two figures stand silhouetted against the dusk. Her fingers slide slowly down his firm belly and pass effortlessly under the elastic in his shorts. He grows firm in her grasp. She raises up on her toes, eyes half closed, lips moist and open. Her tongue darts hungrily into his mouth. Her full, firm breasts slide teasingly back and forth across his bare, hairless chest. Her fingers begin to move slowly back and forth. "Oh yes, yes!" she says breathlessly as he guides her to the bed. "Oh, how I want you, Cathy," he says, rolling passionately onto the sheets trying to press himself into her in the same motion. "Not yet, not yet. I want something else first," she demands sensuously. He looks at her questioningly. She smiles slowly, pushes his head down between her legs.

"You knew her?" Dan asked, barely able to mask his surprise.

"Yeah. Cathy Parks. I lived with her for about . . . oh must have been close to two months." Crawford moved to the door and put his hand on the handle.

"Recently?" Dan forced himself to say the word casually so as not to reveal his eagerness for information.

"Oh no, must be three . . . at least three years ago." For a moment the memory of past pleasures showed in his face. "What a body. And talented." He shook his head in a shudderlike motion, as though suddenly revisited by an old orgasm. "I don't know how they did that trick, or why Cathy was there, but it sure was the last place I expected to see her." With that, he opened the door and left.

v

For three days, Anderson told no one about the picture. But it gnawed at him. He was short with his employees, overly critical, and in one or two instances, verbally brutal. This was the Anderson North they usually associated with those few occasions when the bank found itself veering toward the shoals of the financial sea. Since even the officers knew of no recent or impending crisis—the bank had never been healthier —his behavior was the source of no little speculation.

More than anything, Anderson North wanted—demanded—that he be regarded by the members of his community as someone worthy of public respect. He once compared himself to the World War I memorial to the Soldiers and Sailors that stood in front of the courthouse: While not everyone liked the sculpture, they dutifully paid their respects to what it stood for. To Anderson, the picture was no less a defilement than an obscenity scratched on the stone monument.

The afternoon mail delivery at the bank arrived and among the items addressed to Anderson was a large manilla envelope marked "Personal and Confidential." Anderson slit it open and pulled out a picture.

It was the doll again. But this time the coat and shirt had been stripped away, revealing welts all over its chest. The face was puffy and dark. The eyes were bloodshot and the teeth were gritted as though trying to hold back screams of pain. The long pins had been driven entirely through the body and a small elliptical pool of blood flowed from the stomach. The hands of the doll were clutched helplessly around the pins as if trying to pull them out.

Anderson slammed the picture facedown on his desk. On the back he found words:

> *Choke, choke, choke.*
> *The spirits I invoke*
> *Pain draws near*
> *On wings of fear,*
> *Death to you this year!*

"Who?" he demanded of his empty office. "Who!" And this time only one name came to mind: Crawford Spencer. If that son of a bitch is responsible for this, I'll break his fucking neck.

At that moment, his secretary came in. There were letters to sign and he was late for a meeting with the bank officers. He went through all the motions, but the afternoon was intolerable for everyone with whom he came in contact. By three p.m. the bank was in a general state of turmoil and everyone was greatly relieved when he announced that he was leaving for an hour or so.

Toby Mitchell's office in the courthouse basement loudly proclaimed the need for more files and more space. Pipes painted yellow in a vain attempt to blend in with the low ceiling crisscrossed the office. A water leak from somewhere upstairs had seeped down the cream-colored walls leaving a deltalike wedge of brown stain in one corner. Reports, documents, and records were stacked on every available flat space. One of the fluorescent tubes in the overhead light was out, the other hummed and occasionally flickered. Anderson stood in front of the desk as Toby read the poem and studied the photo under the red, goose-necked lamp that arched over a picture of himself and his daughter taken a half dozen years ago. Anderson shifted his weight from side to side and grew increasingly more impatient.

Finally Toby looked up. "Hmmmm," he said and offered the picture back to Anderson.

Anderson looked at him incredulously. He was incensed.

"Is that all you've got to say?"

Toby took the cigar out of his mouth and said, "What do you want me to say? That it's bad poetry and a good likeness?"

"Don't give me any of your smart-assed answers."

"Who's being smart-assed? What the hell do you want me to say?"

"You can tell me what you're going to do about this!"

"What do you want me to do about it?"

Anderson fought down his anger. "Investigate! I think that's what we pay you for, isn't it?"

"Investigate?" Toby glanced down at the picture. "What is there for me to investigate?"

"Find out who's behind this!" Anderson demanded.

Toby did not respond immediately, but leaned backward in his chair, stuck his cigar back in his mouth, and clasped his hands behind his head. "Anderson, let me tell you something. If a guy wanted to commit a crime right now, this would be the town to do it in. You know why? Because with all I've got to do and with a total of nine policemen—most of whom still can't direct one-way traffic—a criminal would die of old age before I got to him. And you want me to find out who's celebrating Halloween early this year?"

"Mitchell! I swear if this were an elected position——"

Toby cut him off, "I wouldn't run for it!"

Anderson turned away in disgust. Neither man spoke for a moment as tempers cooled.

Toby gestured toward the picture. "Listen, somebody's just trying to get a rise out of you."

"But why?"

"Why do kids make obscene phone calls? Why did that drunk throw a rock through your window over at the bank last year? You're Mr. Big and sometimes people like to take a swipe. It's a way of working off their frustrations."

"I'm glad that I can be of service to the people of Hammin," Anderson said with sarcasm.

"Somebody's taking advantage of the Reeson thing to see if they can scare you."

"But what if there's more to it than that?"

Toby looked at him quizzically. "What do you mean?"

"I mean, what if someone were—" he groped for the words "—trying to get me?" They were no sooner out than he wished he could have them back.

Toby gaped. "You're not going to tell me that Anderson North, the town's leading citizen, believes in this kind of thing?"

"Of course not," he snapped back. "It's just that there are so many damn lunatics running around today . . . well, you never know."

"Anderson, even if I do investigate, I'm not sure where to start. The last thing I want to do is to let word of this get around town. I can see our good citizens drawing lots on the courthouse steps to find the witch."

"You want a lead?" Anderson asked with a cold intensity. "I'll give you a lead. Crawford Spencer."

Toby's jaw dropped and the cigar fell on his desk. "Crawford Spencer? I know he hates you, Anderson, but isn't he more likely just to walk up and punch you in the mouth?"

Anderson responded with a single throaty, "Ha! That chicken-shit hasn't got the guts. This is more his style.

Believe me, I know that bastard and I'm telling you he's where you should start."

Toby considered arguing the point, but decided that he'd rather be rid of Anderson. So he nodded and said, "Okay, I'll check him out."

Anderson grunted a thanks and left.

Back at the bank, Anderson went directly to his office and left instructions not to be disturbed. He locked the door from the inside, then took out a key and opened his private file. His fingers skipped through the tabs until he found what he was looking for.

Dan led his last patient through the reception room, opened the door, and bid the old woman good-bye. He turned back to Carole and gave her his "I'm sorry to make you wait, but what could I do?" look. She nodded to indicate that she understood. The phone rang.

"Let it ring," she urged.

But he'd already picked it up.

"Can I buy you a drink, Dan?" It was Anderson.

"Well, Carole and I——" He didn't have a chance to finish.

"Bring her along, too. I know this is an imposition, but I've got to talk to someone besides the idiots who. . . ." He paused.

This is not like you, Anderson, Dan thought, and waited for him to continue.

"It won't take more than twenty minutes to a half hour. I'd really appreciate it."

"Sure. Where?"

"Hammin Inn?"

"See you in five minutes," Dan said and hung up the phone.

Dan listened to Carole mildly protest the imposition as they walked across the square to the Hammin Inn.

"He said just thirty minutes and I promise we'll

keep him to it," Dan said as he opened the door and followed Carole into the crowded cocktail lounge.

Dan's visits to the inn had been infrequent over the past three years. He knew there were about twenty rooms in the hotel section, but had never spoken to anyone who'd actually stayed in one. The building was old, with only a modicum of charm. The restaurant and bar were located just to the left of the lobby area. The decor was a mixture of pseudo Tudor and imitation Spanish, replete with pressed wood beams, iron fixtures painted bronze, and electrified candles encased in heavy yellow globes. Unusual booths lined the wall opposite the bar. Each was totally enclosed except for a small entranceway.

Dan guided Carole through the tables to the furthermost booth where Anderson sat waiting for them. Before they had a chance to speak, Judy Simpson stepped inside the door to take their orders. Regular patrons of the Hammin Inn expected to be greeted by Judy's nonstop inconsequential banter, peppered, as it always was, with a mildly prurient suggestiveness. A round of drinks never seemed complete until she'd set up one of the customers for a jocular put-down. But this afternoon she seemed detached and merely asked what they wanted.

After she left, Anderson initiated some small talk which Dan observed to be curiously rambling and disconnected. Once the drinks arrived, Anderson seemed to relax a little, finding security in the dark confines of the booth. He made a perfunctory toast, took two long sips, and then told them about the pictures. When he finished, he pulled the latest one out of its envelope and slid it across the table to Dan.

"We seem to be having an epidemic," Dan said.

"What do you mean?" Anderson demanded.

"Crawford Spencer told me today that he got one, too."

"A picture?" Anderson did not try to hide his surprise.

"The way he described it, it was similar to this one."

"Did he say anything about a poem?"

"Yes, but he got his on the phone."

"What in the world is going on?" Carole's voice was full of concern.

Anderson looked away from her, shaking his head, and then gulped the rest of his martini. He looked up and signaled Judy Simpson to bring him another. Then he turned to Dan. His tone seemed to challenge what Dan had told him. "But you didn't actually see Spencer's picture, did you?"

"No."

"Are you sure he got one?" Anderson asked quickly.

Dan looked at him quizzically. "What are you getting at, Anderson?"

"Oh nothing . . . nothing," and he waved his hand as though trying to erase the last several moments of conversation. For a brief instant, Anderson was about to dismiss Crawford as his prime suspect. Then it occurred to him that Crawford might have sent himself a picture as a means of diverting suspicion. He was about to share this thought with Dan, but decided not to. Not yet, anyway.

Carole excused herself to go to the ladies' room. Andersoon lit another cigarette as Dan picked up the picture, examined it again, then flipped it over to reread the poem. Slowly, all the implications, all the memories filed away in his past came flooding back.

He had just turned twenty-seven, with one year of residency behind him and two more ahead. He and the chief of medicine at the university hospital in New York made no secret of their dislike for one another. Dan knew that it was up to him to remedy the situation. So when a medical search group came looking for young doctors who might be persuaded to spend two years

—at the barest wages—staffing medical clinics in West Africa, Dan impulsively seized the opportunity.

He was assigned to the Ivory Coast. He flew first to Paris, then south over the Mediterranean, Algeria, and across the endless Sahara to the capital city of Abidjan. He had three days of briefing and then was driven a hundred miles north in a '47 Plymouth that was in a remarkable state of preservation, to the city of Abengourou. This, Dan discovered, was the major way station for north-south trade. It was at this point that the paved road ended. Travelers going further north were resigned to a ribbon of red dust that cut a twisting path through the dense jungle, then found its way out across the savannas. In the dry season, the harmattan, a dry wind off the Sahara, picked up the dust and strung it out across the horizon giving it a strange red hue.

The village of Biasempia was a hundred miles up the red road, and Dan found it to be as primitive as the pictures he had seen in his predeparture research at the New York Public Library. The mud-walled houses sported thatched roofs. Dirt floors were the norm. The clinic in which Dan would work was a source of local pride. It had a wooden floor and a corregated metal roof which roared back its resistance to the penetrating tropical rains. The village itself was remarkably clean. The people took great pride in their homes and the women could be seen in their long, colorful wraparound skirts cleaning and sweeping every morning. With the exception of a couple of trees, all the vegetation had been removed, giving the village an arid, desiccative appearance. The bareness served as a fortress against the onslaught of insects. Unfortunately, what they had gained against the insects, they lost to the red dust which permeated everything.

Within a week of his arrival in Biasempia, Dan learned that the village had three great loves: music, dancing, and drinking. Each night, the chief, a short man with a large head and a protruding belly, com-

manded the local highlife band to come to his compound and play. Everyone was invited, including Dan.
At first Dan stayed in the background, watching, ob-
serving, trying to get a feel for his new community.
Then one night, without warning, the chief asked Dan
to honor them with a demonstration of his dancing
ability. Sensing an opportunity to gain a measure of
acceptance, he willingly agreed. He called on every
gyration, every contortion that he'd ever attempted or
observed in the New York discos. The rising chorus of
cheers and applause spurred him on, and he literally
threw himself into the effort. He even included what
he recalled of the Hornpipe and a very brief rendition
of a Cossack squat-and-kick step. The chief roared his
approval and joined Dan in his wild dance. Afterward,
he and what Dan presumed were the village leaders
sat and drank a local palm wine until they were all
quite drunk.

It was worth the enormous headache that he nursed
the next day. He was told that in all the years the
French had occupied their country before indepen-
dence, not one Frenchman had ever danced or drunk
with them. His unreserved participation, they said, had
shown him to be a friend.

The villagers soon came to appreciate Dan for
another reason. His general attitude made it quite clear
that he did not possess the missionary zeal or a deep-
seated desire to impose his mores on them. Always,
he behaved like a guest, grateful for the hospitality
and anxious to respect their customs and understand
the nuances of their culture. At times, however, he
found it difficult to mask his disgust for some of their
habits. The Biasempians chewed kola nuts, generating
enormous amounts of spittle. The action was always
the same: a glutinous slug of saliva would be jettisoned
to the ground and then rubbed into the dirt with the
foot. The only restriction seemed to lie in an unspoken
agreement not to spit on anyone else. Every time Dan

witnessed the act, a million germs exploded in front of his eyes. This was one thing he would try to change. It would be a futile effort.

Because of the long French influence, many of the residents spoke the language. It was Dan's proficiency in French that had qualified him for the assignment. He knew, however, that there would be many instances where it would not suffice. So one of his first orders of business was to acquire an interpreter. He was also in need of a houseboy. He found both in a wizened old man by the name of Miizi.

Miizi spoke some English, good French, and several of the native languages. In most matters, Miizi became his encyclopedia, preparing him for meetings with tribal leaders, helping him avoid *faux pas,* and in general guiding him through the social intricacies of the village. Mostly his instructions were simple and direct. Only when Dan inquired about rumors of dark ritual ceremonies or asked for an explanation concerning some comment he'd overheard about jungle witchcraft, would Miizi display his mastery of the evasive answer. On those occasions when Dan's curiosity motivated him to pursue the matter with a battery of follow-up questions, Miizi would simply bring the conversation to an end by saying, "There are many things we should not try to fathom in the jungle." The "we," Dan understood, applied to him.

Sometime during his fourth month at Biasempia, he was brought an old man who appeared to be suffering from severe anemia. The man's condition was marked by pallor, weakness, gastrointestinal and nervous disturbances. Blood tests showed a steady decrease in the red blood cells. To Dan's distress, the man showed no signs of responding to treatment. Perplexed, he sent word by messenger to the chief doctor of the central hospital at Bondoukou, who had a lifetime of experience with native diseases. The doctor arrived three days later, conducted his own tests, and left equally as baffled as Dan. There was simply no detectable virus or amoebic disorder and, other than the condition caused by the anemia, there was nothing medically wrong with the man. Yet, he was most certainly dying.

Afterward, Dan did not try to hide his frustration at having been so totally unable to even temporarily arrest the man's deterioration or hold back his death. All the wonder drugs had been ineffective. It occurred to him that he might have been dealing with a heretofore unknown viral strain. The possibility was even more unsettling. Miizi was especially attentive during this time. When he concluded that Dan's preoccupation with the mystery was showing no sign of diminishing, he decided it was time Dan knew the truth.

"He was the victim of a great enchantment," he began. "The ouanga. The sending of death. We think it might have been one of his wives."

"You mean to say that one of his wives killed him?" Dan asked, his confusion apparent.

"Yes, but not in the way you might think. It was an ouanga, a spell . . . ritual magic."

"I don't think I understand. How did she do it?"

Miizi did not answer immediately. He waited to see if Dan's eyes would betray even the slightest degree of ridicule or belittlement. Dan sensed he was on the edge of a new dimension in his jungle education. He did not object to Miizi's scrutiny. He was prepared to pay whatever admission he demanded for even a glimpse behind what, until now, had been a sealed door.

"The answer is not easy to put in words," Miizi said slowly. "We understand it here and here." He touched his head and heart. "You must too." And so it was that Dan began the long journey to the far side of darkness.

vi

For most of the afternoon, Natalie had had but one objective in mind, and now as the last light of day filtered into Crawford's bedroom she was doing her best to accomplish it. Crawford let her caress him for a while, then rolled over on top of her. She drew him close and stuck her tongue in his mouth. She waited for him. It was no use. He pulled away and rolled back over to the other side of the bed.

"What's wrong?" she asked, putting her hand on his face.

"Nothing." He turned away. "I'm just tired."

Natalie raised up and flopped down on him playfully. "Come to mama," she purred in baby talk. "Let Natalie protect her sweet little fella from that nasty old voodoo hoodoo."

Crawford pushed her off with a sharp, violent shove and got out of bed. "Cut it out!"

Natalie sat upright in bed. She was angry. "Hey! What's with you?"

Crawford said nothing. He walked into the bathroom, turned on the light, and closed the door behind him.

Natalie quickly followed and pushed the door open. She stood in the doorway, legs apart, hands on her hips confronting him. "Look, you're the one who said it was some kind of joke."

"Shut up!" Crawford said, and then permitted a belch to rumble up from his stomach. He looked at himself in the mirror, stuck out his tongue, and pulled down the lower lids of his eyes. Again he belched and reached for the pills Dan had prescribed.

"Hey, maybe the hex is really working," she said tauntingly. "His tummy hurts and he can't seem to get his peter up past half mast. What will the women of Hammin say when they hear their favorite stud won't be making house calls anymore?"

Crawford turned and snarled, "Why don't you get your fat whore-ass out of here! Bill me for your services!"

"You son of a bitch! You rotten son of a bitch!" She slammed the bathroom door, dressed quickly, and started for the front door. She stopped and called to Crawford, who was still in the bathroom, "I hope your goddamn prick dries up and drops off!"

The warm shower beat down on the back of Carole's neck. Long showers were her weakness. From high school on, she had found that the white sound of the spray provided an auditory curtain within which she could shut out the world.

She tried to clear her mind, to put aside the nagging doubt, the questions that had been raging back and forth inside her head since the night at the carnival. The water cascading over her worked a kind of hypnotic effect and for a short period she was able to forget everything and project herself into a peaceful void.

From the outset, she had sensed her relationship with Dan would be a lopsided affair. Dan loved her, she was sure of that. They had both talked of marriage, yet he had not offered, nor had she pressed for a final commitment. Their relationship was not unlike the one Dan tried to maintain between himself and Hammin. She recalled that from the day of his arrival he had appeared to resist permanent entanglements. Anderson North had shown him a dozen houses and several condominiums which Anderson had decreed suitable for "his" doctor. Dan opted instead for a secondhand house trailer, which he towed to a lake just north of town, and set up housekeeping on a piece of land leased from a local farmer. During those first months when their relationship was still mostly professional, Carole had teasingly accused him of buying a trailer so that he could leave Hammin any time he chose. He laughingly replied that she was right.

As the shower continued to envelop her in its wet warmth, she thought about the pleasure of Dan hard within her, his body full on hers, his tongue making small circles around her nipples, sending little shocks of pleasure coursing through her. They were good in bed and pleased each other greatly. Making love in his trailer she felt deliciously naughty and enjoyed exploring his body with her mouth, finding new ways to peak his passion. On warm evenings, she would get up from his bed and swim nude in the lake. Then Dan would appear and they would make love again on the water's edge, feeling very animal, very primal.

Yet, in her heart, Carole felt that he would never—could never—return the love she felt for him. She had been careful of her feelings. She had controlled the well of insecurity that often woke her in the middle of the night, confronting her with the possibility that he might leave her. In the midst of those midnight tears, she would admonish herself severely for becoming so emotionally dependent on Dan. The catharsis would end at daybreak and she would sit in front of her dressing table mirror and restore the countenance that concealed her pain. One day she might lay down an ultimatum . . . one day, maybe. But not now.

The shower started to run cold. She turned around to adjust it, but the hot water was giving out. Must have been in here longer than I thought, she concluded, and turned off the water. Carole opened the shower door and groped for a towel.

Outside the twilight was rapidly giving way to night. The street lights came on. Visibility was minimal.

Carole ran the towel quickly over her body, then

examined herself in the mirror. Dan will be here soon, she thought. Maybe I'll meet him at the door like this. The anticipation of his response brought warmth between her thighs.

Carole slipped into her high-heeled slippers and splashed Dan's favorite cologne over her body. She smiled, realizing that the mere smell of the fragrance would automatically arouse him.

Still nude, she stepped out of the bathroom into her bedroom thinking of the diaphanous negligee hanging in her closet. I'll let it fall off my shoulders the moment he walks in, she mused.

She had left but a single light on in the bedroom before taking her shower. As she passed in front of it, her shadow fell long and dark on the opposite wall. With her right hand she reached for the closet door, her left hand automatically flipping on the overhead light inside.

Like the shock of a thousand shards of ice seeking entry through every pore, her body stiffened. A scream froze in her throat and she reeled back, stumbling over a padded foot stool, falling against the edge of the bed. Her eyes were riveted on the picture of a doll impaled on the inside of her closet door by three long silver needles. Slowly, almost involuntarily, she was drawn back to the picture as though lifted by the grip of her own horror.

The doll was dressed in a nurse's whites, but there were large splotches of blood all over the uniform. The needles had been thrust through the throat, and the face, a mirror image of her own, gaped open-mouthed and wild-eyed into a void of darkness.

Dan heard her screams as he let himself in through the front door. Taking three steps at a time, he ran up the stairs into her bedroom. Seeing him, she collapsed into his arms.

By the time Toby Mitchell responded to Dan's call, Toby had to push his way through a number of curious neighbors who had heard Carole's screams and come over to investigate. Dan had wrapped Carole in her bathrobe and was sitting on the living room couch, cradling her in his arms. As Toby entered, Dan nodded toward the stairs. "Behind the closet door in the front bedroom."

When Toby came down, he was holding the picture by the edges so as not to destroy any fingerprints. His eyes met Dan's as if to ask, "Why Carole?"

Dan had no answer. It made no sense. Anderson, Crawford, and Reeson—he could understand why someone might want to threaten them. But Carole?

At ten, Dan gave Carole a sedative and put her to bed. Then he undressed, climbed in next to her, and wrapped her protectively in his arms.

The neighbors, who had pressed Toby for an explanation—and gotten one—went home, turned on their porch lights, and locked their doors.

Toby Mitchell's style of police work often lacked even a modicum of subtlety. He liked the straightforward approach to things and though his skills as a detective had seldom, if ever, been truly tested in Hammin, he did have a way of cutting to the heart of matters. Several hours before Carole's picture arrived, Toby had found Crawford alone on the country club practice green, bent over his putter stroking a line of balls toward a distant cup. Toby crossed over the gravel drive in front of the white, one-story clapboard clubhouse and walked up on Crawford's blind side.

Crawford inched his feet up to the next ball, glanced toward the hole, which was some thirty feet away, then looked down at the ball. Slowly he brought the club head back.

Just as he began his stroke, Toby bellowed, "If you send any more of those doll pictures to Anderson North, I'm going to cut your balls off." It was a calculated statement designed to strip away—if just for an instant—any facial facade that Crawford might put on to conceal his guilt. What Toby saw in his expression told him that either Crawford had excellent control over his emotional reflexes or he was innocent. Toby suspected the latter.

"What in the . . . !" Crawford's mouth continued to move, but words failed him. Color rose in his face. "Look you . . . you flat-footed schmuck. I think you've got this a little back-assward!"

Toby stared back at him through squinted eyes and said pleasantly, "Oh, yeah? How do you figure that?"

"Because I'm the one that's gotten the picture! I'm the one that gets the phone calls at three in the morning! Are you telling me that North has gotten one?"

"Two." Toby's face relaxed and he reached over and took the putter out of Crawford's hand. He walked over to the line of balls, gesturing for Crawford to give him some room. Barely pausing to line up his shot, he putted the ball across the green. The ball started off well left of the hole, then curled around a slight rise and veered right, rolling up to the lip of the cup and dropping in. He couldn't have made the shot again in fifty tries, but he said shrewdly, "And that, my friend, is why I don't play golf. No challenge."

The abrupt reversal of Toby's attitude left Crawford speechless and he simply gaped as Toby turned his back and headed for the clubhouse. Without so much as a glance back, Toby said, "Come on. Let's get us a beer and talk about voodoo dolls."

Toby spent the next half hour talking to Crawford, and when he left, he felt sure of only one thing: Crawford was as much at a loss for answers as he was. So much for Anderson's prime suspect.

vii

The meeting the following evening was Anderson's idea, and he invited them all to his house. Dan and Carole arrived first, then Toby, and finally Crawford, whose dinner had been confined to that which he could consume from a glass. Rita and Hilda served coffee while Anderson paced up and down delivering a diatribe on the need for action. He concluded by wheeling around so that he stood directly over Toby.

"Last week, I asked you to look into this. You said you would. Now I think there are three of us in this room who have a right to hear what you've found out."

Anderson's courtroom style was irritating to Toby, but not surprising. He'd seen similar displays in the past, although none had had the same kind of personal intensity and urgency as this. What *was* surprising was his sudden demand that Toby tell them what he'd found. He'd already reported to Anderson on his conversation with Crawford. True, Anderson had been reluctant to accept Toby's assessment of Crawford's innocence. But that was certainly no justification for putting Toby on the spot in front of the others. He retaliated with the one weapon which he knew would anger Anderson most. A long pause. Toby took a sip of his coffee, then proceeded to relight his cigar and take several long, thoughtful puffs. He could see Anderson shift his weight back and forth impatiently.

"What have I found out, you asked?"

"I think that was the question. It's been so long since I asked it, I'd just about forgotten," Anderson said caustically.

"Well, the answer, in a word, is nothing."

"I can't say that I'm surprised," Anderson said as he sat down in his chair.

Dan could see that Toby felt the need to defend himself in front of the others. "Anderson, what was there I could do? I had nothing but a picture and a poem to go on. I don't have any way of knowing whether this is something originating in Hammin or . . . elsewhere."

Anderson slammed his fist down. "Well, dammit! I want protection."

"I second that," Crawford said, draining his glass. "How about bringing in the National Guard?"

"What am I supposed to protect you from?" Toby asked with a helpless gesture.

"Good God, man, there's a crackpot out there trying to kill us!" Anderson flailed the air to add emphasis.

"You don't know that. All you know is that you've got some pictures of dolls."

"Mitchell, I don't know how you can sit there and assume that this is anything less than the work of some depraved maniac. What do we have to do? Wait until we have a Manson-style murder before you'll act? If these pictures had come just to me or Spencer you might—" Anderson paused to underscore the point "—I say, you *might* convince me that there's nothing to all this. But when Carole gets one, then I'd have to say we've got a very serious matter here."

Dan reached over and took Carole's hand. It was cold and damp.

"Now wait a minute," Toby began, trying to convey a cool sense of logic. "Let's look at what's happened. There have been pictures, poems, and phone calls. Implied threats, I agree."

"Implied, hell!" Anderson roared. "That poem I got said I would choke to death."

"Be sure to cut all your meat up into bite-sized pieces, Anderson. Too big a bite and—" Crawford clutched his throat and made gagging sounds "—who knows?"

Anderson seethed, but appeared determined not to lose control. Dan wondered how much more he would take from Crawford.

"All right," Toby said, conceding Anderson the point. "I'm not going to say that you're in absolutely no danger. And I'm not going to minimize the fact that someone has gone to an awful lot of trouble and probably a good deal of expense to make up those dolls and photograph them. On the basis of that and of what's happened, I think we're dealing with a very sick, maybe even a deranged person."

Dan saw the shocked expressions on the womens' faces. Toby must have sensed it, too, because he went on quickly, "However, I think the most important and most comforting thing to keep in mind is that there has been no violence. Our dollmaker seems to be satisfied with just trying to scare people."

"But what if he doesn't stay satisfied? What if he does get violent? I want you to act now!" Anderson bellowed. "I want to find out who's behind this and I want it to stop!"

Rita jumped up to try and calm Anderson. "I'm sure Toby's going to do everything he can."

"Well, you've got a lot more confidence than I have." Anderson picked up his drink. He had another thought. "What about Reeson? Are we sure there wasn't some violence connected with his death?"

"Natural causes," Dan said matter-of-factly. "Absolutely nothing in the autopsy report to suggest otherwise."

As Dan spoke, Toby weighed the advisability of adding what he knew of Reeson's death to the conversation. He could tell them about the call from the owner of the building in which Reeson lived. He could describe the pungent odor that assaulted his nostrils as he entered the apartment, and even draw the chalked symbol for which he had no name. He could tell them about the darkened windows and recount finding the entrails of rodents in the garbage pail under the sink. But within that fleeting instant in which decisions are so often made, he decided against telling them. He had dismissed Reeson as a weirdo, a doper, a sorry bit of foul residue from the hippie movement. To tell them what he had seen would only deepen their concern and raise new questions, the answers to which he was sure had died with Reeson.

Anderson poured himself another drink and then sat down across from Dan and Carole. "I'll tell you, the worst part of this thing is walking around town and having people look at you like you've got leprosy."

"And that's bad for the old image." Crawford's words were becoming hopelessly slurred and he laughed both at himself and at the implication of what he'd said.

"I'm glad you're able to find some humor in all this," Anderson said icily.

"The humor, in case you missed it," Crawford said as he topped off his glass with Chivas Regal, "is that Crawford Spencer is standing here in Anderson North's living room depleting his consecrated liquor."

Dan was aware that there was no love lost between the two men. But what he saw in their eyes suggested the dislike was much greater than he had assumed. The situation could not help but grow more ugly. As little was being accomplished, he felt obliged to help bring the meeting to a conclusion.

"I don't think there's much more we can do tonight." He looked toward Toby for support.

"Just a moment," Crawford said, advancing from his position at the bar to the center of the living room. "I would like to make an observation. It seems to me that we have carefully avoided asking the single most important question."

"What are you talking about?" Anderson asked, annoyed.

Crawford's smile was sodden. "I'm talking about *the* question. The one we're all thinking about, but find indelicate to ask." He raised his glass and some of the scotch dribbled down his front. "Since I'm feeling absolutely tactless and totally insensitive to everyone's feelings, I shall ask it."

They waited as he looked at them with a glassy stare.

"Well, goddammit," Anderson barked impatiently, "what is it?"

"Glad you asked," Crawford replied, saluting him with the glass. "The question is this, simply and directly: Are we being hexed? Is someone trying to kill us with witchcraft?"

Dan felt a stony silence engulf the room. Hilda had reentered in time to hear the exchange with Crawford, and Dan saw her eyes dart from face to face.

"Did he really ask that?" Crawford said, playing his own counterpoint. "Of course I did, and I think it's something we should all consider."

"Crawford, you're drunk!" Anderson said, turning away.

"Very observant of you. But drunk or not drunk, I submit the question for debate. Are we the victims of a hex? Are we to be done in by voodoo?" His eyes widened in mock fright.

Carole whispered to Dan, "Let's go. I've had enough of him."

As Toby stood up to defend the others from Crawford's onslaught, Dan could see that Toby was plainly irritated. "Look, knives kill people and guns kill people and a whole lot of other things kill people, but pictures do not."

"True, but not true, my dear Chief of Police." Crawford took two steps toward Toby. "Pictures don't kill, but hexes do."

Anderson was outraged. "This has gone about far enough! Crawford——"

"Wait a minute, Anderson, let's hear what he has to say," Toby interjected.

"No! I am not going to have this derelict from a golf course upset my wife and Carole!"

"My apologies, ladies." Crawford bowed low to the women, then stumbled, off-balance. "Since I seem to have the floor, even if it tends to be a bit unstable——" he paused again to check his balance "——I shall repeat what I was about to say. Let's assume for the moment that we are dealing with a hex. The assumption raises another question: Why us? Why the three of us and the dear departed Mr. Reeson? Why?"

Crawford's head was spinning. Instinct said he needed air. Fast.

"Oh, God, I'm shit-faced! I'm going to throw up." He stumbled toward the door. "You'll excuse me if I call it a night." They watched him go through the door and heard him heaving on the front lawn.

"Maybe we'd better help him," Rita suggested.

"What the hell for?" Anderson retorted. "The son of a bitch can drown in his own vomit as far as I'm concerned."

Dan had already made his way to the door and looked out. "He'll be all right. But I don't think we ought to let him drive."

Crawford's voice filtered into the living room. "Anderson, sorry, I puked on your roses."

Rita shrieked in dismay. Anderson angrily headed for the door.

"Take it easy, Anderson," Dan said, blocking him.

"Let's not make this any worse than it is," Toby added. "I'll drive him home."

"You're not leaving?" Anderson's question was more of an order. "We haven't decided anything. We need a plan!" He was almost pleading.

"All we can do for now is try and ignore this thing.

Don't let's get hysterical!" Toby was backing out the door. He'd had more than enough.

Anderson looked at him incredulously. "And that's it, huh?"

"What do you mean?"

"I mean, that's it! You're calling it quits! Going home!" He was indignant.

"Anderson, for God's sake . . . there's nothing more I can do." Toby turned and hurried down the front walk.

Anderson held the screen open, stepped out on the porch, and called after him, "Well, there's something *I* can do, goddammit!" And he slammed the front door for emphasis.

The village of Kuadii was hardly big enough to rate even a dot on most Ivory Coast maps. It was just fifty miles northeast of Biasempia, but for the effort it took getting there, it might as well have been five hundred. Dan towered over Miizi as they stood in the shade of the thatched eves of the chief's compound. They had arrived the night before and, after confirming his reputation as a "dancer of extraordinary verve and imagination," he had been shown to his bed on the veranda of the chief's guest house.

Exhausted from the day's journey, he had hoped that sleep would overtake him rapidly. Though he'd learned to block out the cacophony of the rasping, grating night insects, he could find no defense against the mind-wracking call of the bush babies. The lemurlike nocturnal animal began every call with a low, moaning sound that spiraled upward several octaves culminating in a strident, piercing cry. This, along with the apprehension he had developed about the event that was to take place the next day, conspired to hold sleep at arm's length. He gained some measure of victory just before dawn. When he awoke, Miizi was sitting on his haunches at the end of the veranda looking out toward the village square. A garish congregation of men in brightly colored togas and face paint milled around the single tree that graced the area. Miizi, forgetting himself for a moment, spoke to Dan in his tribal tongue. It was the first time Dan had ever known him to make that mistake, and he was unsettled by it. Miizi quickly corrected himself and in French suggested that Dan hurry and dress and have a large breakfast, as there would be no opportunity to eat again until that evening.

Dan did as instructed. By the time they arrived at the entrance to the chief's compound, the drums had begun issuing their special invitation to the assembly of witch doctors, who responded by forming two divergent lines—the apex directly opposite from where Dan and Miizi stood. The repetitious drums, the watchful, edgy mood of the villagers had made digestion impossible for Dan. His diaphragm muscles seemed to be resisting all attempts to pass food into his stomach.

The sun stood directly overhead. The temperature, Dan presumed, was well over a hundred, and the humidity level not far behind. He hoped that the tremors of trepidation which were sending chills down his spine would not register on his face. The drums stopped and the imposing figure of the chief appeared. His name was Kaulahu-don-na and he was almost as tall as Dan, but with a far more developed body. He nodded a greeting as he passed, which reassured Dan.

The villagers knew Dan well. He had been there to give inoculations and several times had made the difficult trip to attend to some medical emergency. It was through Miizi's intercession that he had been given permission to see "work in progress." He was to witness the dark rites of an ouanga baptismal, an event of diminishing frequency as other, more direct forms of "private justice" gained increased favor. Miizi had impressed him with the magnitude of the honor and Kaulahu-don-na's trust. As far as he knew, no white man before him could claim witness to what Dan was about to see.

The victim was to be a Frenchman by the name of Jean Tureau. Tureau owned a large kola nut plantation southeast of the village. Dan had met him only once. Tureau, he recalled, was a swarthy fellow with a highly offensive body odor and a generally pugnacious attitude. Their meeting had been brief, and he was thankful for that. It would make what was to come a little easier to tolerate.

It seemed that Tureau had a habit of not paying his employees and of welching on agreements with various village chiefs. It was widely believed, but never proved, that he had played a role in several unfortunate accidents that had befallen those natives who had dared to compete with him by harvesting and selling their own kola nuts. But what finally sealed his doom was an incident involving a young woman whom he'd raped. As he rolled off her, the hysterical girl had scrambled out of his bed and hurled herself through one of the frame windows he had installed as a concession to a wife who had long since left him. The shards of glass ripped at her body. Bloodied and terrified, she ran through the night to her village, careening through the forest until, the village in sight, she could walk no more. In the early hours of the morning she managed to drag herself to the outskirts of the village. Too weak to call for help, the last of her life soaked into the red dust beneath her.

The authorities could do nothing. On the one hand, Tureau held a French passport which gave him certain immunities. On the other, he claimed that the girl had been a most willing bedmate who had, for some unknown reason, gone crazy and jumped through the window. He was not, he insisted contemptuously, to be held responsible for her death.

Dan and Miizi followed the procession at a discreet distance. They left the village to the solemn beat of drums and made their way out past the gardens, across a small stream into the vaporous forest. There, the lower forms of life thrived on the constant heat and grew to enormous size—worms a foot long, scorpions like lobsters, millipedes over eight inches long, and voracious mosquitoes that were at least merciful enough to appear in abundance only in the rainy season.

As Miizi motioned ahead, directing his attention toward the clearing, Dan thought a man was standing sentinel. But as they drew closer, he could see that the figure was lashed to a tree and quite dead. The corpse of the black man had been brought from a neighboring village. He had died a natural death and his family had donated his remains to the service of Kaulahu-don-na. Miizi guided Dan to a vantage point about twenty yards from the corpse. The witch doctors fanned out around the tree and sank to their knees. The incessant drums stopped. In their place was a low, guttural groaning. The baptismal incantations had begun.

Miizi had taken pains to prepare Dan for the ritual, both out of a subconscious dedication to his education and as a measure of protection against a protesting outburst, or worse, a sudden grip of panic that would cause Dan to lose forever the esteem he had gained during his first year.

The corpse was covered with a tarlike substance so that its deterioration in the humid jungle would be markedly slowed. A shirt was presented to the head witch doctor, who had been imported some one hundred miles for the occasion. It belonged to Tureau and was soaked in his own vital juices—which Dan had been told meant that Tureau's sweat had soaked the shirt—and it had been filched before anyone had had a chance to wash it. Next, strands of hair which had been surreptitiously removed from the Frenchman's comb by his house servants were entwined in the corpse's hair. Nail pairings were stuck to his fingernails and a hat like the one Tureau always wore was placed on the head.

The witch doctor stepped back. The groaning sound stopped, only to be replaced by low, venom-filled words which Dan could not understand. Twice he heard the name Jean Tureau, unmistakably. Suddenly, the drums roared into action. The witch doctors sprang to their feet in one fluid motion amid a chorus of shrill, frenzied shouts—calls to the demon gods to consecrate the unholy birth. They rushed the corpse in a constrictorlike movement, and then, as if in the clutches of some unseen force, pulled back. Again and again the movement was repeated until like a fickle wind, they fell into a swirling movement given order by some ancient choreography. An hour passed . . . two . . . and there did not seem to be one less ounce of energy or one less decible of intensity. Dan looked at Miizi for an indication of what to do. Miizi's eyes told Dan not to move. He did not. But by now the small of his back had begun to ache and he found only measured relief by shifting his weight from one foot to the other. Once, he tried to squat to ward off the growing stiffness, but Miizi would not let him. Slowly it occurred to him that he was trapped—bound to this place just as surely as the monstrous doll was bound to the tree. He began to mull over the possibility of escape. Impossible, he surmised. He'd never find his way back. Even if he did, then what? Don't panic, he told himself. I'm going to panic, he echoed silently. In the midst of his growing desperation, it stopped. The baptismal was over and Miizi was at his side saying that they should start back.

Dan leaned backward and then bent over forward to stretch his back. He rubbed the calves of his legs. Miizi looked up at him and smiled. "If you stay with us long enough, my friend, I will teach you how to stand motionless for many hours with no stiffness, no pain." Dan's expression acknowledged his shortcoming.

They followed the exiting procession back the way

they had come. As they left, Dan noticed that several witch doctors had remained behind to begin the magic chants that would focus their malignant hatred through the doll to the person of Jean Tureau.

During the night, the villagers could hear the distant drums sending out their message of death from the clearing. Dan was the guest of the chief for dinner. They ate well and drank enormous quantities of rum and palm wine. In his drunken stupor, Kaulahu-don-na told him things, as Miizi put it later, that no man from outside had a right to know.

Dan left the village the next day and spent the next several weeks participating in what another young doctor from the States described as an "inoculation blitz." He delayed his return to Biasempia and spent a week at the hospital at Bondoukou listening to and working with the noted Dr. Elliston, who had made a lifetime study of endemic diseases in the Ivory Coast. It was during his return trip that he heard the news— Tureau was dead. Of natural causes, he was told.

Tureau's death was confirmed by Miizi. Dan suspected that something other than the ouanga was the cause. The evening of his first night back, he spoke of it. He said that he was prepared to acknowledge the intensity and sincerity with which the witch doctors had gone about the ritual. He was not, however, in any way convinced that the monstrous doll had been imbued with any supernatural powers, or that the baptismal and death chants could in and of themselves cause a man's death. There had to be some other means—poison, an accident, even an errant bullet.

"Think back on the man who died here in your clinic," Miizi said. "Did you find any indication of poison? Were there any bullet holes in his body?"

Dan allowed as how there was no poison . . . no bullet holes . . . no anything.

"You see, my dear young doctor, when the magic is working, nothing else is necessary. The victim will die. It may take longer than with Tureau, but in time, he will die. That I can assure you," he said with a cryptic smile.

Dan approached it from another tact. "Miizi, understand that I am trying to learn. So forgive me if my next question reveals my vast ignorance. I just can't believe there's not something more to the ouanga . . . something you haven't told me. I mean, here was this corpse, baptized and the focus of endless incantations and chants. And miles away, there sat Tureau, who didn't even know all this is going on."

Miizi immediately stopped him. "What makes you think that he didn't know?"

"Well, I . . . just assumed. . . ." Dan looked to Miizi for the answer. "Are you saying that the victims. . . ?"

Miizi nodded his head. A thin, knowing smile crossed his lips. "Yes, they always know."

viii

As always when called to the bank, Charlie Cole put on his gray polyester suit which somehow had refused to wear out even though it was several years past its prime. He sat on the end of the leather couch in Anderson's office. Leaning forward, arms on his knees, his cuffs began to ride up on his legs, revealing several inches of doughylike flesh over his turquoise-blue socks.

Charlie was a very ordinary looking, mid-fortyish man, a fact he claimed helped him in his investigative work. "People tend to forget me as soon as they meet me," he had often said. And it was true. His thinning brown hair, his slightly jowled face, and lack of any prominent features made him virtually invisible in almost any crowd.

Anderson was taking him through the chronology of events starting with the carnival. Charlie listened with vassallike intensity. Anderson noticed that only after he'd completed his briefing did Charlie permit himself to relax and push his bulky frame back on the couch.

"Well, Mr. North, as you might expect, I'm aware of most of what you've told me. But then, so is everyone else in Hammin."

"What do you make of it?" Anderson asked bluntly.

"Well, number one," Charlie moved back to his arms-on-knees position, "I don't buy the prank thesis, okay? Number two, while I don't pretend to know much about voodoo, I do think I know a threat when I see one."

"We're tracking exactly," Anderson said, encouraging Charlie's line of reasoning. "But I want to know Who, and that's why you're here. That piss-poor excuse for a police chief has been about as effective as a one-legged man in an ass-kicking contest. So now I'm counting on you to get to the bottom of this."

"So I presumed," Charlie said in a tone that conveyed both his recognition of Anderson's urgency and his acceptance of the assignment.

He stood up and tried to tuck his hands under his belt to affect a more introspective air, but his belt was too tight so he opted for the pockets of his suit coat. "As you said, the question is Who? and I would suggest—if past experience teaches us anything—that the person or persons behind the threat is probably known to you. Not necessarily someone you know well, but most certainly not a stranger, okay? Think of the people who owe you money, the ones who are behind in their payments. Or the people you've had to foreclose on, or the people you've had to step on."

Anderson's jaw tightened, his eyes narrowed. "You're making me sound like one hell of a nice guy."

Charlie backtracked quickly to hold the damage to a minimum. "I'm speaking figuratively, okay? What I'm trying to say is that there are some people who for one reason or another have got it in their heads that you've, well. . . ." He floundered for words.

Anderson's grimace conveyed his impatience with Charlie's litany of what he had or had not done to people. "Yeah, yeah, I understand. Now get on to your point."

"Well, my point is that we start with the people you know. What I'd like to have you do is make a list of everybody, and I mean *everybody,* you can think of here in Hammin or anyplace else who might—" He paused to preweigh his choice of words—"have a grudge, or who might have indicated some resentment toward you, or someone who'd benefit, say, if you were, ah . . . indisposed."

Dead, is what he means, Anderson thought; the nerve ends in his stomach seemed to come unglued. "Look, I can get you the names, but keep in mind that there were four dolls. How does someone trying to get *me* tie in with the others?"

Charlie stepped over to the desk and rested both hands on it as he leaned forward. "Mr. North, I'm not really all that concerned with them. Okay? I mean, you're the man who signs my checks."

Anderson both expected and enjoyed Charlie's obsequious reassurance. It was one of the characteristics that had motivated Anderson to hire Charlie eighteen months earlier. Anderson had never thought that he needed a full-time investigator—a "trouble shooter," as Charlie put it—to help monitor his financial empire. But Charlie had made a convincing case for his services within the first two weeks, proving his worth by discovering the source of some pilferage in one of Anderson's stores.

Charlie's style was analytical, but plodding; circuitous, but always objectively driven. His manner seemed devoid of any cultural refinements or the studied embellishments that would give one pause to consider if he might be something more than he appeared. But that, Anderson thought, is the key to your success. I wonder if you've cultivated this personality, or did you come by it naturally and then discover you could turn it to your advantage? You don't threaten anyone, Charlie. In fact, most people feel comfortably superior to you and that's their mistake, isn't it? They let their guard down just long enough for you to ferret out the truth or uncover a weakness. You're not the kind of person that I'd ever seek out as a friend, Anderson mused, but you are useful to me, Charlie Cole. Most useful.

It was Charlie who'd uncovered the fact that the Norths' previous maid had been adding to her salary from the food budget. It was Charlie who had presented Anderson with the truth about Rita and Crawford and then convinced Anderson that the most fitting retribution would be to bankrupt the sporting goods store, destroying Crawford's dream and leaving him deeply in debt. And it was Charlie who, for the past eighteen months, had brought Anderson the invaluable asset of an extra pair of eyes and ears. Yes, he was most useful.

Anderson was suddenly aware that his thoughts had been wandering, and he focused on Charlie in time to pick up the substance of his commentary without revealing the lapse. Charlie was saying something about Carole and Crawford. "Of course, logic would seem to dictate that once we find who's behind your threat, we'll know who's behind theirs."

"Which brings me back to the point I was trying to make a moment ago," Anderson said. "There's got to be a link here. It's certainly not blind chance."

"Exactly. And that's why I need the list of names from you. Okay? I plan to get a similar list from Miss Peters and our friend Crawford. If we find the same name or names appearing on all three lists, we'll have some place to start. Okay?"

Anderson shook his head in disagreement. "If it was just Spencer and me, that would make sense. But Carole Peters hasn't got an enemy in the world. Who in the hell could have anything against her?"

"You never know. Sometimes vendettas are purely emotional fabrications. We have to explore every option . . . every possibility. Okay?"

"I agree. You're the boss in this. Do whatever you think best. If you need money, you've got it. But goddammit, let's get to the bottom of this thing!"

"Well—" Charlie looked for some place to put his hands, then dropped them self-consciously to his sides, "—I guess I'll get on with it. And don't worry, Mr. North. I feel very confident that we'll sort this thing out. Okay?" He made a short, jabbing motion which seemed an unnecessary bit of physical punctuation, then turned and left.

Anderson watched him go. Jesus, he thought, I wish he'd quit saying "okay" every other sentence.

The oversized brown envelopes were unmarked. Except for the first-class stamp and Hammin postmark, they gave the appearance of direct-mail solicitation pieces. Anderson was sunning himself by his pool when Rita brought him the mail. Carole met the postman in her driveway as she was about to get into her car. And Crawford, because he'd left early for the club, would not open his until late that evening.

Each envelope contained another glossy picture of their respective dolls. The arms and legs had been twisted and contorted so as to disfigure the dolls. The faces had been carefully and delicately painted to depict a biting inner torment. And the eyes—wide, more prominent than before—stared back with a waxen vestige of horror.

Anderson flew into a frenzy, shouting a string of obscenities and kicking a deck chair into the pool. He tore viciously at the picture and scattered the pieces on the lawn as he hurried toward the house. Rita, not having seen the picture, was at first stupefied by his actions, then in frantic confusion ran after him screaming for an explanation. No answer. He did not even look back at her as he bounded up the back steps and disappeared inside the house. Suddenly, terrified and disoriented, she looked for Hilda . . . for anyone. No one. She fought for a modicum of control, sank to all fours, and began to piece together the fragments of the picture. Inside, Anderson was on the phone calling Charlie. All he got was his answering machine and the sterile instructions to leave name and number, followed by a promise to return the call. Anderson literally shouted his command to come over as quickly as possible.

Carole did not open hers immediately. She placed the envelope and several other pieces of mail on the seat next to her in the car. As she turned into the courthouse square, the first stoplight brought her to a halt. She casually thumbed through the envelopes looking at return addresses to determine the sender and the probable message. A bill from Taylor's department store, her bank card statement, an announcement from the Ladies Auxiliary at the hospital, another bill, and a large brown envelope. She picked the last up and turned it over to see if there might be some identification on the other side. The light changed and she drove on to the next stoplight, made it through on the caution, only to be stopped by a third light.

She slid her index finger under the flap and tore it open. It was the face, the odious, abhorrent face that pierced her frail defenses and sent a tremor rippling through her body leaving a cold chill in its wake. More pins had been thrust into the abdomen.

Green light. She did not move.

The face of her doll was ribbed with pain and what appeared to be a drop of blood had run out of the side of its mouth and trickled across its cheek.

Short horn bleats from the car behind her. She did not hear.

The eyes seemed curiously alive and staring out from the depths of a hundred unspoken fears. Carole could feel her hands tighten on the picture. Blood rushed from her head and she felt nausea clutch at her stomach. And suddenly the car was cold. Ice cold, sitting dead in the sun on a hot June day.

The driver behind her, sensing a problem, got out of his car and walked forward to Carole's. She probably flooded it, he thought. Hey, I think that's Carole Peters. In that instant of recognition, he indulged himself in a brief lascivious spree with the attractive young woman. He leaned toward the driver's side window. The first thing that caught his eye was the picture. He recoiled with knee-jerk suddenness. Catching himself, he looked in again and saw Carole, her mouth open, gasping in short breaths, her eyes locked onto the picture. The man saw her shudder and in that moment he understood the contagion of fear. He would tell about the incident for many weeks to come.

Anderson paced back and forth on his veranda waiting for Charlie Cole. Where is he, goddammit? If there's anything I hate, it's talking to a goddamn machine when you need somebody. Got to find out if Carole and Crawford got pictures. Jesus, what the hell is going on?

"That poor, poor man." It was Hilda's voice. Her tone was tinged with remorse. "It's beginning to take its toll of him." Anderson stepped over to one of the open windows. Through the gauzy filter of the sheer white drapes he could see Hilda on the center-hall phone. "He don't look good at all. Lost most of the color in his face." She paused to listen and Anderson edged closer, his attention riveted. "Well, Mrs. North stuck the picture back together. Oh, it was awful, the legs and arms all twisted up." There was a moment of silence. "I'm not sure what it means. Either he's going to get them broken or they're going to pain him something awful. Oh, somebody has really got it in for that man," she said with concern. Anderson could take no more. "Of course, if they don't take that hex off, he could die," she added.

"Son of a fucking goddamn bitch!" Anderson slammed his fist into one of the porch pillars with such force that he heard the wood crack. A stabbing bolt shot up his arm and he pulled the stinging hand into his midsection and doubled over trying to bury the pain. He bit his lip to fight back tears. "What the hell is going on?" he whimpered. "What in Christ's name do the bastards want?"

Natalie was curled up on the sofa when Crawford came in. He was momentarily startled, but quickly recovered and said with detached matter-of-factness, "Can't say that I expected to find you here."

She looked up at him with a contrite expression. "I came to tell you I was sorry for the other night. I was really off base." She leaned forward and drew a cigarette from a pack on the table. Her loose-fitting blouse, half open, suggested that her body would be offered as proof of her penitence. "I guess sometimes I'm just not as sensitive as I should be."

In all but matters of the flesh, he retorted silently.

"I understand you've been to see the doctor."

"Who told you that?" He was surprised she knew.

She smiled warmly. "Lover, when it comes to you, I make it my business to know things. Are you okay?"

Crawford ignored the question as he opened his bar and filled a tumbler with scotch. "Can I get you something?"

"The usual will be fine. What about the doctor? Did he say you were all right?"

"I get the test results back in a couple of days. Just routine."

Natalie slipped off the couch and nuzzled up to him, forcing her body close. She wedged her legs inside his, cupped her hands around the back of his head, and looked searchingly into his eyes. "You look tired. I can see it in your eyes," she said soothingly. "Let me fix some dinner while you just relax."

It's old home week, Crawford thought. She felt good pressed into him, and they both became aware of his amorous urge. "I think I'd like to fuck your brains out," he said softly.

"Before or after dinner?"

*   *   *

It was over quickly and he lay on his back as Natalie went into the bathroom. He was exhausted. Jesus, she really did me in. I'm getting out of shape. And my goddamn stomach. Maybe Doc is right . . . maybe it's catching up to me. Feel like hell."

"Crawf," Natalie called as she opened the bathroom door, "what are all these pills and things?" She was holding two bottles of prescription medicines.

"Ah, they're nothing. Something I've been taking for indigestion."

Natalie came back to the bed and sat down on the edge. She put one of her hands in his and then stroked his forehead with the other in a motherly sort of way. She did not try to hide her concern. "Crawford, I want to know the truth. Just how sick are you, really?"

Crawford shrugged and smiled. "If you want to play nurse, I volunteer to play patient. Love those massages."

Natalie sat him on the couch in front of the television while she grilled two steaks and prepared a green salad.

A thought struck him. He set down his drink, got up, and headed for the door. "I'll be right back," he called.

Natalie poked her head out of the kitchen. "Where're you going?"

"Forgot to pick up the mail."

The warm night air had inspired the frogs and crickets and other night insects around the lake by Dan's trailer to offer their nightly chorus in a full-voiced fortissimo. On other evenings, Carole had lain in Dan's bed letting the modulated nocturnal serenade carry her off to sleep. But not tonight. There was no pleasure in the sound, only a rasping and scratching that seemed bent on keeping her awake . . . and thinking. From the trailer bedroom she could see Dan as he busied himself in the living area picking up and putting things away. Her depression had set in almost immediately after the discovery of the picture, and little had happened the rest of the day to alleviate it.

She felt secure in his bed. But she wanted him with her, protecting her with his presence, not playing housemaid at the other end of the trailer. She heard the fluttering, pinging sound of fire moths flinging themselves against the screen in a vain attempt to penetrate the wire mesh. The sedative Dan had given her was taking hold and she found it difficult to force any order or discipline on her thoughts. Images were swimming now; she fought to erase them. The crescendo of night noise seemed to swell to a crest that broke over her receding consciousness. Her lips moved in a silent call for Dan. Ping . . . fluta-fluta . . . bizzt. The insects were attacking the screening, challenging the thin metal strands. She spiraled down . . . faster . . . how far to the bottom? Her last fleeting thought was the utter certainty that the insects would somehow manage to penetrate the screen and find her helpless.

Dan stood in the doorway and looked in. Her regular breathing told him she was asleep, but it was too dark for him to see the constricted expression on her face.

Dan had awakened about eight that morning, pledging to give himself over to the number of chores that had piled up. He was waist deep in the lake replacing some boards on the small dock that jutted out into the water when he heard the car. He was not surprised to see Carole coming down the dirt road toward his trailer. She'd said that she'd be over sometime before noon. But the moment she stepped out of her car, even before he could see her face clearly, he sensed the cloud of foreboding that enveloped her. Whatever lingering doubt Dan might have had about the intent and veracity of the dolls, it vanished as he looked at the picture. Miizi's words echoed in his ears, "They always know."

Dan's call caught Anderson moments after Charlie

had arrived. Within minutes Rita, Anderson, and Charlie were standing under the awning that served as a porch for Dan's trailer. Dan and Carole knew Charlie Cole to say hello to, but beyond that he was just one of the people Anderson's dollars had brought into the fold. For the first few moments they all spoke in questions. Seeing they were getting nowhere, Anderson revealed Charlie's assignment. Intending no disrespect for Toby, Dan found some comfort in knowing that now someone would be concentrating on getting to the source.

"I don't pretend to be an investigative genius," Charlie was saying, "but I do pride myself on possessing a good deal of deductive reasoning power, okay? Now, here's where I jump in. We start with a question. Why should Mr. North, Spencer, Reeson, and you, Miss Peters, be singled out as the objects of this threat? Now, let's see what we know? As I understand it—though I haven't confirmed this with Crawford Spencer yet—none of you knew this Reeson fella."

"I think I might have seen him around town," Carole offered.

"But you didn't know him to speak to or anything, is that right?"

"No, I didn't know him," said Carole.

"Okay. Now assuming, as Mr. North suspects, there's a link here, the fact that none of you actually knew Reeson should make my job a little easier."

"How do you figure?" Anderson asked.

"Well, a link would seem to suggest that you all had something in common. And about the only thing I can find in common was that everyone who's received a picture so far——"

"You think there will be more?" Rita interrupted.

"No way of knowing, okay?"

"Let him finish," Anderson snapped. "Sorry, Charlie, you were saying?"

"What I was saying is that everyone who's received

a picture just happened to be in the carnival tent the night of Reeson's death. Now, I find that a most interesting and unlikely coincidence."

"Are you saying that it's got something to do with that psychic?" Dan asked quizzically.

"Possibly, possibly," Charlie said reflectively. A half smile broke across his face. "I understand you folks had a—you'll forgive the expression—*seance* that night."

"And this girl appeared," Rita added. "That's when Reeson ran out."

"Yes, Mr. North mentioned that to me," Charlie said. A thought struck him, "Say you may have sparked something here, Mrs. North." He turned to Anderson, "What was it you told me that girl said?"

Anderson fumbled through his recollection of that night. "I don't know. It was. . . ." he paused.

"I trusted you, I trusted you," Rita supplied.

Charlie's eyes dropped to the ground as he contemplated a new thesis. "Could it be that the words, or more likely the girl herself, might mean something?" He let the question hang for a moment.

Rita plucked it. "You know," she said, looking at Charlie, "Reeson *might* have known her. I remember very distinctly when the psychic was reading him, she asked if he knew someone by the name of Catherine. He denied it. But at the time, we felt sure he knew who she was. Then, not five minutes later, this Cathy Parks person appears. Catherine . . . Cathy?" She accented the question by hunching up her shoulders.

"Hmmmm," Charlie mused. "That's interesting. Almost sounds a little like a set-up, doesn't it? I mean, calling up the name and then having a girl appear. But then, I'm not sure what that tells us."

Dan saw it first. "I think you may have another link, Charlie."

"How so?"

"Let's assume Reeson knew her. You can add me and Crawford to the list."

Anderson's head snapped around. "Crawford knew her?"

"That's what he told me," Dan replied

There was a glimmer of excitement in Charlie's eyes. "Hey, now that's kind of interesting. Interesting that three people should know this girl, okay?"

"Make it four people," Dan corrected.

"Four?" Charlie repeated with surprise. "Who's the fourth?"

Charlie turned to Carole, his face alight with possibilities. "You knew her?"

"Well . . . not really . . . I mean. . . ." Carole stammered

Dan stepped in and explained to Charlie. "The girl was one of my patients, and Carole was working for me at the time."

"But there were hundreds of patients, she was hardly more than a name," Carole explained.

"I don't mean to suggest that you knew her well." Dan sensed that she somehow felt intimidated, and put his arm around her for reassurance.

"This is very, very interesting," Charlie mused. He looked at Carole as he calculated the possible implications of his information. "Even if you knew her only casually——"

"But I didn't," Carole protested mildly.

"Well, let's say for the sake of our discussion, okay, that it was only a passing acquaintance which you may have forgotten. Now when was it, Doctor, that you had her as a patient?"

"Let's see . . . as. . . ." Dan counted back. "Three years ago this summer."

Charlie took out his pad and scribbled some notes. "And Spencer; did he tell you when he'd known her?"

"It seems to me," Dan said thoughtfully, "he said three years ago, too."

Charlie made another notation and was about to go on when Rita interrupted. "Anderson, is there any chance the girl might have worked for you?"

Anderson found himself a chair and offered a second to Carole. His impatience was showing. "Look, aren't we getting a little off the track here?"

"Not necessarily," Charlie protested. "I'd like to pursue this a little further."

Rita prodded Anderson. "With so many employees, she could have come and gone and you'd never have known it."

"Maybe, but I doubt it," he said sternly.

"Might be worth a check in your files, Mr. North," Charlie said.

Anderson shifted his weight around and began to think about a drink to cut through the blotterlike dryness in his mouth. "Look, all I can tell you is that I don't hire circus people to work in my establishments." Anderson glanced over at Dan. "Excuse me, Doctor. I wonder if you could be so good as to prescribe some scotch or whatever you've got for a man in need of a drink?"

"I'm sorry, Anderson. Carole's always saying I'm a lousy host and I guess she's right." He chuckled lightly in hopes of lifting some of the pall that had settled over them. "I've got scotch or anything else you might like."

Carole was helping Dan with the drinks when the phone rang. Getting Dan phone service for his trailer had been one of the more interesting assignments the local phone company had faced in some time.

"I've got to go to the hospital. Shouldn't take me more than twenty, twenty-five minutes. Why don't you all stick around until I get back? There's plenty to drink and Carole knows what's in the refrigerator."

Charlie stood up, "Say, Doctor, would it be too much trouble for you to drop me off on the way?

There're some things I really ought to be doing, and my car is at Mr. North's house."

As Dan spun his car out of the dirt road onto Highway 421, he looked over at Charlie. "Really not much to go on, is there?"

"Well, there are some pieces beginning to turn up here and there." He looked out the window at the rolling countryside. "Got to admit that I like puzzles. Always have. And one thing I've learned about puzzles is that you have to study every piece, okay? You have to be familiar with them and know where they are so that when the time comes to fit this or that piece into the picture . . . you know where to lay your hands on it."

Charlie turned back from the window and Dan sensed that he, as a piece of the puzzle, was now under scrutiny.

"How long you been here in Hammin, Doctor?"

"Little over three years."

"Didn't think you were a native."

"You're not from here either, are you?"

"Nope, although after eighteen months it's beginning to feel like home." Once again Charlie turned his attention out the window. "Not a bad town really. Pace is about right for me, okay? Of course, Mr. North can really keep me hoppin' at times."

"Yes, I guess he can be pretty demanding." There was a pause. "Did Anderson tell you to investigate Cathy Parks?"

Charlie shook his head. "Not really . . . but she is a piece of the puzzle. Why don't you tell me about her?"

"Well, the first time I saw her was not under what you might call the most auspicious circumstances." Dan had not thought about that day for a long time. Now the memory of it began to rush back. "To tell you the truth, it was really very tragic." Dan turned the corner on U.S. 81 and started up The Hill toward Anderson's.

"I really appreciate your going out of your way like this."

"No problem."

"You were saying about this girl. . . ."

"Yeah, well, I got a call. It was mid-June, in the morning. About nine o'clock as I remember. Somebody—a woman, I don't know who—said that there was a girl who had been badly hurt and needed a doctor and that we'd find her at the Sunset Motel."

"The one out on the Interstate?" Charlie asked by way of clarification.

"Right. I got out there and found Cathy. It looked like a few of the cases I'd seen as an intern in New York City. Some butcher had performed a lousy abortion. She'd lost a lot of blood and was in a state of shock. We had her in the hospital for two weeks before she came out of it. Beautiful girl. And I mean the kind of beauty you'd expect to see in one of those television cosmetic commercials. And such a sweet kid." Dan's thoughts wandered off to a private place.

"What happened to her?"

Dan slowed down, put on his blinker signal, and turned into Anderson's driveway. "I don't know, to tell you the truth. And that's always been a mystery to me. She just—" he groped for the right words— "just sort of disappeared."

"You mean she disappeared from the hospital?" Charlie asked as he took out his note pad.

"No, no," Dan replied. "We released her from the hospital in mid-July. Actually, I saw quite a bit of her until about Labor Day. That was when I got word my father was very ill. So I went home. He died a couple days after I arrived. I stayed with my mother and the rest of our family until late in September. And when I came back to Hammin—" he shrugged "—no trace of her. Nothing. Not even a note."

"So you never saw her again."

Dan shook his head no.

"Until that night at the carnival?"

"Hmmmm," Dan nodded his confirmation.

"Now, I've got to say that's strange, okay? Very strange. You know, the more I think about it, the more I think this Cathy person is tied into all this somehow." Charlie opened the door and slid out. "Really think she might be," he said reflectively, and shut the door.

Blank blue eyes fixed on a cold white ceiling, Nourishment flows from a bottle down a tube into her arm. A nurse looks in frequently. Each day at seven a.m., at twelve noon, and at four p.m., Dan comes to stand at the foot of her bed, read the chart, and look. She has been this way for two weeks. A specialist from upstate has been called in. He says there is nothing to do but wait. Each day the question is asked: "Who are you?" The girl never answers.

ix

Toby Mitchell rocked back in his chair, the stub of a cigar clenched between his teeth, and glared with mounting repugnance at the middle-aged woman who sat in his office.

"I realize that you may think I'm just a daft old fool, but I tell you when I looked in her basement window she was going through some kind of ceremony. Now I'm not here to accuse her of being a witch or anything like that—" the woman nervously fumbled with the Bible in her lap"—but with all this hex talk going about, well, I just thought. . . ."

She was interrupted by a policeman opening the door to Toby's office. "Chief?"

"Don't you ever knock?" Toby did not attempt to conceal his irritation.

"Sorry, but you told me to let you know when Charlie Cole arrived."

"Tell him I'll be just a minute."

The woman looked after the policeman as he backed out and closed the door. She turned to Toby. "What I was about to say——"

Toby cut her off with a sharp diagonal wave of his hand. "Look, I don't want to hear any more of this nonsense. I've had it with these stories." The woman was taken aback by his tone and she stiffened with indignation. "Let me tell you something," Toby continued, "it's this kind of busybody, unfounded gossip that ends up causing all kinds of problems. You keep it up and somebody is going to get hurt. And another thing; I don't know if you're aware of the fact, but there is a law in this town that makes it illegal for you to go around peeping in other people's windows."

The woman had taken all she could tolerate. "I never—never have I been treated like this by anyone before in my life!" She stood up and stared at him with burning rancor.

Toby averted his eyes and mumbled something as he began to look through his drawers for another cigar.

"People are right about you! You've been in this job too long!" She lifted her chin, snapped her head away, and hurried for the door.

"Amen, to that," Toby muttered.

His intercom buzzed and he reached over for the talk switch. "Yeah?"

"You want me to send in Cole?"

"Why not?" He let the lever snap back into place and lifted a stack of papers, uncovering a slightly squashed cigar. He looked up as Charlie entered and gestured toward the chair. "Have a seat." His pique was evident in the way he attacked the matchbook. He sucked air through the corona and a flame flared up on the end. "I understand I'm going to have some help? You and Anderson thinking of forming your own little vigilante group, are you?"

Charlie understood Toby's resentment, but his reference to vigilantes brought on a short laugh that he did not try to suppress. "No, but we *were* thinking about getting some volunteers for a posse."

Toby responded with a breathy gaffaw and his vexation faded.

"Understand, Mr. Mitchell——"

"Call me Toby."

"Thanks. Understand, this wasn't my idea, okay? I mean, I work for the man; I investigate things for him. And if I want to continue working for him, well. . . ." He shrugged to show he had no other choice.

"Okay, but does he know what this is going to mean?"

"I don't follow."

Toby stood up, crossed over to his basement-level window, and stared out across the courthouse lawn toward Anderson's bank. "Hammin's number-one citizen, the holder of our municipal bonds," his tone was caustic, "hires a private detective to investigate a possible hex. What more credibility can you give this thing? It's an open admission that the man *believes*."

"Not to argue with you, but I don't see it that way. A threat is a threat, no matter what the form. And my job, as I read it, is to find out who's trying to make things, shall we say, *uncomfortable* for him. If there's criminal intent here, that's your department, okay?"

"Criminal intent? They're going to have to do a lot more than send pictures before I could even get a misdemeanor out of this."

"Well, I can't make judgments on the legality, but I suspect the intent is not all that friendly."

"Damn Anderson North! With you snoopin' around asking questions, we'll have everybody so stirred up. . . ." He threw his hands down in frustration.

"I'll try to keep in the background. Anyway, I don't think many people know what I'm doing. And it'll be a lot easier for me if they don't."

Toby knew he had no recourse. The chances of convincing Anderson to call off his hound were something less than zero. He'd have to live with Charlie Cole. Who knows, Toby thought, he might just stumble on to something. Toby let out a deep sigh. "Do what you have to do. If you get on to anything, let me know."

Charlie nodded his agreement and left.

Toby turned back to the window and watched as a pair of female legs passed by on the walk directly outside his window. He hardly gave them a second thought, which was out of character for him. The old bitch was right, he concluded. I *have* been in this job too long. How many years? Fifteen? Shit, at least that.

He turned, leaned back against the wall, and surveyed his office. What a hole! I ought to have some shelves built. I ought to clean it up! What for? It'll only get this way again. What am I going to do about this goddamn witch hunt? What the hell *can* I do? I've sent for the records, and if they come up zero, then . . . then, he groaned, this thing will just have to play itself out.

Toby aimlessly began to straighten up a stack of papers on top of a file cabinet, then stopped and sat down in his chair. He puffed peevishly on his cigar. He was feeling sorry for himself and he was enjoying it.

Maybe I'll retire in another year and go find my brother and see what he's up to. What's to keep me here? Not a damn thing. Not one goddamn thing!

Toby thought about his wife, who had left him five years ago. She had made it a regular practice to hold Anderson North up to him as the model man and husband. The comparison was odious and grated on him. She'd probably have gone to bed with Anderson if he'd made the offer. Maybe she did. Who knows? Who cares? She's gone. And with her, the sixteen-year-old daughter he adored. For almost three years his only communication with her had been Christmas cards and birthday letters. He felt empty.

He permitted himself a few more moments of somber musing, then decided it had gone on long enough. So he switched it off. The smoke from his cigar curled up around his head. Damn good cigar, he thought.

Outside on the streets around the courthouse, the Monday shoppers paused to look at Anderson's bank and ponder. There was a growing sense of expectancy. Women spoke of it in the checkout lines of the supermarkets. It was the thing one talked about at gas stations as attendants filled tanks. It was mixed in the fetid air of numerous lunch counters along with the grease and onions and other residue odors. Children, even small ones, listened intently as it was discussed over dinner tables. There was a renewed awareness of what to do with spilled salt, and there were frequent admonitions to "Knock on wood." These were not conscious acts, just rediscovered reflexes. A rhythm was surging in the public pulse as ancient and deep-rooted as man's first cognizance of the unknown.

Under the shroud of dusk, cars would drive up The Hill, winding their way past Carole's, then on to the top toward the Norths', where they would slow down and peer out their windows to see if it might be possible to catch a glimpse of something.

Since Anderson held the controlling interest in the *Hammin Journal,* there was never any mention of the new pictures in the paper. But it wasn't necessary. Everyone knew.

At the golf club, people began to analyze Crawford's actions. His words were given a subtext. As his game slumped, there was general agreement that he was not as immune to the implied hex as he claimed.

Crawford sensed their scrutiny, shrugged off the inquiries, and endured their furtive glances. Once, unable to contain his mounting frustration and wanting somehow to strike back at his tormentors, he feigned a fit, throwing himself around the club locker room, making strange animallike sounds, rolling his eyes up into his head, frothing at the mouth, and finally collapsing in a heap. Then, springing to his feet, he grinned at the terrified onlookers and took a bow for his performance. He had meant it as a joke and he told them so, but their laughter was self-conscious.

Carole found that she was becoming the recipient of an increasing number of callers bearing small gifts and anxious encouragement to keep up her strength. Soon after the second picture had arrived, she'd made the mistake of relating the details of a late-night incident—in confidence, she thought—to a young woman she'd known since childhood. Three times the phone had rung. Once at one a.m., then again at two a.m. and three a.m. The first two times the caller hung up as she answered. The third time a raspy voice asked if she was experiencing any pain.

"Who is this?" Her voice trembled. "Who is this!"

"Well, you wouldn't know me. I'm just someone concerned for your health. Have you had any new discomfort of late?"

"No!" she shouted back at the phone. "Now who is this? What do you want?"

"I just wanted to inform you that we're starting to work on your stomach, your spleen, and your kidneys. The pains will come slowly, but they will most definitely come."

With hatred toward her unidentified tormentor, she slammed the receiver down. Then, to ensure that there would be no more calls, she took the phone off the hook.

"Carole." The voice was breathy, distant . . . and female. Carole looked quickly around the room to try to locate its source. Again the voice came. "Carole." Still breathy . . . hollow . . . but nearer, seemingly just outside the windows that overlooked the front yard.

"Who's there?" she cried out, her voice cracking and several tones higher than normal.

She slid a leg out of bed onto the floor. Her pulse seemed to be sending electric shocks of fear through her body. She put the other foot on the floor and started slowly toward the window, consciously approaching it from an angle so as to obscure the view of anyone outside.

Blackness. The light by her bed went out. She froze in her spot, afraid to move. Involuntarily, her body began to shake and she groped her way back toward the bed, feeling for the light. Her hands grabbed the neck of the lamp and she pushed the switch twice . . . three times. Nothing.

Something on the window screen, scraping. For a moment it reminded her of a cat she had as a child that would climb up the screen door on the back porch when it wanted to be let in. Again the scraping, and she realized it was an entirely different sound.

Got to close the window, she thought. Got to get it closed. There was a desperation in her determination, almost as if the mere act of closing the window would wall her from whatever was on the outside. She took two steps toward the window. Something is out there, she cried in _silent_ horror. Her heart raced and there was a strange numbness in her legs and arms. She could barely move.

She took another labored step. It was tearing at the screen now. Another step and she felt something brush against her leg. She gasped and then realized it was only the side of the bed.

It stopped. There was no sound at the window, only the faint wheeze of the wind in the trees. She collapsed on her bed and tried to catch her breath. Got to get help, she told herself. Got to get help.

Then it came—a solid knock on her bedroom door. Unmistakable. A single hard blow. It's not locked, she thought. I've got to lock it.

Again, the heavy sound of a knock on the door. Calling on all her strength, she pushed herself off the bed and slid onto the murky grayness of the floor. She crept on all fours toward the door. A couple more feet, she told herself. She thought she could make out the black silhouette of the door handle. The bolt lock would be just beneath it. She raised her hand to the door knob and dropped her fingers to the lock.

With a rush the door blew open, slamming against the wall. And there, standing over her, the outline of a woman. Faint, but definitely the figure of a woman. Slowly, Carole raised eyes that fought to deny what they were seeing to the pale luminescence surrounding the face. Cathy Parks.

The figure moved toward her and with it came the sound of wind over hollow pipes . . . increasing . . . intensifying into a shrill, high-pitched, strident wail. It was as if the wind had taken the scream of terror lodged in Carole's throat and given it life.

Carole buried her face in her hands and rolled away from the door, crashing into another night table. She found she could not breath as she huddled on the floor, waiting.

Before she blacked out, her last conscious thought was of a sudden silence.

Skeet Fischer, the bartender at the Hammin Inn, was a small, wiry redhead with a large bushy mustache. Gradually, he had become the clearing center for all the stories and rumors surrounding the hex. Business had been good all evening and Skeet considered staying open another hour past the usual closing time. There was at least another hundred dollars or more to be had from the crowd, not counting tips. He looked over at Judy Simpson, standing at the end of the bar by her pick-up station. He caught her eye and made a questioning gesture toward the clock with a quick nod of his head. She understood.

"Oh, God, Skeet, I've had it for tonight. All I want to do is go home and get into a nice cool bath." She slid a tray of drinks off the bar, sidestepped a playful slap aimed at her inviting posterior, and headed across the room.

Skeet contemplated his alternatives and then, as if suddenly reminded of something, turned to the group of men sitting at the bar. "Okay you barflies, last call. Order it now, 'cause we're going to settle up. And by the way, let's show a little respect for me and Judy in the form of some nice tips?"

"Hey, Skeet," a man at the far end of the bar called,

"how about a high-proof potion to ward off evil spirits?" He laughed.

"Barney, the only spirits that are going to haunt you are the ones you've been drinking," Skeet replied.

"Hey," said Barney, "can you imagine old Jake down there getting one of them hex dolls? You stick a pin in him and it's be like tapping a keg."

Jake Geiber, who had achieved something of legend status as a result of consuming beer by the case, responded with a quick flick of his middle finger. The man next to him at the bar took up his defense. "Don't even kid about that stuff, man. You get yourself one of those pictures and you're going to need more than a potion."

"Do you buy this hex business?" asked a short man seated opposite the cash register.

"You bet your sweet ass I do. When I was in the navy, we stopped off in Haiti one time. And I heard some stories from people that had a lot of respect for it." Skeet paused and then leaned over, looked down the bar, and mouthed the words in a loud whisper. "Scared the shit out of me."

"If you want to see somebody really up tight about this thing," said the short man, "come take a look at my wife. You know, she went out and bought herself a rosary and she ain't even Catholic."

"The one I feel sorry for is that Carole Peters," said Barney. "I knew her father real well. Hell, he delivered all my kids. And I tell you, it'd break his heart to look into the face of that girl. I mean, she's aged since this thing started."

"Listen, I'm told that's one of the signs that a hex is taking hold."

"Jesus!" The voice belonged to a bald, middle-aged man who had been quietly nursing a bourbon and water. "I can't believe my ears are hearing this! You sound like a bunch of superstitious old ladies. I'll bet half you guys have started sleeping with the lights on.

Hey, this hex is nothing but a lot of crap! There's nothin' to it!"

"Oh yeah?" challenged a voice. "I'll bet you'd be turnin' that goddamn stool a different color if you got one of those pictures."

"You know what I heard?" said Jake. "Ol' Reverend What's-His-Face is going to talk about hexes in his sermon next Sunday."

"It'll be the first time he's had a full church since Easter."

"Skeet," Barney asked, "what's this about Anderson North hiring a detective?"

Skeet continued to wash glasses in the bar sink. "That's right. He's got that guy who works for him on it—Charlie Cole. Got him out looking for witches full time."

Again the assembly along the bar broke into laughter. But it was a nervous, constrained sound, each man sensing his own vulnerability.

Judy Simpson quietly finished the tally on her bar checks. She had chosen to stay out of the conversation. In the past, she would have been right in the midst of the verbal sparring, throwing in sharp jabs and parrying with playful taunts. Silently, she continued to clear away the tables.

"Were any of you out at the carnival the night they had the seance business?" That from the bald man.

"I was there," responded the short man seated at the middle of the bar, "but I didn't see the show."

"I did." Everyone turned to look at portly Jake Geiber.

"Then you should know, Jake," Skeet said, "that one theory going around has it that only people who saw the girl have to worry about a hex."

Judy was surprised to hear Skeet mention the possible connection with the girl. He had taken her to the carnival that night and recently, in private conversations, had begun to speculate about the relationship between the psychic, the girl, and the dolls. But his attitude and concern had been such that she was nonplussed to hear him bring up the theory of his audience at the bar. Why would he do that, she wondered.

"Skeet," Barney said, sliding off his stool and reaching for his wallet, "you've been hearing every side of this thing for a month now. What do you figure it's all about?"

"Barney, old pal, if I knew that I could walk across that courthouse square to the Hammin National Bank, step right into the office of Mr. Anderson North, and walk out of there a rich man. Who knows what it's all about? All I know is that I'd like to have you guys pay up so Judy and I can lock up and get out of here before sunrise."

Skeet pulled the door closed behind him and checked to be sure it was locked. "Can I drop you off?" he asked, turning to Judy.

A light, misty rain had begun to fall. The square was deserted. Around the perimeter, neon signs in store windows branded their message on the night. A light burned on the second floor of the courthouse. Probably left on by mistake, Judy thought. Off to the right, across the street, a large illuminated cream-colored globe with "Police" in black letters stood lonely sentinel atop a cast-iron pole.

"Where'd you park?" Judy asked in response to his offer.

"Over there by the drugstore." He pointed down the street to the left.

"Thanks, but by the time I walk to your car, I could be home. And it's not raining that hard."

"Feels kind of good, actually. Love a soft summer rain. See you tomorrow."

Skeet turned and headed off toward his car, the metal tips on his shoes clicking on the sidewalk. Judy walked up half a block in the opposite direction to the corner where Taylor Street intersected the square. The prewar buildings that surrounded the courthouse took on a gray, sullen appearance at night. Even the occasional attempt at face lifting with appliqués of decorative brick or painted aluminum siding only served to reinforce the image of a town past its prime.

The storefronts wrapped around the corners and continued down Taylor Street for about half a block. Their doors and windows were drawn tight against the dark. Only the hum of air conditioners ejecting spent air into the street broke the silence. Beyond the stores a cluster of brick apartment houses squared off across the street from one another. Their window frames were painted dark green or black so as to minimize the chipping and deterioration caused by the seasonal ravages of too many years and too little upkeep. Once, the buildings were a symbol of Hammin's confidence in its future. With time, confidence had given way to resignation.

Judy passed the plate-glass store windows shrouded with their faded awnings, then cut diagonally across the street. Her apartment, Number Forty Taylor Street, was almost a full block off the corner.

The light rain was more of a fog now and the thin film of water on the street and sidewalk made everything feel clean. She took a deep breath and expelled it rapidly to cleanse her lungs of the accumulation of smoke and body odors she had ingested during the evening. The single street light at the far end of the block was having little success cutting through the ashen mist.

Footsteps.

Skeet?

No, he had metal tips on his shoes. I just imagined it, she thought.

She turned and looked back in the direction of the

courthouse. The glow given off by the Police globe was barely discernible.

No one around.

She quickened her step a little and started to fumble in her purse for the apartment keys.

Again. Unmistakable this time.

Judy stopped and listened carefully. All she heard was the hum of air conditioners. Then a strange sound began to filter through—wind blowing across hollow pipes, multiple pitches . . . minor key. But there was no wind.

She hurried past the deep, inset doorways leading to other apartment buildings. She did not see the figure before she collided with it full front. Her cry was short and muffled.

"Hey, take it easy. "It's only me."

The face was darkly visible in the gloom. A policeman!

"Jesus, God! I think I've wet my pants. What are you doing out here?"

"What I always do at this hour of the night—checking to make sure everything is locked up. Sorry, I didn't mean to scare you." The mist thinned out briefly and some light fell on her face. "Oh, it's you, Judy," the policeman said. He placed his hand on her shoulder as though to administer a calming balm. It made him acutely aware of how deeply he'd unnerved her. "Say, I really am sorry to give you such a fright."

"Well, for Christ's sake, do you have to creep around like a goddamn mugger?" she scolded.

"Listen, I'm sorry. Can I walk you to your door?"

"No, no," she said, doing her best to regain some composure. "I think my heart is back where it belongs."

The policeman started to back off. He tipped his hat and said hesitatingly, "Well . . . good night." He turned and walked on toward the courthouse.

Judy trudged up the four steps that led to her apartment building entrance and let herself in. The bank of metal mailboxes serving the tenants was on her right. She was still trembling and had to use both hands to guide the key into the mailbox lock. Inside, she found a couple of circulars, a solicitation for a magazine, and a letter with a return address she recognized as belonging to her older sister. She closed the box, opened the inner door, and crossed the small lobby to the stairway. The bulb was out on the first landing and she cursed the superintendent for being lazy, which he was.

Reaching the third floor, she opened her apartment door and turned on the lights. For an instant she recalled the night at the carnival when the psychic, Madame Miranda, seemingly had been able to stand mentally in that very spot and describe her apartment and most everything in it. She closed the door and fastened the chain lock.

Good to be home, she thought, and kicked off her shoes. She dropped the mail on the coffee table in front of the sofa, then opened both windows overlooking the street.

Place needs airing out. Think it's cooling off. It'll be good sleeping tonight.

Entering the bedroom, she stepped over a pile of laundry and went into her bathroom. She flipped on the light and started to run the water for her bath. A box of bubble bath sat invitingly on top of the toilet tank. She sprinkled it liberally into the tub, watching it foam up under the tap.

Her dress slipped onto the pile of laundry as she walked back into the living room to read her sister's letter. This sofa's almost as good as a man, she thought, letting herself sink deep into the stuffed red cushions. The running water in the tub reminded her not to get too comfortable. It'll take a couple more minutes to fill up, she surmised, and slit the envelope open. She settled back with the letter and reached for the chain pull on the reproduction of an old Tiffany lamp that sat on an end table next to the sofa. The gold frame she'd bought for her mother's picture sparkled brilliantly in the shower of light.

Mother was gone.

Judy's doll had arrived.

Her screams ricocheted off the walls and plunged through the windows, masking completely the receding footsteps in the street below.

I think that would be very kind of _____ Gandalf, he
said. "I don't believe we've met, I'm Mr. Muscrelson."

x

Toby stood in Judy's living room holding the gold frame. Carefully, he opened the back and pulled out the picture. As with the others, someone had gone to great lengths to make sure that there would be no mistaking for whom the doll was intended. It had blond hair pulled back sharply off the face. A cocktail apron had been tied around its waist and a small tray affixed to the doll's right hand. One pin had pierced the throat while three others had been thrust up between the legs.

Several of the apartment tenants peered in through the open door. The women pulled their housecoats tightly around them even though the temperature was still in the high seventies. The men jockeyed for position and conversed in whispers.

The door to Judy's bedroom opened and Dan stepped out. He made sure to close it behind him, cutting off the spectators' view.

"How is she?" Toby asked.

"Sleeping. I gave her a shot."

Toby handed Dan the picture. "Nothing like a case of hysteria in the middle of the night." Toby turned toward the people in the hallway. "Okay, folks, the show's over."

A plump, grandmotherly woman in her fifties pushed through the onlookers and into the room. "I'm Emma Ferguson, Mr. Mitchell. I live on two. Would you like me to stay with her until she wakes up?"

Toby deferred to Dan. "What do you think?"

"I think that would be very kind of you, Emma," he said. "I don't believe we've met. I'm Dr. Frederickson."

131

"Oh, I know you, Doctor . . . everyone does," she said with a soft smile. Having gained Dan's permission, she proceeded to park her ample body on the sofa. She'd come prepared: She had her knitting.

"I'll drop back in the morning to see how she's doing. And if you should need me, don't hesitate to call. My home number's in the directory."

"Don't you worry about a thing. I once took a nurses' aid course."

"Terrific," Toby said in an aside to Dan. "She probably thinks that gives her a license to do surgery."

Dan followed Toby downstairs to the street. The call to the station had not come from Judy, but a neighbor in the next apartment. Both he and his wife had been awakened by the screams and immediately presumed the worst. The officer Judy had run into on the street arrived quickly, put in a call for Toby, and indicated Judy needed medical help. The next call went to Dan.

The street was quiet and still slick with rain. And the lights that had come on with Toby's well-announced arrival had been turned out. As he and Dan crossed over to their cars, a cat's meow issued out of the darkness. "Based on the line of reasoning most of the people in this town have been using of late, that meow should mean that we're about to be descended upon by a witch." Toby punctuated the observation with a bubble of laughter.

"You never know." Dan smiled. "Say, did you get a chance to talk with any of the neighbors?"

"Yeah, but they didn't see anybody or anything."

"What about the building super? Somebody must have had a passkey."

"Didn't need one. A five-year-old could force the locks on those doors."

Dan shook his head, perplexed. The addition of Judy to the list did nothing but confound the situation further. Dan remembered her being at the carnival, so at least that much of the pattern was maintained. But he could see no obvious connection with the other four. Unconsciously, he gave voice to his question: "I wonder how Judy fits into all this?"

"Who knows?" Toby pulled a cigar out of his inside jacket pocket. "Give me a good old felony anytime. That I can understand." Toby opened the door to his patrol car and then let it swing closed as he walked down and joined Dan alongside the Pacer. "I gotta tell you, this thing is really starting to get out of hand. I guess you heard about Anderson's putting Charlie Cole on this?"

"Yes, I did."

Toby reached around his back to get at an itch. "Actually, he's the one that surprises me most."

"Charlie?"

"Anderson."

"In what way?"

"Well, he's really become unhinged. And all these years I thought he was pretty rational. Vindictive occasionally, but never like this."

"Well, it's one thing to cope with a business crisis —but this is something else. Let's face it, the man's frightened."

"He really believes he's being hexed."

"He is."

Toby was staggered. "Not you, too!" he said, aghast. "Is everyone in Hammin flipping out?"

For a moment, Dan teetered on the edge of speaking again. He could claim he'd made a bad choice of words and the remark would be forgotten. Or he could open the door to his past and tell Toby what he knew and what he suspected. He chose the latter.

"Toby, I think you've got a much more serious and much more deadly situation here than you suspect."

Toby's eyes were riveted to Dan's. "What are you talking about?"

"Murder. I'm sure I've never told you this, but I did

part of my medical internship in the Ivory Coast and I was assigned to a village deep in the interior. The people in that area believe in and practice voodoo with deadly efficiency. During the time I was there, I saw two men killed by it and a woman brought literally to within an inch of her life."

Toby looked at him incredulously, but said nothing.

"I know it's hard to believe, but there is no doubt in my mind that hexes or voodoo or black magic— call it what you will—work with a deadly accuracy. I know Hammin is a long way from Africa, but I'll tell you this: Much of what I saw happen there is, in one way or another, happening here."

Toby's expression had not changed. "So, what are you saying to me?"

"Simply this: Whoever's behind this knows exactly what they're doing. And what they're doing is trying to kill four people. They've already been successful once."

"You mean Reeson?"

Dan nodded.

Toby cocked his head slightly to the left and for an instant sounded as if he were cross-examining Dan. "But you yourself said Reeson died of natural causes."

"That's right. He did. Cardiac arrest. But I'm willing to give you any kind of odds that it was a hex that brought it on. Now there was nothing in my autopsy that could prove it. Voodoo doesn't leave any marks . . . there's no residue to be found in the blood because it all happens in the mind. It kills because people— despite what they say—believe in it. That belief creates fear, and fear taken to the extreme can kill you."

Toby's mind was befuddled. Not so much by what he was hearing as from whom he was hearing it. "What are you suggesting I do?"

"I don't have any suggestions except to step up our efforts to find out who's behind this." Dan read the confusion and doubt in Toby's face. He recognized it was a pretty big pill for Toby to swallow. "Trust me, Toby. I know what I'm talking about. You've got four murders in progress—right now. And I'm going to do everything I can to help you prevent them."

Toby was at a loss for words. He simply turned away, mumbled "Thanks . . . I appreciate your telling me this," and got into the squad car. "Let's talk more about it tomorrow, okay?"

Dan nodded and turned toward his car. "Good night, Toby."

What's "good" about it, Toby thought. Jesus! That's all I needed was to discover Doc's our resident expert on voodoo. Why the hell didn't he tell me this before? He could have said something the night we found Reeson's doll. And speaking of Reeson, since when is voodoo a natural death?

Toby started his car and made a big U turn in the street. He didn't like what he'd heard. He didn't like it at all, and he made up his mind to give it a lot of thought.

Dan watched Toby's car recede in the rear-view mirror. He was having regrets about what he'd said, but it was too late now. As he wound his way through the mute residential streets, he rapidly played back everything that had happened since the night of the carnival and came out where he'd begun—with questions. Who's behind it? Why are they doing this? Is there a link between the five? How does Cathy fit into this?

No answers.

He thought about what he'd told Toby about the similarities between what was happening here and what he'd seen and learned about the death of the French kola-nut plantation owner, Jean Tureau. In the Ivory Coast, native drums had carried the deadly message. In Hammin, it came by phone and in the form of written poems. In Africa, the rhythms had been orchestrated by the witch doctors. In Hammin, the beat had been set in motion by a person or persons unknown and then carried on the public pulse, which vacillated between abject fear and macabre fascination.

In Africa, the doll had been human; here they were becoming more and more humanlike. In both instances, the slow deterioration of the victims was the same.

It had taken almost a month after Dan had returned to the village of Biasempia from the inoculation blitz and his visits at the Bondoukou hospital for him to piece together the intricacies of Tureau's ouanga. At first, Dan was convinced that he would find some evidence of outright murder. It was inconceivable that the grotesque corpse rebaptized as Tureau could become the actual medium of death. But by the time he had completed his inquiries, the ouanga did not seem quite so incredible. Tureau died, Dan finally concluded, from acute psychosomatic disorders that in a very real way could be linked to the corpse in the jungle forest.

As Miizi had indicated, Tureau knew of the baptismal and of the monstrous doll. Almost immediately after the ceremony, Tureau's foreman, a native that he had come to trust, became distraught and strangely withdrawn. Tureau could not help but notice that the usually jovial, high-spirited man was deeply troubled. Always alert for some kind of treachery, he called the man into his living room and questioned him. At first the foreman seemed gravely reluctant to share his information. Tureau pressed him. The foreman muttered something about the girl Tureau raped. So they're planning some kind of retaliation, Tureau thought. He had to know what, in order to defend himself.

"Tell me, goddammit, you black bastard, or I'll cut your balls off!" he roared.

Hesitatingly and with just the right amount of trembling and fidgeting, the foreman told Tureau that a Great Ouanga had been placed on him. The man's grief appeared deep and genuine when he said, "Monsieur, I fear you will die, and soon."

Tureau, as might have been expected, greeted the news with raucous, mocking laughter. Then anger surged through his body and he kicked open the screen door and strode out on his porch. He reached deep down in his diaphragm for the force necessary to carry his words into the midst of his native workers, who had gathered by one of his sheds for their evening meal. He, Jean Tureau, was not afraid of any superstitious mumbo jumbo.

"Bring on your devil demons!" Tureau shouted. He swung around, grabbed the cowering foreman, and with all his strength, rushed him down the long porch and propeled him off onto the ground. "Go tell those witch doctor bastards that I piss in their faces with contempt. I fear no jungle magic."

But what he did fear was the possibility of assassination by more conventional means. So he took to wearing a revolver on his hip and carrying a high-powered rifle whenever he left the security of the plantation compound.

As the days went by, more reports reached him of the ouanga, and he asked some of his workers to see what they could find out. They came back with hideous, detailed descriptions of the corpse. They pictured for him what they'd heard of the clearing in the jungle, the endless incantations. The following day, word came that the doll was wearing one of his shirts. Upon checking, Tureau found that a shirt was indeed missing.

The servants in his house became oversolicitous, consoling him. If he belched at dinner, which he frequently did, they would nod to one another as a kind of confirmation that the ouanga was taking hold. A cough would bring on inquiries about how he felt. They made sure he would overhear their conversations about his ordained fate.

Tureau began to notice in himself a general lassitude

and a steady increase in gastrointestinal distress. He suspected poison. He sent samples of his food for analysis to the Bondoukou hospital. It came back negative. He called in a doctor to locate the cause of his distress. The doctor found nothing, but suggested that Tureau seemed tense, tired, and slightly neurotic. When Tureau told him of the ouanga, the doctor nodded his head ominously and prescribed a long vacation away from the plantation. Tureau responded by saying that he wasn't going to be driven from his home by this native nonsense.

That night at dusk, he became aware of the sound of distant drums. The servants informed him they carried the message of his death and that each day they would come closer, squeezing out his life. He dismissed their interpretation with ripe obscenities. They would not be dissuaded and told him of other cases similar to this. His cook frequently remarked about his languid pallor and his maid regarded him with a long, sympathetic face. Tureau's temper hovered constantly at the flash point. He sought help from the local magistrates. They derided his concerns and mocked his "belief in that nonsense." He disclaimed any belief, but feared for his life nevertheless. He was told to find the corpse and then the police would arrest the guilty parties . . . for stealing his shirt.

Tureau made up his mind to find the doll and destroy it. He questioned his field hands, but all they could tell him was that it was deep in the jungle in a secret place that only the witch doctors knew. And when he sought out the witch doctors, they were not to be found.

The drums drew closer. The beat was always the same: simple and repetitious. Tureau found he was beginning to have difficulty keeping food down and grew weaker. His house maid reported she'd heard a cord had been tied around the neck of the corpse and each day it was being drawn tighter. Did he feel any

constriction in his throat? Did he find his wind pipe
clogged? Until then, he had not. "I hear it in the
drums," she told him. "They're cutting off your air."
By the following morning, Tureau had become very
conscious of his breathing and noticed, or thought he
noticed, an occasional tightening in his throat and chest.
The more he thought about it, the more frequently he
found himself stopping to take deep breaths to try to
relieve the creeping sense of pressure.

In the days that followed, he ranted and swore,
accusing all his servants of poisoning him. He demanded to know who was guilty. He brandished his
pistol at them, fired shots at their feet. But always, they
responded with commiseration and pity. There was
nothing they could do, they said, but make his last
days comfortable.

Fear was consuming him. The drums beat day and
night. When his attention was diverted, the natives on
the plantation added to the din by pounding out the
rhythm on trees, on metal oil drums, on the side of
his house. It was closing in, inexorably. Dan learned
that in Tureau's last hours, his raving ceased. He lay
on his bed paralyzed with keen cognizance of his impending death. He died, shriveled into a fetal position,
huddled in a dark corner of his bedroom.

Upon analyzing the factors surrounding his death,
Dan concluded that the doll, in and of itself, had no
supernatural powers, although he recognized that the
natives believed it did. It was, he decided, a symbol,
something for everyone, including Tureau, to focus
attention on.

Tureau's demise came about as a result of what
psychiatrists call a compulsive neurosis which had been
externally induced through autosuggestion. The initial
suggestion of his illnesses, of course, had come from
the natives. In time, the suggestions had taken root in
Tureau's mind and tapped some very real, if latent,
fears. The drums and the corpse were all part of a

major orchestration to provide reminders . . . inducements to keep him thinking. In the face of this constant reinforcement, he became aware of his visceral organs and every pain or twitch became a source of concern. Once having accepted—even subconsciously—that the ouanga might be having some effect, he began to generate his own worries. Fear began to eat at him, and at that point, his fate was sealed. Like people suffering from psychosomatic illness, it was the mental fiction that caused the physical deterioration.

It's all here in Hammin, Dan thought. The same pattern. Except in place of Tureau's servants and plantation workers, Carole, Anderson, Crawford, and now Judy have the good people of Hammin to provide the constant reminder of the hex. Instead of the repetitious drums, they have the constant buzz of whispered rumor and speculation. Dan felt the burden pressing down on his shoulders. Only *he* understood what was really happening. He and whoever had initiated the hex. In the jungle, he had been taught how to break an ouanga. But that required knowing the source.

As he sped along 421 to his trailer, he wondered if he should tell them what he knew. It might help them cope with it, he thought. After all, they're rational, intelligent people. Correction. They're frightened people —that makes a big difference. And I won't be able to answer the two most basic questions: Who? and Why?

Dan took his foot off the accelerator and began to brake for the dirt-road turnoff that led to the lake and his trailer. He swung the steering wheel to the right and automatically prepared himself for the jarring ruts and bumps to come.

At that moment, a pair of headlights broke the night at the point where 421 met the horizon. The driver was pushing his small van up toward its limit. He was late and there were several stops to make before dawn. In the back of his truck were large canvas postal bags of

mail for the people of Hammin and several towns beyond. The white-and-blue truck with the red trim
flashed by Dan's road and on into town.

In one of the bags there was a letter addressed to
Toby Mitchell. The contents, once known, would tear
at Dan's guts and begin a chain of events that would
put everything into an entirely different perspective.

xi

The headlights of Charlie Cole's car washed over the front of Anderson North's house as he pulled into the drive. He got out and lumbered up the front steps, crossed the porch, and rang the bell.

Hilda answered the door. "Oh, it's you, Mr. Cole." Her eyes searched his face expectantly. His expression told her nothing.

"G'evening, Hilda. Mr. North home?"

"They're both here. Come in." Hilda ushered him to the double doors leading to Anderson's library. Anderson was in his bathrobe, tilted back in his recliner. Rita was busying herself at the desk, answering some letters and occasionally glancing over at the television which, at Anderson's insistence, was playing without sound. They both looked up a little surprised to see Hilda standing in front of them. She had a cat-like way of entering rooms that Anderson numbered among her many irritating habits.

"Mr. Cole is here to see you."

As Charlie entered the room, Anderson brought his chair to a sitting position. "Where have you been for the last two days?"

"Didn't you get my message?"

"Yeah, something about following up a lead. But you didn't say anything about being gone for two days. Have you heard about that Simpson woman?"

Charlie nodded, "Yes, about an hour ago when I stopped for dinner. It was the number-one topic of conversation."

Rita looked at Cole with great distress and let out a mournful sigh. "Oh, Charlie, I wish you could find out what this is all about. I swear, it's destroying Anderson."

"Rita!" Anderson snapped. He turned to Charlie. "Well, what did you find with this lead of yours? And where have you been?"

Charlie sat down in an overstuffed chair and pulled out his notebook. "I've been to a carnival."

"The same group that was here in Hammin?"

"The same. Took me about five dollars' worth of phone calls to track it down, but I found them up in Hendersonville. It occurred to me that the time had come to have a talk with Madame Miranda. This business of all the victims being at the show that night was just too much of a coincidence—plus this girl that everyone but you, Mr. North, seemed to recognize. . . ."

Anderson stood up to fix himself a drink and Charlie paused. "Go on, I'm listening."

"Well, the first night I decided just to see the show and do a little nosing around. It was pretty much the same as you people described it, except there wasn't any seance. I've got to hand it to that woman. I know mind reading is a lot of nonsense, but I sure couldn't figure out how she did it."

"Look, Charlie, I don't want every detail. Just tell me what you found out." Anderson gulped down his drink.

Charlie flipped through the pages of his note pad. "The psychic's real name is Pauline Baoukas and she's got an assistant by the name of Homer Vivian. Strange bird, that one," he added parenthetically. "Anyway, on the second night I went backstage after the show and asked about the seance. She said she does them occasionally when the spirit moves her—sorry, no pun intended. That night in Hammin she felt an overwhelming, almost demanding urge to hold the seance. Claims that when she does one of those things, she's totally unconscious and that as a medium she has no control over who appears or what happens."

"Bullshit!" Anderson said bitterly. "It was some kind of effect."

"You don't have to convince me, okay? I even tried to get this Homer character to open up. But all he'd say is that the materialization was real and that if my friends saw a Cathy Parks, then that's who they saw. I'll give that guy one thing—he's loyal. I offered him up to five hundred dollars to tell me the truth, but I couldn't budge him. Insisted it was authentic."

"It's always nice to hear about a loyal employee," Anderson said with sarcasm, "but what else did you find out?"

"The woman did recall one other name. It had come to her very strongly that evening, but she never got around to mentioning it." Charlie shifted uncomfortably in his chair.

"Whose name was that?" Anderson asked.

"Yours."

"Mine!"

"Anderson's!" Rita said simultaneously.

A queasy feeling made Anderson sit down on the arm of the recliner. "Aside from this woman's knowing my name, what you're telling me is that you've really come back with nothing."

"I wouldn't say that. I've come back with what I regard as a more complete picture, okay? I have to work a lot on instinct, every investigator does. And my instinct says that she's a very big piece of the puzzle."

Anderson walked over and put his hand on Charlie's shoulder. "Look, don't misunderstand me, you've got my complete confidence. You haven't failed me before, and I know you won't now."

Charlie looked up at him gratefully. "I appreciate your saying that. And don't worry, we'll sort this all out, okay? You can bank on that."

"Come on, I'll walk you out," Anderson said, opening the double doors.

Charlie dutifully followed him down the hall and out onto the front porch. He was about to separate the steps from the darkness when Anderson stopped him.

"Look, Charlie, as you dig further into this, ah. . . ." Anderson fumbled for words. "Look, as you find things . . . now don't misunderstand, but I'd like to screen anything you dig up."

"Mr. North, you know that my information is for your eyes only."

"I know, I know. I guess what I'm saying is that I'd like to reduce Rita's exposure to all this. So I'd appreciate from now on if you'd give me your reports in private."

"I understand, Mr. North."

"What's your next move?"

"I think maybe it's time I had a talk with Crawford Spencer."

"Bastard," Anderson muttered.

Charlie responded quickly, "If you don't want me to talk with Spencer, just say the word."

"No, no. Go ahead. Don't let my prejudices influence your investigation."

"Well, I'll be going now," Charlie said somewhat lamely and hurried off the porch.

Anderson retied the belt on his robe and jammed his hands into the pockets. Charlie's lights blinded him momentarily as he backed out. He stayed on the porch for several minutes. I think maybe I know *why,* he said to himself. I just don't know *who.* But the prospect of knowing brought no satisfaction, only the heavy dread that a past indiscretion might surface.

The lake in front of Dan's trailer was a flat gold mirror. Only the frothy lapping on the sandy edge gave the lie to its glasslike surface. The July afternoon had been pleasantly warm. Dan and Carole had devoted most of their time to weeding his organic vegetable garden and bringing some order to a flower bed run riot. Toward evening he did two Cornish game hens on his charcoal spit and assigned Carole the task of concocting a sauce for the birds and creating something original in the way of salad dressing. Anything to keep her mind occupied. That, in total, had been his objective for the day. His success had been sporadic. From time to time, Dan could see her start to slip into the morass of uncertainty and doubt, then fight her way out.

By dusk they'd finished their coffee and adjourned to the end of his small pier with a bottle of Grand Marnier. Their backs rested against a large board that Dan had installed for the purpose of making sunset watching more comfortable. The sky turned from crimson to gold to cameo pink to azure. The evening had not cooled as expected and Dan felt rivulets of perspiration coursing down his body. He slipped off his pants and shirt and slid into the water.

Softened by wine and the liqueur, Carole did not hesitate to doff her shorts and blouse and follow him. They swam together in perfect unison toward the middle of the lake, then turned around and headed back to the short stretch of sandy beach and lay on their backs to take in the pebbly sky. There was a long silence. Dan was afraid Carole had lapsed back into her despondency.

"Do you want to talk about it?" Dan asked.

Carole did not respond immediately. What was there to say? All she could do was recount the fear, reask the questions, and find no satisfaction or comfort in either. She could tell him of an incident several days before. She had been on the street by the courthouse late one afternoon doing some shopping and noticed she was being followed. It was a little girl of about eight, a patient of Dan's named Deanna. The little girl was weeping and Carole beckoned to her. The little girl walked up, rubbing her eyes with the back of a grimy hand. Carole bent down and held out her arms. "What's wrong, Deanna?" she asked comfortingly.

Her little chest heaved up and down with each sob. "Oh, Miss Peters . . . please don't die, please don't die!"

Carole had absorbed the full impact of the blow. She blanched, stood up, turned, and walked briskly down the street, giving all the appearance of having some urgent business. At the corner she turned and saw the little girl, still sobbing, being led away by her mother. Her thoughts spun out in all directions with frenetic abandon. I don't know what I'm doing. Where am I going? What should I do? Tears welled up and spilled over, but it was dusk and the few people on the streets could not see them.

The knot of despair throbbed with increasing intensity as she found her car and got in. She drove home, went inside, climbed the stairs to what had been her mother's and father's bedroom. As a child, waking from a nightmare, she had run on tiptoe down the hall to their room and snuggled in between them, their bodies a fortress against the terrors of the night. She found herself once again climbing into their bed, so many years vacant, looking for the solace of long-ago comforts. She wept unashamedly into the pillow until exhaustion brought on a merciful, dreamless sleep.

She could tell Dan about that. But to what end? There was nothing to do but wait and hope that she could last until this silent horror had run its course. Again, she heard Dan asking, "Do you want to talk about it?"

"No," she said with a firmness that surprised her. "I want to talk about us." She turned her head toward his and tried to read his eyes through the veil of darkness. "What am I to you?" she asked with intensity. "What am I really?"

The questions caught Dan completely by surprise. "I don't understand."

Carole recalled the promise she'd made to herself not to push, to let him come to her in his own time. But promises didn't seem to matter now. "Why aren't we living together? Why are we keeping up this ruse of celibacy?" Her voice was growing more strident now. "Why am I living in that big empty house when I should be here?"

Dan grappled for an answer. "Well, I didn't want people to talk."

"Fuck people!" she shouted. In all her life she had never used that word. She tried not to register her own surprise.

Dan jerked to a sitting position. His mouth opened but nothing came out.

"I understand you, my darling, better than you think." She was totally in control now. "I know you don't want to be tied to anything. You want to feel that you can pick up and walk out of Hammin any time you please. You want to delude yourself into thinking that you owe them nothing and they owe you nothing. Pay as you go. But it doesn't work that way. You've given too much and we've accepted. You've let us need you, depend on you. And that's a commitment. You could say that you've never asked me to love you. You could say that you've never asked me to come share your bed or lie with you on this beach. And you'd be right. I've done it of my own free will. But what we've shared transcended the physical a long time ago. And you know that. You've given me a part of you and I've accepted . . . as you wanted me to. That's a commitment. I want to live with you, Dan, married or otherwise—I don't care. Or I want to be free of you. I know I can never have you totally. My mother taught me that. But I can accept it."

Drained from her outburst, Carole turned away. She

had said it all and left no retreat. The thought sobered her and brought on a shiver. Then she felt Dan's arms take her.

"You're right," he said tenderly. "I have made a commitment. And it's one I want to keep."

She leaned back into him, but did not give him her face. I'll find a Justice of the Peace tonight, he thought. He caught himself. No. I'm sure this is right. We should be married. But I want to feel this way in the cold light of morning. We'll wait till August. Silently, he laughed derisively at himself. You goddamn coward. You've been a bachelor too long. But another voice inside said, Yes, but it's hard to give up. It's so easy this way. The first voice answered back, But I don't want to be alone. I don't want to lose her. And who says we have to stay here? Why would marrying her tie me down? It wouldn't. In a very real way, it would probably set us both free.

"August 26th," he said.

"That's my birthday," Carole said, turning to him.

"Let's make it our anniversary, too."

"I'm not asking you. You don't have to."

"I know."

Later they went back into the water to wash off the sand. The more Dan talked about getting married, the more he found the prospect appealing. His banter was light, and Carole found his mood contagious and laughed at his growing delight. He was a little boy with a new toy he had thought he wouldn't like, but then discovered it to be his favorite.

As they talked in bed, Dan took no notice of Carole's steady, pensive retreat. His last waking thought was one of contentment. For that reason, he was not prepared when he awoke early the next morning to find Carole up, dressed, and saying, "About last night— let's not set a date just now."

Her words swept away any thoughts of going back to sleep. "What? But I thought——"

"Consider it a woman's prerogative to change her mind. I love you, Dan." Her voice was sullen and she averted his searching gaze. "I just need time."

Dan laughed through his confusion. "What is this, a role change?"

"We'll talk about it," she said, starting down the hall to the living room end of the trailer. "I've got to go now or I'll be late."

"Late for what?"

She was out the door. If she heard him, she gave no indication, but hurried for her car. Had Dan been able to see her face, he would have refused to let her go without an explanation. The impassive exterior she'd shown him was graying with pain. All night she had lain there by his side, fully awake, chasing memories that refused to be driven off . . . or forgiven. At dawn, she told herself there was no way she could marry him and live on the edge of a lie.

xii

The Hammin Inn had never been busier . . . nor quieter. Like the others, Judy became the focus of stolen glances. Questions papered the faces of the patrons. There was a genuine sympathy and occasionally quiet offers to be of help. And yet, beneath their compassionate exteriors, they were glad. Glad it wasn't them. However, this "Better you than me" feeling did not sit comfortably, and Judy detected a sense of guilt in her friends that she could not understand.

Work at the inn was rapidly becoming intolerable for her. At those times when she would be out in the kitchen, she could hear Skeet Fischer bawling out customers for some thoughtless comment or intruding question. She appreciated his concern, but it only added to her gnawing despondency.

The morning after she found the picture in her apartment, she awoke to find Emma Ferguson looming over her with a benign smile. Until that time, the rotund, grandmotherly woman had been no more than the occupant of 2C. Dan arrived as promised, relieving Mrs. Ferguson, and sat with Judy for over an hour, calming her, reassuring her. He told her of Anderson's decision to bring in Charlie Cole and pointed out that there had been no violence nor was there likely to be any. After his second cup of coffee, he left, telling her to call any time she felt the need to talk.

Judy thanked him, but knew full well that she would not call. Not him. She would keep her own counsel. Later that afternoon, Judy found herself sitting alone in the Hammin Inn. It was too late for the lunch crowd and too early for the cocktail hour. Skeet was out front on a ladder washing windows. Judy aimlessly nursed a tomato juice and lit another cigarette. The pay phone on the wall behind her rang. She turned, leaned back, and took the receiver off the hook.

"Hello, Hammin Inn."

The voice on the other end was soft and melodious. "Judith, Judith, turn to clay. In fire of fever waste away." She dropped the phone and made a dash for the front door.

Skeet tried to comfort her, but Judy tore off her apron and went home.

Outside the air-conditioned bar, the sidewalks were giving up the heat of the day. The air was very still and extremely close. Beads of perspiration broke out on her forehead. Her breath came short and for a moment she felt as though she might suffocate.

She passed several people—Hammin Inn regulars —on the way to her apartment. Either they didn't notice her or had the decency not to stare or comment. Whatever the case, she was grateful.

Inside the building, Judy headed quickly for the stairway. The steps all seemed to be two feet high. She grasped the railing with her right hand, leaned forward a little, and pulled herself up. A cool bath, she thought, a cool bath.

A door cracked open slightly on the second floor. Eyes watched as the blond head emerged above floor level. Judy stepped onto the landing, swung around, and headed for the flight of stairs leading to the third floor.

"Hello, Miss Simpson." The greeting came from the darkness behind the door.

Startled, Judy wheeled in the direction of the voice.

Emma Ferguson swung open the door revealing her rotund silhouette. "I'm sorry, Miss Simpson, if I frightened you. I saw you from my window. Home early this evening for a change?"

Judy nodded and started to turn away.

"Have you got a minute?"

"I'm very tired," Judy said, trying to beg off any invitation that might follow.

"Well, I'm not surprised with all that has been going on. You must be under quite a strain. Terrible what a thing like this can do to a person. But if you'll step in, I promise to keep you only a moment."

"Another time, maybe. Thanks."

"There might not be another time . . . for you," Emma said flatly.

Judy furrowed her brow and squinted into the dark recess where the woman stood. "What are you talking about?"

"Come in," Emma beckoned. "I think you'll find what I have to say most helpful."

Judy hesitated, then reluctantly let herself be drawn into the apartment. Emma stepped aside to let her pass, then closed the door. The living room was strangely vacant—a throw rug on the floor, simple furniture, and no pictures on the walls. It was the antithesis of what one would have expected to find in the apartment of an elderly single woman.

She offered Judy a straight-backed chair with a simulated needlepoint seat. "There now, just make yourself comfortable." Emma crossed the room to a small table on which she'd already placed a tea pot and two cups. The second cup told Judy she'd been expected. "I was just about to have a little tea. Would you care for some? It's good and hot."

Emma picked up the pot and carefully poured herself a cup. "I've been worried about you since that night. And I've noticed that this hex business has been taking its toll, Miss Simpson." She sat down slowly in a wooden rocker across from Judy. "Yes, I can see that it's been taking its toll."

Judy stood up. "Look, I've had a long day. . . ."

Emma's smile faded and she began to rock. "I know

a woman. She helps people like you." Emma paused to let Judy's curiosity peak. "She's a witch."

"A witch?" Judy scoffed.

Emma was not put off. "This woman practices only white magic. She's an exorcist. She knows how to break spells and hexes. I'm sure she can help you."

Judy's impulse was to get out of the room as fast as possible and enclose herself within the comforting confines of her own apartment. "Look, I don't need any help . . . I'm fine. Now I think I'll go on upstairs." Judy turned toward the door, aware that the woman's eyes were boring into her back.

"Go ahead," Emma said. "I understand. You think it over. When you're ready, let me know and I'll make the arrangements." Her rocking picked up in tempo. "Whenever you're ready, I'll be here."

Judy closed the door and mumbled, "Jesus, God! She wants me to see a witch." Her laughter rose as she climbed the stairs. It ebbed just on the edge of hysteria.

The officer on duty in the station was tilted back in his chair, feet up on the desk, reading a well-worn copy of a slightly pornographic novel. At intervals he sucked on a sixteen-ounce Pepsi. The outside door swung open and Toby entered, shooting the officer a look that brought his feet off the desk. The policeman put away the book and sat up, trying to project a semblance of officialness. He straightened up the papers on which his feet had been resting and watched Toby give the soda machine the side of his fist as a prod to ensure that it would yield a bottle.

"Oh, Chief, this came in for you from the state."

Toby snapped off the cap with the opener, then turned to see what the officer was talking about. Toby took the official-looking envelope and read the return address. "I've been waiting for this."

"It came in a couple of days ago."

Toby stared at him in disbelief. "Were you trying to keep this a secret, or is this your week to obstruct the postal service?"

"Gosh, Chief . . . it's been sittin' right here. I figured you'd seen it."

"Forget it," Toby said, entering his office. He tore open the envelope expectantly. Inside were the results of his penchant for tying up loose ends. The night Dan and he had found Duff Reeson's doll at the hospital, Toby had made a mental note to run a routine check on Madame Miranda and Cathy Parks. Two days later, he'd sent a formal request to the state's R&I for any information they might have on the two women. Almost as an afterthought, he'd included the name of Duff Reeson.

Toby pulled the neatly folded pages out of the envelope and sat down behind his desk. There was nothing on a "Madame Miranda," and that disappointed him. But Reeson's and Cathy's records made up for it. He scrutinized the data for a long while, trying to unravel it in terms of the dolls and the hex threat. The information made interesting reading, but he could not make a connection. He picked up the phone and, after two tries, finally got through to Dan at his office and asked him to stop by.

As Dan walked in, Toby got up and cleared off the only other chair in his office. "Have a seat."

"What's this all about?" Dan asked.

"Well, it occurred to me that maybe there was more to Reeson's death than we suspected. And it also occurred to me that the girl, Cathy Parks, might figure into all this somehow. So I ran a check through R&I and they came up with some very interesting reading material."

Dan's eyes fell on the computer printouts in Toby's hand.

Toby held up the first page. "Duff Reeson. Seems he spent a good deal of time upstate. Police picked him up, ah—" Toby adjusted his glasses "—three different times as a suspected narcotics pusher. According to this, nobody was able to make anything stick." Toby handed Dan the page.

"He wasn't on the stuff himself. I checked for that during the autopsy."

Toby held up the second page. "*He* may not have been, but a friend of his was. Cathy Parks."

"I don't believe it! Not possible," Dan said with total conviction.

Toby handed him the printout. "See for yourself. They busted her twice for possession, and the record indicates she was an addict. Her third bust was for possible trafficking, and they booked her in the Monroe County jail. Look who put up bail."

"Duff Reeson," Dan read. The report confirmed everything Toby had said.

"You'll notice she had a court date for sometime in March of that year."

Dan stared at the page incredulously. "I can't believe this. March. That was only—" he counted on his fingers "—just six months after she disappeared." He read the report again, looking for an explanation. "All this happened to her in six months? My God!" Suddenly he turned defensive. "Something's wrong. She wasn't into any of this." He dropped the paper back on Toby's desk, glad to be rid of it. "There's got to be a mistake. It can't be the same girl. She couldn't have changed that much in six months."

Toby said nothing and showed no expression as he handed him the next page. It had a front- and a side-view mug shot. "You tell me. Is this her?"

It was not the Cathy he'd known. Oh, the features were the same, but the pictures seemed to reflect only a mask drained of all the life that had made her what she was to Dan. "That's her," he said softly. "I don't understand." He looked at the picture again. He felt something go out of him. And it was lost forever.

The depth of Dan's reaction came as somewhat of a surprise to Toby. He had not known Dan that well three years ago, and he certainly was not aware of any relationship Dan might have had with one of his patients. But the distress etched on Dan's face made it clear there was more between him and Cathy Parks than Toby would have presumed. That discovery disturbed Toby. He wasn't immediately sure why, nor could he specify exactly what it was that bothered him. Yet something told him there were questions to be asked, if only he knew what they were.

"You said she had a court date," Dan said, placing the mug shots on the desk. "Were you able to find out what happened?"

Toby picked up the last piece of paper. "Well, she was supposed to be in court on March 10th, but she never made it. This item is dated March the 5th." Toby read the words with almost as little emotion as the computer that had printed them. " 'Parks, Cathy. Age 22. Cause of death, overdose of barbiturates. Ruled suicide by the medical examiner, Monroe County.' "

They have spent the entire Labor Day together roaming the vacant meadowlands across the lake from Dan's trailer. She is running toward the top of a low rise. Her laughter lifts into the air like a handful of leaves in the wind and drifts down to where Dan sits on the blanket finishing the last of their picnic.

It has been six weeks since she left the hospital. The lines of the doctor-patient relationship have blurred. Only recently has he begun to try to analyze the nature and origin of his feelings toward her. There is a physical magnetism, of course. She has a beautifully pro-

portioned face—high cheek bones, classic American-girl nose, blue eyes that have the ability to come alive with love. A slender, lithesome body . . . the stuff of which fantasies are born. There is also a certain inno-cence, slightly brittle at the edges, but nonetheless there, inviting Dan to play his role as protector. She is also, for him, the quintessence of the mysterious woman. Everything about her before that morning in the motel is a void. He has never pressed her for an explanation. Never asked, Who? In a curious way, he feels to probe her past would be like asking the butter-fly about its previous life as a caterpillar. In the reality of now, it does not matter. Later, perhaps.

Dan pours the last of the Fumé Blanc and watches her pull down the bough of an apple tree on the crest of the rise. She lets the limb snap back and runs toward him. Her yellow cotton skirt billows up, reveal-ing firm, slender legs. Her happiness cascades over him as she presents the booty from her foray on some unknown farmer's tree. The wine and the proximity of her face make his thoughts swirl. His pulse beats faster. He borders on the kind of delirium most often reserved for first loves.

As recently as three weeks ago, his regard for her had been mostly paternal, due both to his professional role and the gulf of twelve years which separates them. That has vanished now and their relationship is rush-ing to that point in time which demands decision: to be lovers, or to be acquaintances with a history of private memories.

She looks up at him expectantly. Her eyes dance over his face, looking for a sign, an indication that the decision has been made. His hands slide onto her arms. She is warm and soft to his touch. He has not intended to fall in love with her. He has promised himself to resist any entanglement. Yet her love, his passions, and the ardor set free by the wine demand that he draw her face to his, that he make a commitment and consummate it there in the verdant field.

He forces himself to mentally step back, to weigh the gravity and the implication of his choices. Cathy has suffered in that void before he met her. This he has detected in unguarded comments and vague inferences. She is not to be sacrificed to the instincts of the moment. He cares too much for that. Now must be forever, or not at all. Her breath is coming faster. Her hands slowly rise and cup his face. He teeters on the edge.

A thunderclap. A gust of cool wind. The decision is held in limbo.

Cathy looks over his shoulder. "It's going to rain," she says. Dan glances off to his right. A small three-sided shed, abandoned by the animals that must have grazed here sometime in the past, offers them a place to wait out the storm. In a flurry of motion, they pick up the picnic things, the blanket, and run for the shelter. Its fourth side opens to the lake and they press themselves against the back wall to deny the sheets of rain. "I love a summer storm," she says. "Everything smells so sweet afterward." There is a glow on her face that comes from deep inside.

The rain and the reprieve have sobered him. He needs time. What does he really know about her? This is just a mutual intoxication, an infatuation growing from our personal needs. We must let it develop. See where it goes. Why am I fighting this, he asks himself. Why don't I just let go? I can't. It would not be fair to her. I must be sure. She cannot take any more pain. I must be very gentle. But my God, Cathy . . . I think I really love you.

He takes her hand and his touch ignites a smile that flows over her face. Lightning crackles across the sky. She feels secure with him. And in that instant of time that comes but rarely and flees so rapidly, he envisions them marrying, having children, and living forever as they are in this moment.

Another streak of lightning. Together they turn to watch the astral pyrotechnics. Neither can know that these are to be their last hours together.

xiii

Mondays, during the summer, the country club was closed. The caddies had their run of the golf course and the grounds people tried to perform one-day miracles on the greens. Crawford Spencer lived just off the fifteenth hole in one of a clump of Alpine-style condominiums. He sat on the raised wood deck that jutted out from the living room and watched as one of the caddies arched a beautiful six iron to the heart of the green, leaving the ball about six feet from the cup.

"The putt will tell me how good he is," Crawford mumbled.

"What?" Natalie said, looking up from her magazine.

"Nothing. Just talking to myself."

Since their reconciliation—if one could call it that —Natalie had been a constant presence in his life, administering to all his physical needs. She was stretched out on a nearby chaise longue clothed only in a sheer gown that did nothing to conceal her ample body. As she leaned back, closed her eyes, and lifted her face to the sun, Crawford imagined himself rising slowly out of his chair and gently descending on her. He tried to feel her pulsing under him, hear her rapid breathing and encouragements and commands. Fantasies were not the norm for Crawford, but he had hoped that it might excite his languid passions. The mind was willing, but nothing else was.

He turned back to the fifteenth hole in time to see the caddy leave the putt a foot short of the hole. No guts, he thought to himself. Gotta charge that hole.

He glanced down at the tray on the table in front of him and picked at the remains of the brunch Natalie had prepared for him. It was cold.

"Well, I can't lie here all day. I've got to do some shopping or we won't have anything to eat tonight." With that, Natalie got up and went inside. There was a domestic tone in her voice that Crawford found offensive. But he said nothing.

Within a few minutes, Natalie reappeared, dressed, car keys in hand. She gave Crawford a kiss on the cheek and left. He did not watch her go, but stared aimlessly across the rolling fairways. The sun was directly overhead, bearing down and inviting sleep. He must have dozed, for the next thing Crawford knew his name was being called from below the porch deck. He gathered his senses and leaned forward to look over the railing.

'So this is the way golf pros spend their Mondays," Charlie Cole said, smiling up at him. "I was going to give you a call, but since I was in the neighborhood I thought I'd drop in and see if I could catch you."

"You want to come up and have a beer or something?" Crawford's offer was indifferent at best.

"Love it." And with that Charlie went inside, climbed the short staircase, entered the living room, and made his way through the large sliding screen doors to the deck.

"In the cooler." Crawford pointed to a fiberglass ice chest by the railing. "Help yourself."

Charlie pulled out a beer and then sat down next to the circular table that Crawford and Natalie used for meals. He took a long drag from the can, set it down, and mopped the edges of his mouth with the back of his hand.

"Is this social, Charlie? Or has North decided to foreclose on my mortgage?"

Charlie smiled. "Well, I am actually here on business, but nothing like what you're talking about. I guess you heard that Mr. North has got me looking into this hex. It was supposed to be on the Q.T. but in this town nothing is secret for long."

"Yeah. I heard the day after he'd put you on it." Crawford looked at him with a half smile on his lips. Charlie was a bit of a bore, but a tolerable one. Throughout the sporting goods store bankruptcy proceedings, Charlie had provided the bridge between Anderson and him. And Crawford felt that Charlie sympathetically, if not actively, sided with him. For that reason, none of Crawford's resentment and vindictiveness toward Anderson had spilled over onto him.

Charlie rambled on for a few moments, seeming to be trying to find some way to bring the conversation around to the purpose of his visit. Finally, he gave up looking for a smooth transition and broke in on himself.

"Let me tell you why I'm here, okay? I've got some theories about this hex business, but I need help in trying to fit the pieces together. I wonder if you'd mind my asking a few questions." Charlie went on quickly to add some clarification to his request. "This is just for my own information, okay? I mean, you understand, I'll be discreet."

Inwardly, Crawford was amused by what he read as Charlie's embarrassment at having to play his role as investigator.

"Ask anything you like." Crawford grinned. "Of course, I can't promise to answer everything. I mean, I have some very staid reputations to protect."

Charlie gave him a knowing look. "So I've heard." Charlie took out his note pad and flipped open the cover. "As of right now, all my thinking pretty much centers on the girl that 'appeared' out at the carnival, okay? My instinct says she fits into the picture somehow."

Crawford was skeptical. "You really think so?"

"Well, let's just say that I'm speculating at this

point. But let me just run this thing out on a line and see how it hangs."

Crawford nodded his acquiescence.

Charlie picked up his book. "Doc Frederickson tells me you recognized the girl. That true?"

"Yeah, I did. And I might add, she was about the last person I expected to see that night."

"Where'd you seen her before?"

"We went together for a while."

"Went together, huh?" Charlie made a notation on his pad. "You must have known her pretty well."

"I thought I did. But the Cathy Parks I knew wasn't the type to work in a psychic act like that."

"Then you don't think the materialization was real?"

"Ah, come on!" Crawford said sarcastically. "Are you kidding?"

Charlie offered only a slight smile in reply. "How long ago was it that you went with her?"

"Hmmm . . . three years."

"I'm sure it's hard to remember details that far back, but do you recall the last time you saw her? The month will do."

"June."

"First or last half of the month?"

"First part, I'd say."

"First part," Charlie echoed, writing it down. "And you met her when?"

Crawford thought for a moment. "Must have been sometime in April of that year."

"Not one of your longer courtships, was it?"

"Listen, anything over a month is a long time for me."

"Was this Cathy from around here?"

"Tell you the truth, I don't know where she was from. I met her at the bus depot. A lot of the supplies in our pro shop and caddie house are sent in by bus. They have this express service for small packages; when something comes in, they give me a call and I go down and get it. That's what I was doing the day I met Cathy. Must have been late afternoon. I walked in and saw her sitting there in the waiting room all alone. Now one thing you don't see in Hammin very often is good-looking women hanging around the bus depot. So when I picked up the package, I asked the agent about her. He said she'd missed her bus and that the next one wasn't until the following morning. Well, to make a long story short, I introduced myself. We talked, and then I offered to put her up for the night. I mean, she couldn't have stayed there."

"Sounds a little like the fox taking the chicken back to his den for protection."

"Yeah, and she was the fox. Jesus, that girl could fuck. Hell, we didn't get out of bed for three days."

Charlie seemed to force a smile. Then he raised his hand slightly to interrupt. "Three days? Didn't you say she had a bus leaving the next morning?"

Crawford chuckled. "She missed it."

Charlie plodded on with his questions. "Had she been visiting in Hammin?"

A quizzical look passed over Crawford's face. "You know, I haven't the foggiest idea. I guess she must have been passing through. Otherwise she probably wouldn't have been there all alone."

"Why didn't you ask what she was doing here?"

"I'm not so sure I didn't. Seems to me it was more a matter of her not telling me. In fact, as I think back, she was sort of at loose ends, if you know what I mean. It was one extreme or the other. One day she couldn't get enough of me, then just like that she'd get depressed and I couldn't even so much as talk to her, much less get her in bed. Finally, I decided the hell with her. I didn't need all that hassle."

"So what happened?"

"We split."

"Do you know where she went?"

"She took a room across town some place."

"Was that the last time you saw her?"

Crawford didn't answer, but stood up and walked over to the railing, then looked back at Charlie askance. "Why is it that I get the feeling that this is turning into an inquisition? Are you trying to tell me something?"

Charlie broke into short spasm of laughter. "You should be the detective. Just goes to show, you should never try to be too clever. Let me level with you. What I was trying to do was see if you knew about her being pregnant."

How in the hell did he find out about that, Crawford wondered. "Yeah, I knew."

"Was it yours, do you think?"

Crawford looked away and purposely made his answer oblique. "You'd think a twenty-two-year-old woman in this day and age would have been on the pill or something. Especially one that had been around as much as she had."

"I guess you also know about Doc Frederickson finding her in that motel out on the interstate?"

Crawford's head snapped back and his eyes bore down hard on Charlie. "What are you talking about?"

"He found her in the Sunset Motel. Apparently she'd had an abortion and somebody hacked her up pretty bad. The way he described it, she almost died."

Crawford blanched and sat forward in his chair. "I never heard a thing about that. Honest to God, I never knew a thing about it."

It is a soft June evening. Crawford stands at his bar fixing drinks for Rita North. She has resisted his suggestion to sit out on the deck. It is her first time here and she fidgets and speaks in nervous, short sentences. Crawford is mildly amused, but his comments seek only to reassure her. No one can see her there. No one will find out. Anderson will never know.

The doorbell rings. Rita tenses, stands up, and looks

*for someplace to hide. Crawford is not expecting any-
one. He tells her to wait in the bedroom as he walks
down the short flight of stairs to the entrance alcove.
Again the bell rings. Anderson? No, he's out of town.
Crawford opens the door. Cathy! It's been almost three
weeks since he saw her last. His immediate thought is
that she is going to ask if she can come back. She
doesn't.*

*"I'm pregnant," she tells him. Immediately, Craw-
ford challenges the implication that it's his. "There was
no one else," she responds. "No one." "I have company," he says. "Let me call you tomorrow." She will
not be put off. "No, you have responsibilities." Crawford denies them. "You should have been more careful." Marriage is out. They both know that. Long
silences fall between words. Got to get her out of here,
he thinks.*

*Finally, Crawford suggests an abortion and tells her
that he can have it arranged. Cathy resists the idea,
but Crawford asks her to consider the alternatives.
"It's early still. It would be very simple. Think it over,
Cathy, and call me in the morning. And don't worry,
I'll pay for everything. Now, I'm sorry to have to rush
you off, but I've got company." She lowers her head
to hide the hurt and desolation. "You should have told
me you weren't using anything," he says. "You should
have told me."*

*Cathy does not call the next morning . . . or the
next. But on the third day, she calls and asks him to
make the arrangements.*

Crawford looked at Charlie quizzically for a long
moment and then challenged him. "Are you saying
Cathy is behind all this? Is she the one sending the
pictures?"

"Not very likely," Charlie said matter-of-factly. "I
might have considered that possibility before this
morning. But according to some information Toby

Mitchell showed me a few hours ago, Cathy Parks is dead."

"Dead?" Crawford was dumbstruck.

"Apparently she O.D.'d. She and Reeson were both involved in drugs." Charlie flipped back several pages in his note pad. "According to what I've learned so far, you, Carole Peters, and Reeson all either knew or had some relationship with this girl."

"What about Anderson?"

"He didn't know her. But that doesn't mean there couldn't be some kind of indirect connection, okay? As far as the Simpson woman goes, I haven't had a chance to talk with her yet."

Crawford's face tightened. He saw some things that gave Charlie's theory credibility. "Do you think someone is out for revenge?"

"Hard to say. But revenge is a pretty common motive."

"But why me? So I slept with the girl. That doesn't justify someone coming after me. Hell, she must have slept with a lot of guys."

"But you got her pregnant."

"I never said I did."

For the first time, Charlie showed some impatience. "Come on, Crawford. You knew she was pregnant and you said you saw her before the abortion. You don't think she set it up all by herself, do you? Doesn't seem logical that a girl new in town would know where to go for help."

"All right, so I gave her a name," Crawford said, slapping his hand on the table.

"Of a doctor?"

"No, of someone who could make the arrangements. . . ."

"So now you've got a conscience," Judy Simpson said, spitting her words angrily at Crawford.

"You said it would all be taken care of," he shot back.

The kitchen in the Hammin Inn was deserted and Charlie Cole stood by the entrance to the main room to be sure they were not disturbed.

"I asked you to stick around, didn't I? I told you she'd probably need someone afterward."

"I gave you six hundred bucks!"

"And that was supposed to wash your hands of it? Is that it?"

"I gave you six hundred bucks for a doctor, goddammit! Not for some do-it-yourself method!"

"You're not going to stick all this on me!" Judy shrieked. "You got her into it!"

"And I paid you to get her out!"

"Hey, you two can settle your differences later," Charlie said, moving in between them. "I'm not interested in accusations. I only want to know what happened in the motel room!"

Judy buried her face in her hands and crumpled into a chair. "I don't know," she said, whimpering. "Something went wrong. The girl panicked. I couldn't control her. She started to scream. Everything was so mixed up. And I couldn't stop the bleeding."

"For six hundred dollars, you almost killed her. For six hundred lousy dollars." Crawford hammered his disgust and loathing into every word. "I paid for a doctor!"

"The hell you did! You paid for an abortion! And I'd done it before."

"On what?" Crawford asked with a sneering, mocking laugh. "Dogs?"

"You rotten bastard! You rotten no good bastard!" Her body constricted and the veins stood out on her neck. She jumped up, spun around, and grabbed for one of the butcher knives held by a magnet on a rod over the cutting block. In one motion, she pulled it down and threw it at Crawford with all the strength she could muster. He ducked and the knife careened off the far wall, falling harmlessly to the floor.

Crawford exploded with rage and lunged at her, swinging first with his left and then his right. The first blow smashed into her chest. The second caught her on the side of the head and sent her sprawling to the floor.

"You goddamn cunt! I ought to smash your face in!"

Charlie grabbed for Crawford's shirt and jerked him back. "Unless you want to face up to assault and battery charges, you'd better get your ass out of here!"

"She tried to kill me! That stinking cunt tried to kill me!"

"You're lucky she hasn't had more practice. Now get out of here before she takes another shot."

Seething with anger, Crawford slowly backed away. He turned to leave and struck the door with such force that it swung all the way around on its spring hinge and slammed into the wall on the other side.

"You okay?" Charlie asked as he helped Judy to a chair. A welt was rising on the side of her face and she clutched at the spot on her chest where Crawford's first blow had struck. Charlie went over to the sink, wet a towel, and gave it to her. Tears flowed down her cheeks and she seemed to be having trouble breathing. "You want me to call a doctor? Maybe something is broken."

Judy shook her head. "I thought I could do it. I used to assist the doctors in a clinic in Chicago. It was all so simple."

Charlie watched her dab the towel against her cheek. "If you think you're going to be all right, I'll be going." She nodded. With that, he turned and left.

Judy slumped in the chair. I should never have stayed here after that. I should have left. Why didn't I leave? She recalled the agony she had endured throughout that summer. Her first impulse had been to run; she had gone so far as to pack her belongings and withdraw her savings from the bank. Then it occurred to her that she could deny any charges Cathy might make. It would be a matter of her word against that of a girl no one even knew. She could express great shock and indignation at the accusation. She could claim that she'd never met the girl and that as a cocktail waitress she didn't know the first thing about abortions. Judy felt confident that her medical experience would never be uncovered. The possibility that Crawford might say something never entered her mind. She decided to wait it out and act as though nothing had happened.

Several days later, she overheard a conversation at the bar about "some girl in the hospital who was suffering from shock and hadn't said a word in a week." For a couple of days, Judy let herself be lulled by the delusion that Cathy might be suffering from amnesia and would never be able to recall any of what happened. But she made sure to develop an alibi for her whereabouts on the morning of the abortion and she rehearsed over and over what she would say in a confrontation with Cathy, the police, or both.

Upon hearing that Cathy had come out of shock, Judy waited for two days, alone in her apartment, for the knock on the door that would most certainly come. It did not. Apparently, she reasoned, Cathy had decided not to say anything or she had actually suffered some kind of memory loss. The lack of any accusation brought on a short period of giddy relief which was soon shattered by the prospect of yet another possibility: Maybe the girl was planning to blackmail her. . . . But weeks passed and there was nothing.

Then one day late in August, as Judy was leaving a small apparel shop on the square, she saw Dan and Cathy across the street walking toward his car. Cathy caught a glimpse of her and Judy saw the signs of recognition. Their eyes hung together for a precarious moment and then Cathy turned away and got into the car. She's seen me, Judy thought. Maybe she's telling Dan about me right now. Maybe he's going to get out of the car and confront me. Maybe he'll tell Toby Mitchell. Dan's car pulled away and, again, nothing.

The following October, Judy chanced to hear a remark about the girl Dr. Frederickson had been seeing. She'd disappeared, went the report. Left town. And even Dan didn't know where she'd gone. It was over. Judy was free. Cathy left with her secret. During the intervening years, Judy pushed the memory of the early morning in the motel room and the subsequent weeks of mental torment deep into the recesses of her mind.

It was all but forgotten.

Until that night at the carnival.

And now this blow-up with Crawford. It would all come out, she was sure of that. Everyone would know. And they would understand, as she understood, the *why* of the hex.

Sitting there in the kitchen, her face throbbing with the pain of Crawford's blow, a thin plaintive wail issued up from deep inside, ripping through the protective veneer, baring her inmost self to the strident terror of things yet to come.

xiv

Dan sat across the desk from Toby Mitchell, staring vacantly at the police chief's dirty linoleum floor. Charlie Cole, leaning against one of Toby's file cabinets, was providing a detailed account of the confrontation between Crawford and Judy Simpson. As Charlie talked on, Toby found his attention divided between what he was hearing and Dan's effort to give the appearance of being a dispassionate listener. Toby noticed a pronounced tightening in Dan's jaw as Charlie revealed Crawford's role in the abortion. When Charlie recalled Judy's description, Dan leaned forward in his chair, elbows on knees, in order to conceal his face from the other two men. Once again, Toby found himself speculating about Dan's relationship with Cathy. No question that there was something between the two of them, he mused. *I wonder if he was ballin' her?*

"Doesn't surprise me about Spencer," Toby said when Charlie had finished. "He's always had the morals of an alley cat. But Judy Simpson performing abortions?" He shook his head incredulously. "Jesus! That's really hard to believe."

"I'm telling it like I heard it, okay?" Charlie moved some folders off the remaining chair in Toby's office and sat down. "Can she be prosecuted?"

"Hell, yes, assuming we can get corroboration." Toby paused. "Which won't be all that easy without a victim or a witness to testify."

"I don't think you'll need one. My reading is, she's ready to confess everything."

Toby tilted back in his chair, fished a toothpick out

175

of his shirt pocket, and performed some light dental work on his right rear molar. "Well, goddammit, this is all getting out of my league. I'm going to drop this mess in the lap of the state attorney's office. Hell, let them handle it."

Cathy is wearing a pastel dress and a blue ribbon in her hair. She stands by her bed looking out the hospital window. Dan enters, she turns, and her smile showers him with warmth. He sits casually on the side of the bed and, after glancing at the door to be sure their privacy is complete, reaches over and takes her hands in his. "You've never told me where you're from," he says. "I rent a room over on Barker Place," she replies. He rephrases his question. "I mean, where are you from originally?"

Her eyes sparkle with silent laughter. "I'm from Paradise."

Dan laughs and tells her that he's not in the least bit surprised.

"Pennsylvania," she adds. "There really is such a place."

She has come far in the month she has been here, and Dan tells her that as a condition of her release from the hospital she must promise to come see him twice a week at his office. She protests that she feels fine and doesn't need any more treatment. Dan smiles and says that the visits are for his benefit—he wants an excuse to see her. "Do you really need an excuse?" she asks. Her voice is soft and the words float on love. His eyes fall away from her for just a moment. "No, I suppose I don't."

She takes a step closer and he resists the unspoken invitation to take her in his arms. He is, after all, her doctor.

"You know, it seems to me," Toby said analytically, "that we come out of all this with a pretty clear motive for this hex business. Knowing what we do about Reeson, Spencer, and Judy Simpson, we don't have to stretch too far to assume someone is out for revenge."

Charlie nodded his agreement, "No question. In my own mind, this Parks girl is the link between the three of them. But I run into a problem when we come to Mr. North and Carole Peters. Anderson tells me he'd never seen the girl before that night at the carnival." He paused a moment to consult his note pad. "Of course, Miss Peters knew her."

Dan jumped to Carole's defense. "Carole didn't know her. I mean, she knew who Cathy was, but that's only because Cathy came to my office a couple times after she was released from the hospital. It takes more than having someone pass through your waiting room to say you know them."

For a moment, Toby considered voicing his agreement with Dan, but he held back, deciding to see what he could read in Dan's mounting agitation.

Charlie shifted uneasily in his chair as he prepared to pursue the matter further. "Were you and Miss Peters . . . ah . . . I don't mean to get personal, okay? But were you going with Miss Peters at the time?"

"No. She was working for me."

"But you weren't," again he paused, "romantically involved?" Charlie quickly followed with an apology. "I'm sorry, that's none of my business."

"You're right," Dan said, not trying to conceal his irritation. "But the answer is no. We really didn't start going together until after she came back to Hammin this past winter."

"She'd been away?" Charlie showed no knowledge of her year's absence from Hammin.

"Yes, after I settled into her father's practice she went back to St. Louis."

"What do you think brought her back?"

Dan had never really given the question much thought. "Well, her roots are here and. . . ." He shrugged and his expression made no secret that he'd had his fill of Charlie. Abruptly, he stood up and stepped over to the door. "I've got to get back to the hospital." And with that, he left.

Toby looked after him, a bit taken aback by Dan's uncharacteristic sudden departure, and then it occurred to him that except for a kind of working familiarity, he really didn't know all that much about Dr. Dan Frederickson. And that began to bother him.

Anderson North's eyes were glued on some distant point outside the bank window as Charlie sat in his office repeating, once again, what he'd learned.

"So what does all this tell you?" Anderson asked.

"Well, it certainly stands up as a motive. Someone close to the girl—her family, for example—might be out to avenge her death."

"But Reeson caused that," Anderson said by way of countering Charlie's surmise. "Didn't you say Mitchell's report indicated that he'd got her onto drugs?"

Charlie nodded.

"So if what you say about revenge is correct, how do you fit me into the picture?"

"To tell you the truth, Mr. North," Charlie seemed intimidated under Anderson's cool scrutiny, "I hoped that you could tell me."

"But, I told you, I didn't even know the girl," Anderson said with even intensity. "And she never worked for me or any of the companies or businesses I'm connected with."

"Well, I'm sure you'd know better than anyone."

Anderson nodded his concurrence. "I checked it out personally." Anderson's unblinking gaze seemed to be challenging him to advance another supposition.

Charlie dropped his eyes to his note pad. "Well, that does make things a little more complicated, okay? But right now, I've got nothing else to go on. Except, of course, the psychic. I'm still not convinced that she doesn't figure into this some way."

Anderson got up slowly and came around to the front of his desk so that he was towering over Charlie. He was taking command. "Tell you what, let's not worry about establishing links between the five of us anymore. Let's concentrate on finding out who's behind this."

Charlie started to protest. "But how am I going to——"

Anderson cut him off. "Let me finish. Let's assume that you're right. The girl and maybe the psychic are the link. Maybe it *is* revenge for real or imagined wrongs. That really doesn't make too much difference as far as I'm concerned. What I want you to do is forget about chasing the ghost of this girl and start concentrating on people."

Charlie edged out of his chair and stood up. "I could go back to Madame Miranda. . . ."

"One more thing. You may be right about her family being involved. Try to find out where she's from and where her family might be." Anderson walked Charlie to the door and clapped him on the shoulder. "I want to get to the bottom of this, Charlie . . . and soon."

There was just the slightest trace of panic in Anderson's face.

"Don't worry," Charlie said reassuringly, "we will."

By three o'clock that afternoon, most of the lunch crowd had left the Hammin Inn. Judy sank wearily into a chair and emptied her pocketful of tips onto the table. Skeet Fischer slipped out from behind the bar and made a perfunctory attempt at sweeping up. His heart apparently wasn't in it, and after a while he walked over to the front window and stared out. After several deep drags on a cigarette, Judy began to separate the tips into individual piles.

The pay phone on the wall behind her rang. Slowly, she raised up out of her chair and walked over to it.

"Hello," she answered flatly.

The voice was breathy and cold:

> *"Judy, Judy has a knife*
> *For a price she'll take a life.*
> *But now the price is on her head,*
> *Ten to one she'll end up dead!"*

Judy slammed the receiver back onto the hook, drawing the attention of several people in the room.

"What's wrong?" one asked.

"My God, look!" a woman shrieked. "She's bleeding! She's bleeding!" she screamed, pointing at Judy's legs.

Momentarily stunned by the scream, it took Judy a second to realize what was happening. She felt the sticky warmth flowing down her thighs. Her white skirt was slowly turning crimson red.

"Help me!" she screamed in sudden hysteria.

Skeet and several others dashed across the room.

"I've got to stop it! I've got to stop it!" Her shrill terror-filled cries ignited a rampant fear that swept through the room. Several people ran from the bar while others, clawing like animals, ripped away her dress.

Slipping on the bloody floor, she pushed through the groping hands toward the restroom. She slammed through the door and started splashing water from the washbasin onto her naked thighs.

"Where's it coming from?" she cried in desperation. "I can't tell where it's coming from!" She pulled down her panties and pushed a handful of paper towels hard against her crotch.

A sudden pain shot up the back of her neck. Her body reeled and she groped for support. The entire room seemed to be spinning . . . shaking . . . coming apart. For a moment she felt she would lose consciousness, then hands helped her sit down on the toilet seat. Her head sagged forward and came to rest on the toilet paper dispenser.

"I'll call a doctor," she heard Skeet say.

"No, no!" Judy pleaded. "No, I'm all right."

Voices in the bathroom cascaded down around her. "What happened?" "Where'd all the blood come from?" "She'll die if we don't get her to the hospital!"

Slowly, Judy opened her eyes. The bleeding had stopped, but her thighs and calves were streaked with rivulets of red. Legs were pressed all around her. Suddenly the room filled with a stomach-wrenching stench. Judy raised her head slightly, gagged. For but an instant, through the bodies that surrounded her, she caught a glimpse of the restroom mirror. And in the mirror, the ashen face of Cathy Parks.

"I'm so goddamn horny," Natalie said, throwing down her magazine, "that I'm about to climb the walls." She looked over at Crawford, who remained barricaded behind the afternoon paper on the far side of the deck. "Won't you at least try?" she pleaded, crossing to him. He held the paper resolutely between them as she knelt at his feet and started to massage his inner thighs. "Come on," she purred suggestively, "let's see if Natalie can't get it up for her baby."

"Cut it out!" he said sharply, getting up and walking into the living room. He sank into the sofa and took several deep breaths in hopes of uncorking some of the tension that had gripped him since the altercation with Judy.

Natalie followed and sat on the edge of the sofa. She looked at him with kittenlike tenderness and slowly ran her hands up across his chest to his shoulders. "Try to relax, huh?" she said soothingly. "You're just a bundle of nerves."

Crawford closed his eyes and submitted to her

manipulations. Her hands worked on the back of his neck and then slid down to his pectorals. The motion was circular and he felt the bow-string tightness start to leave his chest area. His sleep had been fitful, his appetite sparse, and Natalie's frequent attempts at seduction and his flaccid response, plus his new perspective on the hex, had drawn his temper to razor-edged sharpness.

Natalie's hands moved to his stomach and then down to his groin. "Oh, how I need it," she murmured.

Crawford jerked to a sitting position and swept her hands away. "For God's sake, leave me alone," he whined.

"Oh, come on, try," she begged.

"When I'm ready."

"When you're ready?" she echoed sarcastically. "Maybe we should make an appointment. I've got needs, you know. I happen to like to have sex occasionally."

"Occasionally?" Crawford guffawed. "My God, if your brain was as active as your cunt, you'd be a genius!"

Natalie bristled and stood up, backing away from the sofa. "I'm going to pretend I didn't hear that, Crawford Spencer. I'm going to make believe those words were never spoken. You have no right to talk to me like that. Not me. You forget who's been here cooking for you and babying you for the last six weeks. I've put up with your moods and your fits and your depressions. I've listened to you belch and fart and never said so much as one word. Now I'm going to repeat what I've been saying for the last week just one more time. You had better get some help. Psychiatric help. Because I'll tell you, whatever's wrong with you is not in your prick, it's in your head!"

"Would you get off that crap about a psychiatrist! I am not going to any fairy-assed shrink and have him tell me I hate my mother."

"Okay, so don't go. Just sit here and tear yourself apart. But don't count on little Natalie hanging around while you do. I'm not going to live in this—this *convent* much longer. I've got needs and I'll find somebody who can satisfy them."

"Well, that's just fine, you fucking whore," Crawford hissed. "Go out and sell it on the street, why don't you. Advertise in the goddamn paper. You're beginning to bore the hell out of me anyway."

"I'm boring the hell out of *you?*" Natalie fired back. "What do you think living with you is doing to me? It's dull, Crawford—dull, dull, dull!" she screamed.

"You know where your bags are. Pack 'em and get the hell out, then. Nobody asked you to come and live here."

Natalie snarled at him. "So this is the way it ends, huh? Well, I'll say one thing, I'm getting out of this a hell of a lot better off than that Cathy Parks did. At least I won't need an abortion."

"Shut up about her!"

"Oh, sensitive, are we?" she asked with sing-song derisiveness.

"Shut your fucking face!" he shot back.

"You want to hit me like you hit Judy Simpson?" She put up her fists. "Big strong Crawford Spencer can beat up any woman in town."

Crawford started across the room after her. Natalie quickly ducked into the bedroom and locked the door. Crawford raised his leg and kicked at the door with the bottom of his foot.

"Go ahead, break it down," Natalie called from the bedroom. "Show me what a he-man you are!"

Furious, Crawford picked up a lamp and hurled it across the room. Then he kicked over a coffee table, propeling dirty cups and saucers across the floor.

"That's terrific." Natalie opened the door a little and peered out. "We must learn to control ourselves."

"Five minutes, whore. Five minutes and out!"

Natalie laughingly turned back into the bedroom.

Crawford lurched down the stairs and out the front door. He hit the driveway, legs churning, and ran full out to the fifteenth fairway. He'd not gone more than three hundred yards when he pulled up, gasping for breath. He sank to his knees, his body writhing and twitching. His heart pounded convulsively.

"I'm going to have an attack!" he wheezed. "I'm going to have an attack." He fell on his back and then quickly rolled on his side as his stomach constricted and forced up a stream of vomit.

"Oh, my God! Oh, my God! Got to get control of myself."

By eight o'clock that evening, he was on his third tumbler of scotch. The first had burned, refusing to make peace with his indigestion. The second had brought on a degree of numbness, and the third promised oblivion. Already he was regretting his fight with Natalie. She'll come back, he thought. "Maybe," he added aloud, feeling despondent and alone.

There was a definite pain in his testicles. He'd noticed it for several days now. He pushed himself up out of his chair and found some difficulty in navigating his way to the medicine cabinet. But the bottle of medicine Dan had prescribed was empty.

He belched and the acid that accompanied the gas left a burning sensation in his throat. "Shit!" he said aloud and headed back for the deck and his scotch. He gulped the drink and stared apprehensively at the thickening darkness.

The phone rang.

"Whoever you are," he called out as he walked over to it, "come on over and let's have a party." Crawford reached down and took the receiver off the cradle. "Hello."

The sound of wind blowing across hollow reeds.

"Hello?"

The voice came back husky and with a strange, broken cadence. "We enjoyed your little performance on the golf course."

"Who is this?" he barked angrily. "Come on, goddammit, identify yourself, you chickenshit."

"We're getting there, aren't we, Crawford? A few more pins . . . a few more weeks . . . and it'll be . . . all . . . over."

He slammed the receiver down and rushed over to the bar to fix himself another drink. "I'll be damned if I'm going to stay here and rot with this thing. I'll be goddamned if I will!" He tossed down a shot. "I'm going to leave this fucking town and this hex so far behind that there's no way it'll find me." He wheeled around and shouted at the phone, "And you can take your needles and stick 'em up your ass!"

For the next hour, while fighting his way through an alcoholic haze, Crawford struggled to bring some order to his financial records to determine what he could pull together in the way of cash. The results were gravely disappointing.

"Six hundred and fifty dollars. Jesus! Is that all I've got? That won't last me a week."

He staggered into his bedroom and crawled into bed. He gathered in a pillow and propped up his head. "What am I going to do?" he muttered. "What in the hell am I going to do?" With sudden swiftness an idea took shape and he resolved then and there to adopt it as his plan of action.

Anderson North would pay his way out of Hammin.

xv

Judy Simpson stared at the small blue flame as it slowly curled its way around the bottom of the tortoise shell, drawing its life from the liquid cradled inside. A thin column of smoke rose up, permeating the room with a pungent, acrid odor.

Emma Ferguson had introduced the other woman only as Hilda, saying that she had had much experience in breaking spells. Sitting there, hands linked to the other two women, listening to the dismal monotone chants, Judy felt at once ludicrous and apprehensive. The surroundings of her own living room, cast as they were in the dim light of a single candle, seemed curiously unfamiliar and foreboding.

Except for one or two early-morning trips to buy food, she had not left the apartment for over a week. Emma had served as her information conduit. There had been reports of a man asking questions about Judy and her activities over the last few years. Apparently he had been looking for substantiation of the abortion she had performed. Emma said that word had it, he was from the state attorney's office. Now, as three years before, Judy waited for the knock on the door.

Emma had also become Judy's mirror, sympathetically pointing out the telltale signs of strain. Suggesting rest. Noting a perceptible loss of weight. Wanting her to see a doctor. And finding frequent occasions to promote a visit by a witch skilled in white-magic antidotes. Judy experienced gastrointestinal distress. She found herself spotting well in advance of her period. And there were night sweats, drenching night sweats that made it necessary for her to shower and change the sheets sometimes as often as twice a night.

Once, she found herself in a kind of half sleep, imagining her own death. She saw her mother holding out a hand, welcoming her beyond. Her father smiling as he had when, as a young woman, she had returned home for visits and holidays. It had all seemed so real, so full of promise. She felt herself lift out of her body and ascend to a position well above the bed. Her parents beckoned, pleaded with their eyes for her to follow. She was alive, but dead. There was no pain, no sense of self . . . a peace she had not experienced since, as a small child, she had sat between her parents on their front porch swing, feeling their love press around her.

Then, with savage abruptness, it was over. Her body convulsed into a sitting position. She threw off the covers and switched on all the lights in her bedroom and living room. Then turned on the television and the radio, opened the window to feel the night breeze —anything to confirm life. In the morning, she called Emma. She was ready. The arrangements were made for that evening.

Judy sensed she had seen Hilda before, but she was not sure when or under what circumstances. No matter.

Hilda said little. What she did say was in the form of requests and instructions.

"I'll need a flat surface."

"Will this do?" Judy asked, pointing to a small round dining table.

"That will do fine," Hilda responded, her voice flat and cold.

When it was cleared, Hilda produced a small container of a white chalk substance from her handbag. She unscrewed the cap and with studied deliberation, began to form a pentagram—two circles surrounding a five-pointed star.

Judy stood away from the table, her hands clasped tightly in one another. She watched as Hilda placed a tortoise shell, possibly four inches long, in the center and poured in a bluish liquid. Emma lit a candle and placed it on one of the points of the star. Both women seemed coolly efficient, though Emma frequently glanced up at Judy with a confident expression.

"Emma," Hilda said when everything was in place, "you and Miss Simpson can sit down." Hilda stepped over to the window and closed the venetian blinds, plunging the room into dim candlelight.

Hilda paused for a long moment before approaching the table, as if she were waiting to be moved by some unseen spirit. Finally, she sat down, took the candle from its holder, and touched it to the liquid in the tortoise shell. It sputtered and hissed momentarily, then caught fire.

"We must join hands," Hilda said, extending white bony fingers to Judy. Slowly, Judy reached over and clasped the old woman's hand. It was ice cold and sent a tiny shock up her arm. Emma's hand was warm, damp with perspiration. Hilda glanced at both women, then locked her gaze on the flame. "At no time break the circle. No matter what happens, do not let go of my hands." There was a deadly serious command in her tone.

The incantations began.

Emma had described the ritual to Judy earlier, explaining that when the shell cracked in half, the hex would be broken. She could not predict how long it would take. Minutes. Possibly hours.

Judy stared at the shell expectantly. Hilda repeated the sing-song incantation again and again, but at no time was Judy able to make any sense of it other than to assume it was some primitive chant. From time to time, Judy glanced up at Hilda, noting the growing intensity in her expression. Her hand seemed to grow wetter and Judy had to secure her grip several times.

There was no air circulating in the room and it seemed to Judy that the temperature was soaring. The flame was having a hypnotic effect and Judy caught herself nodding twice. Both times, Hilda's chant ceased and she shot her a harsh, reprimanding look.

Judy could not begin to estimate how much time had passed. Her arms became heavy and the smoke began to scratch at her eyes and burn the membranes in her nostrils. Her mouth felt parched.

Emma's earlier confidence had dissolved markedly. Perspiration cascaded down Hilda's forehead. Her voice cracked with creeping hoarseness.

The incantations continued. Repetitive . . . unintelligible . . . no relief from the steady, sing-song cadence.

Pain gripped Judy's upper back and neck. Her head began to throb unmercifully. She could not take much more. She searched the two women's faces for some sign, some indication that they shared her fatigue and were ready to stop. But she felt their hands tighten around hers with viselike intensity.

I think I'm going to throw up, she thought. My God, why doesn't it crack? Why doesn't it come to an end?

And then it did.

Like eggs cracking under foot, the entire shell shattered into a hundred little pieces.

Hilda dropped Judy's hand and jumped up, staring open-mouthed at the table.

"Hurry! Hurry!" she shrieked, and started to brush off the chalk pentagram. Emma picked up the cue and did the same.

"What's wrong? What's happened?" Judy cried, her nerves suddenly raw and exposed.

Hilda stopped and backed away from the table. Her face was filled with abject horror. "It's too strong," she said huskily. "The hex is too strong. I can do nothing. Nothing!" Her body seemed to quiver, driven by fear.

Judy turned to Emma for comfort and found her weeping, totally spent.

Slowly Hilda picked up her bag and walked to the door. She turned back momentarily. "I . . . I. . . ."

Judy spun in her chair, hoping for a reprieve. There was none.

"May God have mercy on you," Hilda said with finality and left.

The street lights flickered through the leaves, throwing patterns on the sidewalk in front of them. The night air was sweet with the promise of rain. Their footsteps echoed rhythmically off the concrete. There was no other sound save the single hollow chime from the courthouse clock as a reminder of the hour.

"Shall we start back?" Carole asked. Her voice was thin and flaccid.

"I didn't realize it was so late," Dan said. They turned and walked by the dark houses standing mute witness to their passing.

"I'd so looked forward to this summer," the words seemed to drift aimlessly from her mouth. "And now it's almost gone. I sometimes wonder. . . ."

Dan waited for her to finish the thought, but she only looked away as though trying to hide her face from him.

"We can fight this thing, Carole," he said with a firmness that revealed only the edge of his deep frustration. "You've got to let me help you fight it. Believe me, I understand what you're going through, but we can fight it." The words rang hollow in his ears, echoes of hours and hours of appeal to her intellect, to her determination, to their future together. And as before, she simply nodded her head in agreement, which he knew was little more than a weak attempt to appease him.

"I love you, Carole, more than anything else in the world. If you won't fight for yourself, do it for me."

Tears welled in her eyes. "Oh, you don't know how much I want to, Dan," she said, turning and pressing herself into his arms.

For a moment he felt that at last he might have sparked the will to fight. But it was fleeting. With curious abruptness, she pulled away and said, "We'd better get back. You need your sleep."

It was these sudden vacillations of attitude that frustrated and confused Dan the most. He had always thought of Carole as a strong person; he could not fathom her almost total lack of desire to maintain even minimum resistance. Thank God she only had headaches and vague pains. He might not be able to cope with serious physical manifestations.

He was not ready to predict or even speculate on how far down she would go. He knew that in many cases of extreme neurosis, patients had lost the use of a limb or become convinced they had suffered a crippling stroke. There had been those that died, too. He was also aware that often where diagnosis showed no physiological disorder, severe neurotics had been cured by simply being jolted out of the neurosis. While the nature of this psychological jolt differed according to the patient, the resultant rapid reversal of the condition was generally the same. Dan decided that in Carole's case, the jolt would have to come from her taking part in what Miizi had once described as the ritual of turning the magic backward.

Dan had been witness to it only once during his two years in the Ivory Coast. It occurred almost a year after the death of Tureau and, while far less dramatic, provided another dimension to the curious power of the ouanga. The incident involved a local villager by the name of Abdolulaya and his two wives. As Dan discovered early in his stay, Biasempian law permitted a man, on his wife's approval, to take on a second, a third, or as many wives as he felt he could afford. Unlike some polygamous societies, the wives lived in separate households and could demand the husband treat and support all wives equally. If, however, a man decided to take another wife against his first wife's wishes, she had the right to sue for divorce.

Dan was told that it all began when Abdolulaya decided that his growing wealth afforded him the luxury of a second wife. His choice was a woman much younger than his first wife and, by village standards, far more attractive. The first wife objected strenuously to Abdolulaya's intentions, but he was adamant. He suggested that she either agree to let him have a second wife, or begin divorce proceedings. At length the woman agreed, at least outwardly. To have initiated a divorce would not only have left her without a husband, but her husband's family could have demanded repayment of the "bride price" which they had given to her father when Abdolulaya received permission to marry her.

The first wife let the second marriage take place and for a while it seemed that the husband had achieved harmony in both his households. Dan recalled that when he attended the wedding fete—which tradition held must last three nights—the first wife danced and sang and seemed to have an inordinately good time. In retrospect, he realized it was only a facade, for the woman had decided to kill the new bride with jungle magic.

Abdolulaya made his living as a safari guide and the first wife waited until he had gone on one of his longer trips before starting the ouanga. With the help of her sister and a friend, a piece of cloth was stolen from the second wife's house. The baptismal took place in a cave deep in the forest. First, they wrapped a small wooden doll in the cloth and placed it on a crude altar. As the incantations were spoken, chicken blood was smeared on the doll and pins were thrust into the abdomen.

As with Tureau, the second wife was made well

aware of what had happened. She was told that a doll
had been baptized in her name, but no one seemed to
know who the witch might be. The first wife went to
her to offer comfort and commiseration and to ensure
that she had daily reports of the ouanga's progress.
The second wife was quite certain that she would die
and her condition steadily deteriorated as accompani-
ment to her belief.

Fortunately for the second wife, Abdolulaya returned home early from the safari. Immediately, he
suspected his first wife and made up his mind to wring
a confession from her. His methods were anything but
subtle: He simply beat her until, terribly battered, she
admitted all and revealed where the doll had been
hidden. The man retrieved the doll and called on
Miizi to help him perform the unbaptism.

"We are going to further your education tonight,"
Miizi announced one evening. "We have talked about
turning the magic backward and now you will have an
opportunity to see it firsthand."

Miizi led Dan to the second wife's house, which was
located on the other side of the village. Inside, Dan
found the woman on the floor, lying on her bedding.
She appeared very weak and in considerable pain. Abdolulaya squatted next to her. The doll lay in the
middle of the floor concealed under a white cloth.
Miizi said a few words in the tribal tongue to the man,
then motioned for Dan to sit down. There was more
conversation, mainly about the girl as far as Dan could
tell, and then Miizi began his preparations. A small
fire was built on the mud floor in the middle of the
room and a bucket of kerosene was placed at Miizi's
side. As Miizi began the first of several incantations,
he removed the cloth from the doll. Dan saw the woman cringe and turn her head away, burying her face in
her hands. Miizi barked something to the husband,
who went over to his wife, cradled her upper body,
and held her head in such a way that she was forced

to look at the doll. Assured of her attention, Miizi continued.

The rhythm of the chant changed to a sharp staccato. Miizi picked up the doll and began to pull the pins. One by one he held each up for the woman to see. The wife's eyes were riveted on the doll. When the last pin was out, the tempo of the chant was again changed. Miizi raised the doll over his head, then thrust it into the kerosene for a moment, pulled it out, and dropped it into the fire. Smoke billowed up quickly, filling the room. It occurred to Dan that even if Miizi succeeded in breaking the hex, he might cause them all to die from smoke inhalation. The chant stopped and everyone stared at the fire as the doll was quickly turned to ashes. Miizi looked up at the girl and said something which Dan thought sounded like "You are free." Whatever the exact words, the wife's face brightened and she smiled at her husband.

Her recovery started almost immediately. Just as before the ceremony she had been certain she was going to die, now she was convinced that she would get well. It's really all so basic, Dan thought. If the power of suggestion could make someone sick, then that same power, turned around, could provide the cure. The unbaptizing ritual, performed as it was in front of the victim, became the psychological jolt needed to reverse the process.

As Dan rolled over his memories of the unbaptizing, he felt sure that with a little preconditioning, with the proper set-up, he could convince Carole and the others that pulling the pins and burning the dolls would end the hex. He would carefully explain to them what he'd learned in Africa. He would document the success of the ritual from his own firsthand experience. Then he would explain the ritual of the unbaptism, every detail. He would omit nothing. And then, while they all looked on, he would begin the chants and incantation . . . pull the pins and burn the dolls. They would accept it and in a matter of days they would be well because they understood fully, comprehensively that the hex had been broken.

It could work, he thought. Done right, with preparation, it would work. Suddenly, the realization hit him. He had just assigned himself the task of playing witch doctor.

There was only one problem—he had to find the dolls first.

xvi

The page for Dan came over the hospital intercom. He handed the patient chart to the nurse beside him and walked out into the hall where he picked up the phone off the nurses' desk.

It was Charlie Cole. He seemed rushed and his conversation was short and somewhat cryptic. From what little Dan could decipher, he gathered that Charlie had gotten onto something that might lead them to discover who was behind the hex. He and Carole were to meet Charlie later that evening at Charlie's house.

Charlie Cole rented a clapboard, 1900-vintage farmhouse on the outskirts of town. As they drove up, Dan and Carole were surprised to see several cars already in the drive. Dan recognized Anderson's and Crawford's, but not the third. He thought about having to face Crawford now that he knew about his relationship with Cathy. He quickly made up his mind to say nothing and to keep conversation with him to a bare minimum.

As they stepped up on the porch, Charlie came out to greet them. His expression was serious, expectant.

Dan put his hand on Charlie's arm and stopped him. "Before we go in, what's this all about?"

Charlie spoke in a low, hushed voice. "Well, Mr. North and I have come to the conclusion that Pauline Baoukas may hold the key to all this!"

"Who's Pauline Baoukas?" Dan asked.

"The psychic, Madame Miranda. Baoukas is her real name, okay? Anyway, I've hired her to give us a private performance tonight. She refused at first, but a

197

thousand dollars changed her mind. Now, you know and I know that that materialization at the carnival was some kind of optical trick. It had to be. What we want to find out is why she chose this Cathy Parks. That woman's not going to leave here without telling us what she knows. You can count on that." Charlie looked at both of them as if waiting for any questions. "Well, come on in."

Carole pulled on Dan's arm. "Dan, I don't want to stay for this," she said, cowering. "I'm really not up to it. You go."

Charlie stepped toward her and placed his hand gently on her shoulder. "Miss Peters, I really think you ought to stay. The more people we have confronting this woman, the better our chances————"

She cut him off. "I really don't feel well." She started to back down the steps.

"Well, I have a couch inside. Maybe if you were to come in and lie down. . . ."

Dan interceded, "I don't think she has to be here, Charlie. In fact, I'd rather she weren't."

"Well, it's up to you, of course." Charlie's face showed his disappointment.

Dan reached into his pocket and gave Carole his car keys. "Why don't you take my car. I'll have Anderson drop me off when this is over."

Carole took the keys and headed for the car. She did not bother to look back. The men stood on the porch, watching her leave. Then Dan followed Charlie into the house.

The foyer was long and narrow, leading to a staircase in the back. To the left, through an arch, was the dining room. To the right, double wooden doors opened onto the living room. Charlie pushed open the doors and motioned for Dan to step in. The interior generally reflected Charlie's lack of decorative skills. The furniture was a mix of Victorian reproductions and nondescript 1930s utilitarian. It probably came with the house, Dan thought. There was a heaviness to the room that was accentuated by the maroon drapes and the dark gray carpeting.

Anderson stood up as Dan entered the room and held out his hand. "Glad you could make it, Dan. Where's Carole?"

"She wasn't up to it."

"Poor kid," Anderson said sympathetically. "Well, there was really no need for her to be here anyway."

Dan turned to Charlie. "Where's Spencer? I saw his car in the drive."

"In a bottle somewhere," Anderson spat.

Charlie smiled. "That's not too far off. He's in the kitchen mixing himself a drink. Can I get you one?"

"No, thanks," Dan answered. "And the psychic?"

"Upstairs," Charlie said, gesturing with his head. "She got here about five and asked to take a nap. Said it would make her more receptive." He rolled his eyes to underscore his disdain.

"You think anything is going to come of all this?" Dan asked.

"God, I hope so," Anderson responded. "Did Charlie explain what we're going to do? We've asked her to put on a—Jesus, I can hardly bring myself to say it— a seance. Charlie told her that we want to contact this Cathy Parks again. Now, we figure she'll go through her mumbo jumbo and then tell us she can't make contact or that her vibes aren't right, or some such horseshit. That's when Charlie here will go into action."

"And do what?" Dan asked quizzically.

Charlie smiled knowingly at Anderson. "Well, let's just say Madame Miranda is going to have an opportunity to star in two performances tonight."

Dan frowned. "If this woman does have some connection with the hex, why did she agree to come here tonight? I'd think this is the last place she'd want to be."

"Money," Anderson said. "The way we see it, this

woman is not our dollmaker. Someone paid her to stage that materialization."

Charlie nodded. "So I told her that I represented a group of people who were most interested in psychic phenomena and that we'd pay up to a thousand dollars for her to try to contact the girl that we saw at the carnival that night. I also told her—and I think this may have been one of the things that sucked her into coming—that we'd give her the thousand whether she succeeded or not."

"One last question, then I'll get off it," Dan said, feeling a little self-conscious for possibly making a problem. "Why bother with the seance? Why not just bring her in and lay our cards on the table?"

"We could do that, okay? But my instincts say we should let her go through with her seance . . . let her fail . . . let her think she's had us, and then hit her. I think I might catch her more off guard that way, okay?"

"You're the boss. I sure as hell hope it works."

"Charlie, your bourbon's lousy," Crawford roared as he came into the room and flopped down onto the couch. "Well, when does the spook show begin? A command performance by our very own Madame Miranda."

Dan looked closely at Crawford and saw the ravages of the hex etched in his face. The wan complexion, the hollow eyes festooned with dark bags reminded him of Reeson that night at the carnival.

"I'll go get Madame Miranda," Charlie said as he left the room.

Crawford stood up and followed him out the door. "Need more ice for this," he said, holding out his half-empty glass.

"Look at that drunken bastard." The words flew out of Anderson's mouth like spittle. "Smug, arrogant son of a bitch!"

At first, Dan thought the outburst might be a prelude to some new information about Crawford, but it quickly became apparent that it was little more than a release of Anderson's bitter hatred for the man. Dan was surprised to find that the surge of bitterness and loathing he'd felt toward Crawford when he'd learned of his involvement with Cathy had lessened considerably. The rancor had given way to measured compassion.

Dan decided to get Anderson's mind off Crawford. "You know, the more I think about Charlie's little ploy here, the more I think he might really be onto something. That woman has got to be involved in this."

Anderson seemed to let down. He looked tired and terribly vulnerable. "She's got to be," he said with a touch of desperation in his voice. "She's got to be. I've been over this thing a hundred times in my head. I've laid out all we know and every time I come back to her and. . . ."

Anderson appeared to cut himself off.

"And?" Dan echoed curiously.

"And . . . and beyond that, I don't know where we look." Anderson looked down at his hands which were clinched in tight fists. Dan noticed that Anderson seemed to be having some difficulty in straightening out his fingers.

"By the way," Anderson said, looking up. "I've got to come see you. I'm wound up like a mainspring. This fucking hex has put ten years on me."

"Come around tomorrow," Dan said, and then turned as Crawford banged through the doors on his way back into the room. His glass was filled to the top with bourbon and there was no sign of ice.

"Gentlemen," Charlie said, following Crawford in, "I'd like you to meet Pauline Baoukas. I think you know her better as Madame Miranda."

The woman gave the men a forced smile, which

Anderson returned with a cold stare. Crawford lifted his glass as a silent greeting.

As the woman crossed the room to a chair near the front windows, her assistant, Homer, slipped in and stationed himself behind the sofa that Crawford had commandeered. Dan noted that he was dressed exactly the same as the night at the carnival—black suit with narrow lapels, thin bow tie. Dan saw Crawford look up at the gaunt, skeletal figure towering over him and then reveal his discomfort by sliding off the sofa and half crawling to an overstuffed chair across the room.

Dan's attention turned to Madame Miranda and he thought back to the night he had seen her working against the blue astral background. She seemed different to him somehow. It was her hair, he decided. She'd done it differently. That evening she wore a long gown, while tonight she was in a regular knee-length dress. Her legs were thick and heavy and her feet seemed to swell over the sides of her low-heeled shoes.

The medium looked up at the men and, with a studied, regal wave, signaled for them to sit.

They formed a rough circle, Dan to her right, Charlie on her left, Crawford and Anderson directly in front of her. There were no casual informalities or social banter.

She glanced over at Charlie. "I thought you said there were to be six?"

"Can't you perform with five?"

"Yes, of course. But I was just curious."

"The woman wasn't feeling well, so she went home."

Dan could not find any significant reaction to the information as she glanced around the room demanding the eyes of each person for a brief moment.

"I understand that your interest is in psychic phenomena and that you're curious about the girl. . . ." She looked over at Charlie. "I believe you said her name was Cathy."

Charlie nodded. "Cathy Parks."

Dan tried to read through Charlie's expression, which reflected a combination of awe and intimidation. *I hope what I see is part of your act, Charlie, or you're not going to get very far with this woman.*

"You understand that I was in a complete trance at the time and had no conscious awareness of what was going on. I can assure you that you saw what you saw."

Homer moved to the side of the couch. "Miss Baoukas is going to try to contact Cathy again. We must make it quite clear that Miss Baoukas can not guarantee results. If the spirits aren't willing to come, they won't."

"Do we hold hands?" Crawford guffawed.

Dan watched the medium raise her eyes and meet Crawford's. The look was long and cold, but it was Homer who answered the question. "That won't be necessary."

Charlie got up and started to turn off the lights. Homer produced a candle and holder from his pocket, lit it, and set it on the floor in the middle of the room.

Charlie waited for Homer to return to his place behind the sofa, then turned out the last light. Dan could see the woman staring hypnotically at the flickering flame. Her eyes glowed unnaturally with reflected luminescence. Slowly she began to rotate her head much as Dan remembered her doing at the carnival. Again the breathy, humming sound emanated from deep inside her. Dan looked around the room at the others. Charlie was watching her intently, as if trying to detect a flaw in her performance. Anderson's eyes darted from the candle to the woman, to Charlie, and back to the woman. Crawford had slipped down further into the chair with the drink perched precariously on his chest.

They waited.

The woman's head continued to rotate and the humming sound seemed to intensify. Dan guessed that at least five minutes had gone by. He saw Crawford start to close his eyes and then catch himself and gaze at the woman.

The psychic's head stopped and fell forward on her chest. The room was totally silent. Dan shifted uneasily in his chair and glanced over at Charlie, who caught his eye and nodded as though indicating that at any moment she would have to admit failure.

The floor started to creak as if the old house were yawning. A thud sounded upstairs. Dan looked up at the ceiling but saw nothing other than the shadows projected by the candle.

Something in the basement. Timbers stretching. A distinct bang on the far wall. The room was coming alive with sound. Dan looked over at the medium. Her head was now back off her chest, her mouth hung open.

Wind over hollow reeds. . . .

Anderson twisted in his chair and looked around the room. Charlie kept his eyes riveted on the woman, and Crawford started to push himself upright in the chair. A look of expectancy crept across his face. Where's Homer, Dan asked himself, and then strained to peer beyond the rim of the candle's light. Homer was behind the couch, standing motionless, staring blankly at the medium.

The sounds grew louder. The wind over hollow pipes began to spiral up to a higher pitch. A cool draft. The candle flickered, sputtered . . . and went out, plunging the room into total darkness.

Almost immediately, Dan became aware of a glow, a billowing phosphorescent mist above and behind the psychic. Dan felt transfixed in the chair. His body trembled with the build-up of anticipatory tension. My God, if this is some kind of trick. . . . He did not finish the thought. Slowly, the amorphous glow began to draw inward, congealing, taking on dimension.

A face.

"Cathy!" The name leaped from Dan's lips. He gasped for air as he fought against the pounding in his chest.

Her eyes stared at a spot on the far wall. Her face was chalky white. There was just the slightest movement around her mouth as though she were trying to form words. And then, "I trusted you." The voice was high and thin and seemed to wander across a minor tonal chord. It was not the voice Dan remembered. Similar, but not the same. Yet, there was no question that the face was hers. Lined, drawn, gaunt, but still hers.

"My God, I see it but I don't believe it!" Crawford said as his drink tumbled off his lap. The glass rolled along an exposed section of wood floor until it clunked to a stop.

"Believe what you see, Crawford," Cathy said; her gaze still unblinking, unaltered.

"This is some kind of trick!" Anderson snapped. "Charlie, get the lights."

Charlie did not move. He seemed mesmerized by the apparition.

Dan saw Cathy's face turn toward Anderson and look at him with despondence. "Hello, Anderson. It's been so long since we first met in New York. You weren't fair, Anderson. You told me you were divorcing Rita." Her voice had grown dark and funereal and echoed with pain.

"I don't know what you're talking about," Anderson protested with uncharacteristic vehemence. "Where are the goddamn lights?"

Anderson started to push himself up out of the chair when suddenly a hand clamped down on his shoulder, pressing him back. "Please," Homer warned with a low but intense sharpness. "No lights until Miss Baoukas returns."

"Don't deny me, Anderson," Cathy said in a disconsolate tone. "Once was enough." There was a pause, and Dan noticed Cathy's eyes fill with tears. "If you hadn't said you'd marry me, I would never have come to Hammin. Remember? It was in the spring."

It is February in New York. A cold winter rain whips down between the tall buildings. Cathy stands in the lobby of an ornate building at Fifth Avenue and Fifty-third Street. On the street the wind turns umbrellas inside out. People dash along the sidewalk, leaping over puddles, seeking refuge in doorways, waving futilely at cabs with Off Duty lights boring bright holes in the sheets of rain. Cathy steps outside and presses against the building.

A cab pulls up to the curb. Through the fogged windows she sees, silhouetted, the familiar enactment of a passenger reaching forward over the front seat to pay the driver. The rear door opens and she dashes across the sidewalk. She grabs the door handle and glances across the top of the cab. A man is about to get in the other side. "How far you going?" *he asks as the rain runs off the rim of his hat. He is middle-aged but very distinguished looking.*

"All the way down to the West Twenties," *she answers back.*

"Let me share this taxi with you, and I'll be happy to pay the fare." *She hesitates. A gush of wind pushes a wall of rain in front of it.*

"Come on, make up your minds," *the driver barks.*

They both slide in and close the doors. "I'll even sit way over on my side," *he says laughingly.* "Anyway, I'm too wet to be dangerous."

It's a warm face, she thinks, and a genuine smile. She feels immediately at ease with him. "Where are you going?" *she asks.*

"To the Waldorf."

"We can swing over on Forty-eighth and pass right by there."

"No, no," *he protests.* "It was your cab. We'll drop

you off first. Anyway, this is about the most pleasant thing that's happened to me all day. My name is Anderson North."

As always when it rains in New York, the traffic slows to a crawl. They ride together for almost half an hour. She tells him that she has been in New York for a little over a year. She is trying, with little success, to make a living as a model.

She's wet, but gorgeous, Anderson thinks as he listens to her. She opens her raincoat—a calculated gesture, he believes—exposing her blouse which reveals that she is not wearing a bra. Innately he knows that with little effort he can have company in bed tonight. To ensure his success, he begins a not-so-subtle effort to establish himself as a man of substantial means. Before long, they have managed tacitly to establish that each has something the other wants.

The cab pulls up in front of her walk-up on West Twenty-third. He tells her that he's dining at "Twenty-one" this evening. Would she be so kind as to join him so that they can finish their conversation? "I'd love to," she says, and her eyes tell him that all his expectations will be fulfilled.

She dazzles him in bed. He has never felt more virile, more dominant in his life. Her seeming insatiability excites him more than Rita ever has. In the days that follow, she can't keep her hands off him. Even in public she titillates him by finding discreet ways of unzipping his pants and sliding her hand into his shorts, holding him until he becomes hard.

At the beginning of their affair, Cathy regards Anderson as little more than good company and a first-class meal ticket. After a year in a fifth-floor walk-up, barely able to make ends meet, she readily accepts the role of kept woman. After a while, she finds herself more and more attracted to him. He is handsome, charming, he takes her to the best places and introduces her to a world she's only read about. In time, *she finds herself in love, responding to his tender entreaties, touched by his considerate gestures, and overwhelmed by his stream of gifts.*

Often during foreplay, at the height of his passion, he tells Cathy how much he wants to marry her, but the divorce, he says, will take a little time. Rita is fighting it, he contends, even though there has been no love in their marriage for years. "I've even moved out of the house and leased an apartment near the bank," he tells her, "but still Rita refuses to face up to the facts." Cathy assures him that she is content to wait so long as she knows he loves her and that one day she will be Mrs. Anderson North.

Occasionally, Anderson actually believes he will ask Rita for a divorce. But in reality, he knows that he cannot. He has built his empire on her money and Rita's father, an aged shadow of a man who refuses to die, would bring Anderson's world crashing down if he were to leave her. All he can hope is that Cathy will continue to believe that he is doing everything possible to get free. He is determined to extend his affair as long as possible.

The idea comes to her as an impulse. She will go out to Hammin and surprise Anderson on his birthday. He has told her repeatedly how dreary it is there without her.

When she lands at the airport, she discovers that she is still sixty miles from Hammin. There is a bus, she is told, that will take her there. And so she arrives on a warm afternoon in April, gets off the bus, and heads directly for a pay phone. Anderson has never given her the number of his apartment, so she calls the bank.

"Is Mr. North in?" she asks when his secretary answers.

"I'm sorry, he's gone for the day," the secretary answers.

"Do you know where he can be reached?"

"Probably at home," she says. "He and his wife are leaving for a short vacation this evening. May I be of help?"

Anderson tells Rita that the call is from the bank—there's been a bit of an emergency with an important client. He finds Cathy waiting for him in front of the bus station. From the look on her face, he knows there is no way to salvage their relationship. All he can do now is try and find some way to prevent Rita from finding out.

His explanation begins even before she has closed the car door—he has not asked Rita for a divorce because she has been ill and. . . . Anderson's explanation is lame and his impromptu performance contradictory; it accomplishes nothing, only revealing the depth of his lies.

Her first impulse is to strike back. To get even. She'll tell Rita everything. She spews out her anger, lacing it with threats until, her energy spent, she slumps morosely in the seat. After a while, her hatred slowly begins to turn inward and she silently rebukes herself with a virulence she does not deserve. To have been so stupid . . . to have had so blind a trust in him. I have been nothing more than his whore. Bought and paid for. Subconsciously, she calls up the image of her father the night he caught her petting with a high school boy friend. His Protestant fundamentalism brought forth images of wanton depravity. Of sin without remission. He cursed himself for his failings as a father and loudly bemoaned the passing of Cathy's mother, who he was sure would have prevented this transgression. It was a terrible scene that lingered for over a week, leaving Cathy bowed, contrite, and filled with guilt.

The memory is vivid to her now and she pits her strength against it, driving it down, pushing it back, blocking it out. She stops crying. She has achieved a certain level of numbness. "Take me back to the bus *depot," she commands, and Anderson complies. He offers her several hundred dollars to cover expenses back to New York. She turns her back on him and walks into the waiting room. It is empty except for the ticket agent behind the cage. There will not be another bus until tomorrow.*

She will wait.

"Well, well, Anderson! Surprise! Surprise!" Crawford's taunt sailed out on the buoyant delight of discovery.

"Shut up, Spencer!" Anderson seethed.

"A little kink in the pious armor."

"Shut your face, Spencer! I'm warning you!" Anderson's body coiled and Homer stepped in once again.

"Please! Please! Control yourself for Miss Baoukas's sake."

Dan glanced back at Cathy. Her eyes were vacant, focused at some point well above their heads. She showed no awareness of the exchange taking place in front of her.

Crawford was not about to be silenced. "Anderson, don't you see? This is where it all comes out. This is where we discover the real you." He was enjoying himself immensely. "It's confession time, Anderson. Oh, how those little indiscretions come back to haunt you."

"I'll smash your fucking face in!" Anderson roared as he lunged toward Crawford.

Crawford avoided Anderson's flurry of wild punches by quickly slipping to the floor. Dan grabbed Anderson's arms, pulling him back as Crawford sought the relative security of the dark behind the chair.

"Look!" Charlie shouted, pointing toward Cathy. "It's fading! It's going!"

As the glow faded, Cathy's face seemed to disintegrate.

Dan called out, trying to hold her presence. "Cathy! Cathy!"

She was gone and the room was plunged into total darkness again. Dan felt Homer brush by him as he rushed toward the medium.

"Charlie, turn on the lights," Dan shouted.

Charlie groped for the wall switch and ran into a table, knocking over a lamp.

Crawford's jeering laughter careened off the walls. "I wonder what the people of Hammin are going to say when they hear about the sexual exploits of their moral leader."

Charlie found the switch and for a moment everyone was partially blinded.

The medium groaned.

"Doctor!" Homer shrieked. "I think she's having a heart attack!"

Dan let go of Anderson to help the woman.

Anderson snarled with animallike rage as he tried to reach Crawford.

"Don't get me wrong, Anderson," Crawford said, darting back and forth, adroitly managing to keep a piece of furniture between them. "It's great to know you're human!"

Dan felt for the woman's pulse. It was racing. Her breathing was rapid and her body twisted and turned as though she were suffering some kind of pain. Dan could not begin to determine the source.

"I'll kill you, Spencer! If I get my hands on you, I'll . . ."

Charlie wrapped an arm around Anderson's shoulder trying to contain him.

"Let me go!" Anderson's shrill command was followed with an elbow to Charlie's midsection, doubling him over. Anderson spun away and dashed for the front door.

"Don't go now, Anderson," Crawford called. "The party's just begun." He whirled around, threw his head back, and hooted. "Oh, I've waited a long, long time for something like this! Oh, God, that felt good!" Crawford staggered out to the foyer and opened the front door. "Anderson! I've got you now, you cocksucker!"

His words were answered with spinning wheels, kicking up gravel, and then a short screech as rubber met concrete.

Crawford's laughter faded as he got into his car.

"What do you think, Doctor?" Homer asked, looking over his shoulder.

The woman's breathing was back to normal and the pulse was slowing down. She fluttered back to consciousness. "I think she's going to be okay. Here, help me put her on the couch." Together the two men lifted her up. Charlie got a pillow ready for her head.

"Don't worry," Dan said as the medium opened her eyes. "Everything's all right, you're going to be fine."

Within a short time, Pauline Baoukas was sitting up sipping on a glass of bourbon. She answered Charlie's questions, but the answers told them nothing. As Charlie began to circle back over some previous points, the woman stood up and announced she was leaving and instructed Homer to collect her thousand dollars. Charlie produced it from his pocket and gave it to her. She handed it to Homer and signaled for him to follow.

Dan and Charlie stood on the front porch and watched until their car disappeared into the night. Charlie turned back toward the house shaking his head. "Mr. North is going to have my ass. And Jesus, I never expected anything like that to happen. How in hell did she do it?"

"I don't know," Dan answered pensively.

"Goddamn, that was enough to give a man religion. Look at me." He held out his hand and spread his fingers. "I'm still shaking. I'd give anything to know how she pulled that off. And the worst part was that I didn't get anything out of her. The whole damn strategy went out the window. Didn't tell us one goddamn thing."

"No but Cathy certainly did," Dan said, turning around and leaning up against the railing.

"Yeah. Think of that," Charlie said reflectively. "Anderson had an affair with her. He knew who she was all along." Charlie looked up at Dan. "You know, he really had me convinced that he didn't know her. I'll bet Crawford Spencer is going to have a field day with this. It'll be all over town."

Dan nodded his concurrence, but he found he was having a difficult time bringing any order to his thought processes. Nothing wanted to stay stuck down for very long. "I know what I saw," he said in slow, measured tones, "but I don't believe it."

"Well, you knew the girl. Was it her?"

"All I can tell you is that it *looked* like her. The voice was different, I'm sure of that."

"Whatever it was, that woman's got one hell of an act." Charlie rocked back in the chair and put his hands behind his head. "You know, it could be that she had an accomplice. Maybe someone was outside a window with a projection device or something. Tomorrow morning, I'm going over this place inch by inch."

"And if you don't find anything, what will that tell you?"

"That she's either extremely clever or that I'd better reassess my belief in the supernatural." He underscored his answer with a light, self-deprecating laugh.

Dan found nothing more to say except to ask Charlie for a ride over to Carole's so that he could pick up his car. As they drove through the courthouse square, Charlie broke a long silence.

"You know, Anderson had an idea that I'm going to follow up on. He said that I should try to find the girl's family. If revenge is the motive, they might be very likely candidates."

"How long do you think that's going to take?" Dan asked with a touch of impatience in his voice.

"Hard to say," Charlie answered simply as he stopped in front of Carole's house.

"Well," Dan snapped, "all I can say is that we'd better find our dollmaker soon, because we're running out of time." He got out of the car and slammed the door.

Inside, Carole was huddled on the sofa in the fetal position. She looked drawn and tired as she asked him what had happened. He felt it best to sidestep the question, so he told her things didn't work out as planned. She let out a deep sigh and lowered her head to her knees.

"I'm not going to make it, Dan. I don't think I'm going to make it."

"Yes, you are," he said firmly. "Yes, you are." And with that he picked her up and carried her up to the bedroom. He gave her a sleeping pill and sat by her bed until she fell asleep. Then he went back downstairs, let himself out, and locked the door.

The night was sticky and close. Dan parked his car by the trailer, got out, shed his clothes, and left them on the hood. He walked down to the lake and waded in. He swam a few strokes, then turned over on his back and floated. A cloud cover made the sky a black pit.

If that was really Cathy, he thought, why didn't she say anything to me? She recognized Crawford and Anderson, but not me. It's almost as if all she wanted to do was reveal her relationship with Anderson. All the links are falling in place. Let me think. Anderson must have been seeing Cathy when he was negotiating with me to come to Hammin. Must have met her on one of his trips. I can understand how she would have fallen for him. Anderson can charm the shoes off a person when he makes up his mind to it. And then for some reason she followed him here. That must have shaken him. What was it Charlie said? Oh yeah, Crawford said he'd met her in the bus depot. He's followed by Judy Simpson . . . and then me. Still can't figure how Cathy fell in with Reeson. Maybe that's one of the things I don't buy about tonight. If it had really been her, she would have said something about leaving. I'm sure she would have. No, that wasn't her. I don't know who or what it was . . . but it wasn't her.

Dan recalled that several months after Cathy's disappearance, he had concluded that their relationship would never have worked out. Beyond the physical attraction and the emotional intimacy that her original condition and recovery had created, the kind of things so necessary to the fabric of a day-to-day, year-to-year living-together just weren't there. That didn't mean he cared less, it was just that after her disappearance . . . with time . . . the pragmatist in him had risen to subdue the romantic. Then, that night at the carnival, the sight of her image called up the sense of loss, the unsettled enigma of her disappearance. It had awakened old feelings. And while those feelings did not impinge upon or diminish his love for Carole, he found himself confronting the same melancholy that one might experience when, after many years of silence, news comes that an old love has died.

Dan pulled up his knees, forced his feet to the bottom, and stood up, turning toward the far side of the lake. A little less than three years ago, he and Cathy had picnicked on the hillside. He strained to try to see the little three-sided shed which had sheltered them from the rain, but it was too dark.

Dan tilted his head back and shouted as loud as he could, "Caaaaatheeeee!" Her name arched up over the water only to be consumed in the dark folds of the distant meadow.

xvii

The sun hiked up over the redwood enclosure that formed the railing around Crawford's deck and pierced the morning grayness in his bedroom. He glanced over at the clock. It was a little before six. His tongue was a wad of cotton and he sucked and worked his mouth back and forth to generate saliva. Crawford rolled over on his back and stared up at the white void of his ceiling. He played through the events of the preceding evening and tried to rationalize what he'd seen. Unable to arrive at a satisfactory explanation, he directed his thoughts to more immediate concerns. With reluctance, he began his morning inventory of physical discomforts. The legs: leaden. Stiffness in the joints. No change. Testicles: dull ache. Would have to make evaluation after he'd urinated. Stomach: bloated and painful to external pressure. Chest: moderate tightness. No different from yesterday. Final check: He raised his head slightly. The pincers of pain drove through his temples, meeting in the thalamus, exploding outward and shooting down the back of his neck. His head dropped heavily to the pillow and he waited for the waves of agony to ebb.

Crawford had, from time to time in his thirty-nine years, given occasional thought to the circumstances of his demise. In his twenties, he had alternately pictured himself at some ripe age giving-it-up after having satisfied the voracious appetite of an enticing young creature or, failing that, cashing in while involved in some daring adventure of indefinite description. But as he neared forty, he hoped for the familiar comforts of clean sheets and the good fortune to go off in his sleep. And in recent weeks, he had found himself confronting, with disturbing regularity, the specter of his mortality.

His initial plan, to finance his escape with several thousand dollars from Anderson, had been conceived through the veil of an alcoholic haze. Upon more sober analysis he found it flimsy, uncertain, and lacking the necessary degree of coercive inducement. No point in trying to use his affair with Rita North for blackmail if Anderson already knew about it. And Rita was, he felt, in many ways as victimized by Anderson as he had been. But all that did not matter now that Anderson's affair with Cathy had been revealed.

That bit of information would be his negotiable bond, his collateral for a sizable loan to be carried for an indeterminate length of time. He permitted himself to smirk as he imagined the consternation Anderson must be experiencing realizing that he, Crawford Spencer, might have already begun to spread the news.

He stood up and made his way into the kitchen where he fixed himself a Bloody Mary and put on a pot of coffee. The anticipation of his plan pumped adrenaline into his system and he felt better than he had in days. He showered, shaved, and dressed.

He waited until eight o'clock to place his call.

Rita answered the phone. "Hello?"

"Hi Rita, did I wake you?"

"No, no, I've been up for some time."

"Is Anderson there?"

"He's in the shower, but he should be out any second. How are you doing?" she asked with sympathetic concern.

"As well as could be expected."

"It's horrible, this hex thing, isn't it?"

"Yeah," he mumbled.

"Crawford, what happened last night at Charlie Coles'?"

"What do you mean, what happened?"

"Well," she seemed to catch her breath. "Anderson came home and—I've never seen him so upset. Wouldn't say a thing to me. Just locked himself in his library. What went on there?" Her tone begged for an answer.

Just as he'd suspected, Anderson had said nothing. Good. That meant he was primed.

"Crawford? Crawford, are you still there?"

"Yeah, yeah . . . I'm sorry . . . had to catch something on the stove. Actually I'm not sure what happened. I left early, so there's really not much I can tell you. He didn't say anything, huh?"

"Nothing. Oh, Crawford, I'm so worried," she lowered her voice, "for *everyone*. You are taking care of yourself, aren't you? I mean, do you need anything?"

The timbre of Rita's voice echoed of other times. Crawford thought he detected a trace of the old desire, and he smiled with satisfaction at the remembrance of the magnetism his mere touch had held for her. Rita had just entered the first throes of her change of life and in an effort to counter the increasingly frequent emotional depressions—and to get her off his back —Anderson had insisted that she take golf lessons. Her need wasn't diversion, but rather reinforcement of her sexuality. Crawford provided that along with her golf lessons. Because of his attention, Rita bloomed. Her bouts of despondence were fewer and far between. She started dressing in ways that accented her full and still firm figure. But by late fall, instead of appreciating the change, Anderson accused her of behaving like a capricious twenty-year-old in heat. During the winter, he ignored her altogether.

Rita confided in Crawford that Anderson seemed to be totally unresponsive to her needs. To further complicate her life, an overactive imagination caused her to suspect that Anderson might be seeing other women. As his business trips to New York became more frequent and prolonged, she found herself searching his laundry for lipstick or long hairs—anything that might confirm her suspicions. There was nothing, but she felt sure. During the spring, she found herself alone for as long as ten days to two weeks at a time. At first, she tried to resist her own feelings about having a retaliatory affair. After a while, she let them flow freely. In May, she resumed her golf lessons. Crawford was attentive; his hands constantly found reason to touch her shoulders, her arms, or to grip her waist. Their conversations were rife with double entendres. They both knew the final decision was hers.

It was a soft June evening. Crawford stood at his bar fixing her a drink. She had resisted his suggestion to sit on the deck. It was her first time in his house and she found herself fidgeting and speaking in short, nervous sentences.

Anderson was in Chicago and would be there for several days.

There were more drinks, meaningless talk, and soon she found herself warm and relaxed. Sensing the appropriate moment, Crawford simply took her hand and led her to the bedroom.

The affair, episodic as it was, lasted the summer and then Rita nervously ended it. They had been discreet—or so she thought. She had come and gone under the cover of darkness, avoided his windows, and stayed off his deck. And yet, people knew.

Somehow the rumor of Rita's affair with Crawford eventually reached Anderson North. It was the only reason Crawford could think of for Anderson's destroying the dream Crawford had wrapped in the sporting goods store.

As Crawford listened to Rita's voice on the other end of the line, he remembered their meetings fondly. He was tempted to say something that would signal his regard for her, but let it pass.

"Here's Anderson now," Rita said.

Crawford heard her tell Anderson who it was. There was a sharp, "What's he want?" followed by the deadness of a hand being placed tightly over the mouthpiece. After a moment, the background sounds of the room could be heard and Anderson followed with a rapid, guarded, "Yeah?"

"That was quite a little show you sponsored last night. Wouldn't have missed it for the world. But say, I do have one little suggestion. Next time, be sure you get a look at the script first."

"Why don't you stick it up your ass!"

"I'll take that under consideration."

"Good-bye!"

"Hold it! Wait a minute. We've got business to discuss. I want a mutual-benefit arrangement."

"What are you talking about? Get to the point."

"Not on the phone. This is something we should discuss in person."

"Spencer, I wouldn't discuss the time of day with you."

"But you'll discuss this, because right now I've got you by the short hairs. I'll be over in thirty minutes."

Crawford hung up before Anderson could reply. I've got him on the defensive, he thought. Now all I have to do is keep him there.

Anderson was standing on his front steps when Crawford pulled into the drive. Crawford made no move to get out of the car. It would be better to make Anderson come to him. The two men glared at each other for a long moment, then Anderson walked toward the car and leaned over to look in the passenger side window.

"Get in," Crawford said with a short, crisp firmness that was intended to reinforce his offensive position.

"I can hear you just fine out here."

Crawford leaned over, pulled up the handle, and pushed out the door. "I don't think we need to advertise our meeting to your neighbors."

On that point, Anderson seemed to agree and got in.

Immediately, Crawford put the car in reverse and backed out of the drive.

"Where the hell do you think you're going?"

"I thought we'd take a ride," Crawford said coolly. "This way, we'll be sure not to have any interruptions."

Crawford turned onto U.S. 81, headed over the summit of The Hill, past the churches, the park, and the cemetery, and then down the hill, past the small tract development, picking up speed as the road flattened out across the open farmland.

"I'll come right to the point," Crawford said. "I've decided to leave Hammin, for good."

"That's the best news I've heard in a month. Now turn around and take me back home."

Crawford ignored him and continued, "I'm not going to sit here and rot with the hex. And anyway, I need a change of scenery."

Anderson looked at him warily, "So when are you leaving?"

Crawford stared straight ahead and permitted a smile to creep across his face, knowing full well that it would unsettle Anderson. "Well, that depends on our mutual-benefit agreement." He enunciated each word slowly and distinctly. "Paradoxical as it may seem, we need each other. Now what could Anderson North ever need from ol' Crawford Spencer, you ask. I think you know the answer. You need me to keep my mouth shut. Because if I should . . . inadvertently tell people about what happened last night and in the telling let it slip that you had indulged your secret lusts in an amorous adventure. . . ."

He purposely left the resolution of the sentence hanging, then quickly stole a glance to assess Anderson's reaction. Satisfied with his progress he continued. "Well, you know better than I what that little revelation would do to your reputation. A lot of people in this town would not take kindly to the knowledge that their moral and financial patriarch had feet of clay. No, sir. If I were in your shoes, I sure wouldn't want folks to know that I'd been fucking my head off with a girl young enough to be my daughter."

Anderson's sweat glands seemed to burst open and his body drew up taut. Bitter rage ran rabid just beneath the surface. Crawford sensed it and wondered if maybe he'd pushed him too close to the edge. An irrational, defensive outburst would do him no good at all. What he needed was rational acquiescence anchored soundly in Anderson's instincts for self-preservation. There was no backing up. Crawford knew he had to continue to play out his hand.

"Now what is it that you can do for me?" he asked, trying to sound more like a barterer than tormentor. "No mystery to you, I'm sure. I need money. And you've got money. I'd say that your half of our mutual-benefit agreement would be worth, oh, about fifteen thousand dollars. "You might be interested to know how I arrived at that figure. It's roughly the amount I lost in our little joint business venture. I can't prove it, of course, but we both know that you screwed me in the deal."

Crawford waited to see if his assertion would draw a comment from Anderson. It did not. "You know, when you think about it," he said reflectively, "you're going to come out a lot better in this than I did in our bankruptcy. I barely crawled away with the clothes on my back, and here you're going to walk out with your good Christian reputation intact and you'll barely miss the money."

"You forget," Anderson said without changing his expression or taking his eyes off Crawford, "there were other people in that room last night. You're not the only one who knows about me and the girl."

"That's true. And I've taken it into consideration.

First, there's Charlie Cole. You own him. He's not going to say anything. Then there's Doc. Too much of a gentleman to tell tales. Finally, there's the medium and her creepy assistant. What do they care about you and your sex life? So that leaves me . . . and I'm your problem, because you don't own me and I'm certainly not a gentleman."

"You really are a low, slimy, ass-licking son of a bitch!"

"That so? Think of it, Anderson, for fifteen thousand dollars this slimy son of a bitch will be out of your life forever and nobody will ever know about Cathy." Crawford looked confidently at Anderson, who was sagging a little. The first indication of resignation, Crawford thought. He went for the close. "I presume we have a deal?"

Anderson turned away and stared out the window. After a moment of contemplation, a sneering smile curled his mouth. "No deal! No fifteen thousand! Not so much as one goddamn cent!" Anderson snorted a laugh. "I really thought you had me boxed in. I really did. And you were right, I worried about it all last night. But you dumb bastard! You showed me the way out. You opened the door and I'm going to walk through it and slam it in your filthy face!"

Crawford was stunned by the abrupt turnabout, but he tried not to let it show. "You're a lousy poker player, North. I'm calling your bluff."

"Then let me lay it out for you. As you said, you're the only one I have to worry about. The others won't say a thing. That means it's your word against mine. And I think it's safe to say my word carries a hell of a lot more credibility than Hammin's unanimous choice for motherfucker of the year." Anderson turned away and laughed, "Go ahead, say what you want. Sure it'll cause me a little problem, but in the end, people will believe me." Anderson's smugness filled the car. "Now you can take me home."

Crawford's foot pushed down on the accelerator.

"Let's not play games, Spencer," Anderson said, glancing at the speedometer.

It's not going to work, Crawford thought. He's right. I've let the bastard off the hook. And even if I could make people believe me, what good is that? It's not going to get me out of Hammin. He felt tremors of panic spiral down through his body. Maybe if I sell all my furniture . . . I've got three sets of clubs. They should bring several hundred each. No! Goddamn it! That son of a bitch is going to pay! He owes it to me, and he's going to pay! I'm not going to crawl out of Hammin while he laughs his ass off.

"All right, Anderson, try this one on. What if I could prove beyond question, and I mean so that everyone in Hammin would believe me beyond any doubt. . . ." He took a quick, sidelong look at Anderson. "What if I could prove that three years ago, I was fucking the hell out of your wife right under your goddamn nose. I'd have everyone in Hammin laughing their asses off at you."

Anderson's lungs exploded with a bansheelike yowl. His hands shot up toward Crawford's throat as he lunged across the seat.

"Look out! Jesus Christ!" Crawford brought up his elbow to blunt some of Anderson's thrust. He shot a glance down the road and saw a blue pickup truck approaching in the distance.

"You rotten asshole bastard!" Anderson spat as he drove his right hand into Crawford's ribs and grabbed for his hair with the other.

"Let go of me, goddammit! You'll get us killed!" Crawford's foot slammed down on the brake, but it slipped off as Anderson's knee kicked into his thigh.

"I'm going to kill you with my bare hands!" Anderson shrieked, his eyes bulging with fiery rage.

The blue pickup was bearing down on them.

"I can't steer!"

The car swerved across the median line. Crawford managed to yank the wheel back in time to miss the pickup. Again his foot went for the brakes. Anderson landed a crunching blow on the bridge of his nose and blood gushed over his mouth. The steering wheel kicked as the right front tire dropped off the pavement onto the shoulder. Crawford jerked his head back to avoid a wildly thrown right. He cocked his elbow and launched it viciously into Anderson's chest, knocking him back across the seat against the door. The right wheel slipped into a deep rut, pulling the car further off the road, pushing the worn shocks beyond their capacity, throwing both men's heads hard against the roof.

Crawford fought to bring the car back to the left. Suddenly, he felt the steering wheel spin free as the front of the car rocketed off the shoulder, over a drainage ditch, slamming into a tree. Anderson's body was catapulted head first into the windshield while the gear box on the steering shaft was forced backward, ramming the steering wheel into Crawford's chest, flattening his breast bone, crushing his lungs, and severing his spinal cord.

The driver of the pickup had pulled up after the near miss. Now he spun his truck around and rushed back to the mangle of twisted metal. He got out, ran up to the driver's side window, and immediately turned away gagging on his own vomit. Wiping his mouth with the back of his hand, he forced himself to go around to the other side. Through the bloody mess he recognized Anderson North. He was unconscious, but still breathing.

Using his CB, the trucker called for help. The state troopers arrived first. Just minutes later, Toby Mitchell screeched his squad car to a stop. He and Dan Frederickson jumped out. The ambulance was right behind them.

"Over here!" Charlie Cole was standing there, waving his arms frantically.

Dan leaped across the drainage ditch and ran over to where Charlie was kneeling beside Anderson. Dan made a quick inspection. Pulse strong. Good possibility of multiple fractures. Definite break in the right forearm. His lungs seemed clear, so apparently they hadn't been punctured. But his face. As Dan looked down at the lacerated skin, the long, deep gashes laying open the meaty flesh, the pulverized nose and the misshapen jaw, it occurred to him that nobody would ever again suggest that he looked like Cary Grant.

Anderson groaned, then opened his eyes, trying to focus through bloody slits. "You're going to be all right," Dan said with calm reassurance. "You're going to be all right."

Dan helped the ambulance attendants lift Anderson onto the stretcher. They carried him across the ditch, fastened the stretcher on the metal rolling frame, and slid it in the back of the ambulance.

Dan followed and sat down beside Anderson, reaching for his medical bag. The driver closed his door and looked back at Dan. Dan nodded, "Let's go."

Toby and Charlie watched them disappear in the distance. Turning around, they saw that the state troopers had freed Crawford and were laying him in a rubber body bag. Toby shook his head as they zipped it up. "Jesus! They must have been doing over seventy. Where in hell were they going? And what were they doing together in the first place?" Another question flashed into Toby's head and he turned to Charlie. "Say, how did you get out here so fast?"

"I was following them. I got a call this morning from Mr. North. Said he wanted me to come over right away, okay? He said something about Crawford coming to see him and he wanted me around just in case."

"Just in case, what?"

"I don't know. That's all he said. Well, when I got there Crawford was pulling out of the driveway and Anderson was with him. So I thought I'd better follow them. I stayed about a quarter mile behind until we got well out here on the flat. Then Crawford took off. He must have been doing eighty, and that car of mine groans when it pushes sixty-five. When I got here. . . ." he made a gesture of futility.

"Poor bastards," Toby said with a sigh. "Well, I guess there's nothing more to do here."

"Hey, Chief!" the shout came from one of the troopers. "Come take a look at this." The man was standing next to Crawford's car. As Toby and Charlie approached, he gestured inside toward the back seat.

They peered into the dim interior. There, lying in a pool of blood on the back seat, its body broken and twisted, its face split open, was Crawford's doll.

xviii

The news of Crawford's death and the discovery of the doll had been like a massive infusion of adrenaline in the public body. It was not that interest in the hex had waned, rather it had settled on a high plateau of watchful expectancy. The accident had provided new substance and inspired a rash of new speculations, especially around the bar at the Hammin Inn. There were those who gave the dolls animate powers and for substantiation pointed out that only one doll had been found at the crash site—Crawford's. They argued against someone's planting it in Crawford's car, saying that no one could have anticipated the accident. Even if they had, there would have been no way of knowing which, if either, of the two men would survive. No, they concluded, the dolls had mystical powers.

"I can't buy that," Skeet Fischer said in response to one of his patrons who voiced support for the theory.

"Then how'd it get there?" the man challenged.

Skeet shrugged and shook his head.

Toby was seated at a nearby table. One of his police officers, Amos Zipp, sat across from him, watching him consume his evening meal. Zipp had been listening intently to the conversation at the bar; he turned to Toby and found himself repeating the same question, "How did it get there?"

"How did what get where?" Toby asked while trying to coax some peas onto his fork.

"The doll you found in the back of Crawford's car. How did it get there?"

"I don't know, but I've got it on my list to think about just as soon as we get Spencer in the ground."

Toby had arranged for a local undertaker to bury Crawford with the promise that he'd be paid out of whatever Crawford left in his estate.

"Where they going to put him?" the policeman asked.

"Up on The Hill."

"The Hill?" Amos voiced his surprise.

"Yeah. Carter Langly donated a plot."

"You don't say? He wasn't all that close with Crawford. I wonder why he'd do a thing like that?"

"He said it was the least he could do for the man who helped him take twelve strokes off his handicap."

A smile revealed the policeman's nicotine-stained teeth. "Well, I guess that's one way to get yourself firmly planted in Hammin's high society."

Toby looked up at him and groaned his rejection of the man's pun. He pushed his plate away and reached for the coffee. "I'll tell you one thing for sure, Anderson North is going to pee in his pants when he finds out. His family is buried up there and I don't imagine having them spend eternity with Crawford Spencer is going to sit too well with him."

"From what you told me, North is damn lucky that we're not layin' him out, too."

The door to the Hammin Inn swung open and another policeman stuck his head in and looked around.

"Hey, Jack! Over here." Amos waved to get his attention. "Looks like something's up," he said, offering an interpretation of Jack's expression and uncharacteristic haste.

Toby did not bother to turn around, but concentrated on achieving the right balance between sugar, cream, and coffee.

"Hey, Chief. . . ." Jack said, pulling up a chair and sitting down.

Toby raised his hand to cut him off. "Why aren't you watching the station?"

"I don't have to. The place is full of reporters. Must be six or seven of them. One came all the way from Chicago. They want to ask you some questions about the hex and about the accident and all."

"How they find out about that?"

"I don't know. But they've already interviewed the trooper who found the doll, and I guess he told them they should come see you."

"And you left them in the station? By themselves? *Kee-ryst*, man! Did you invite them to look through the files while you were out!" Toby quelled an urge to rip off the man's badge. "Get your ass back there and throw 'em out!"

"I already tried that. They said they wouldn't go until they talked to you. They seem real determined," he said, obviously somewhat in awe.

Toby thumped his fist down on the table. "Look, nitwit! You're a cop! You've got a badge! Order them out and if they don't go, lock em up!" Toby quickly thought better of that bit of direction. "No . . . no, don't do that. Just tell them I've gone for the day and you don't know where to reach me."

Jack stood up and was about to leave when he saw them coming in the front door. "Uh oh. Here they come."

The reporters spotted Jack and made their way across the room to where Toby and Amos were sitting.

"Which one of you is Chief Mitchell?" one of the reporters asked as the rest surrounded the table.

The question surprised Toby momentarily until he realized that his penchant for dressing in civilian clothes gave no clue to his identity. Immediately seizing the opportunity, he stood up and looked at Amos Zipp sitting across the table from him and said, "Chief, I guess you've got company, so I'll be running along. See you tomorrow."

The policeman did a double take and sloshed his coffee into his lap. When he looked up again, he was surrounded by the reporters hammering him with questions.

As Toby hurried out the door, he knew that sooner or later he'd have to face them. But at least now he had some time to order his thoughts and formulate an official position. As he walked across the street toward the courthouse, he permitted himself a couple of minutes to savor his facile escape.

"Hell, I think that just about made my day."

Dan stood at the end of Anderson's bed examining the chart. It was a perfunctory gesture, for he knew exactly what he'd find. No change. Condition: stable. He looked at Anderson's right leg in its heavy cast, trussed up off the bed on a pulley arrangement. Dan had put casts on both arms as well, and bandaged his entire head, leaving holes only for his mouth, nose, and eyes. Dan was aware that beneath the layers of gauze Anderson was listening to the nurse's motherly sounding report on how well "her patient" was doing.

"Dan." The sound came out in the wheezy alto of a boxer who's been hit on the windpipe once too often. Dan stepped over to the side of the bed.

"Dan . . . you got to help me." Anderson's speech was constrained and clenched. Dan had had to wire his jaw closed after he'd reset the jawbone. Anderson would have to live with that for weeks.

Dan laid a reassuring hand gently on Anderson's upper arm. "You're going to be all right. Nothing to worry about. All you have to do is try and rest."

"No . . . the hex . . . it's gonna kill me." He gurgled, trying to clear his throat. "I know it now. Tell . . Charlie. Got to get dollmaker . . . before it kills me."

"Anderson, you don't have to worry about that. Nothing can harm you here. I promise you that."

"Don't let the . . . doll . . . get me."

Dan left the hospital a little after eight and drove over to Carole's. He found her in bed, under a stack of covers, shivering even though the room temperature must have been eighty. Dan sat on the edge of the bed and pulled her up into his arms. She wept quietly, but said nothing.

My God, he thought as she pulled away, she's dying a little more each day. Panic rippled through his body. Until this moment, he had assumed that he could somehow reverse the power of the hex . . . that he would save her. Suddenly he found himself confronted with the reality of it all: Carole might die.

On impulse, he picked her up out of the bed as though snatching her away from the grip of death, and carried her down to his car.

"I think it's better if you stay with me." Dan ignored her protest, realizing she was too weak to pursue it. Once at the trailer, he put her to bed and then climbed in alongside, pressing his body close to hers.

By ten, Carole was asleep and Dan listened carefully to every breath and sensed every movement. He prodded his mind to come up with possible treatments, ideas of what he might do to save her. Always he came back to the same answer: Find the dolls. And find them soon. Time was running out.

The phone rang in the far end of the trailer.

Dan eased himself out of bed and hurried down the small hallway, hoping that the ring would not awaken Carole. He lifted the receiver off the hook before the fourth ring and glanced back toward the bedroom. He heard her stir and thrash a bit as she rolled over, but there was no indication she'd awakened.

"Dan, I'm sorry to bother you so late." It was Rita.

"That's okay. What's the matter? Anything wrong? I've got a nurse with Anderson around the clock."

"No, no . . . it's not that. I just wondered. . . ." She paused, and Dan sensed indecision in the silence. "You know they're burying Crawford tomorrow?" It was a rhetorical question.

"Yes, I know."

"Are you going to the funeral?"

"I really hadn't thought about it."

"I think I will. I mean . . . well, I don't suppose anyone else will be there. But he *was* a friend. Once. Before he and Anderson——" She cut herself off and Dan thought he heard a catch in her breathing that suggested she was choking back tears. "I'm sorry, Dan, I really don't know why I called to tell you this."

Dan understood the implied request. "Would you like some company?"

"Oh, it's not necessary. . . ." She quickly reversed herself. "I hate to put you out. But I want to go, and I'd rather not be alone."

"I understand. I'll pick you up in the morning."

"Thank you, Dan. I just really think . . . somebody ought to be there. He was. . . ." There was an extended silence, then, "Good night. I'll see you tomorrow."

Dan waited until he heard the click at the other end of the line, then hung up. He walked over to the trailer door, opened it, and leaned against the door frame taking the sweet night air deep into his lungs. His thoughts raced back and forth over a dozen different questions and problems that had no resolutions.

Another piercing ring startled him and he reacted with a leap toward the phone.

Rita again? The hospital?

It was neither. The caller had a message, a message that provided the answer to what had become one of his most important questions. But with the answer came a wave of despair, the intensity of which sent him reeling out of the trailer into the night.

xix

A heavy rain during the night had left The Hill obscured by cloud and mist. Wet tree trunks, turned dark, stood out as silhouettes against the shroud of gray.

Rita, dressed in black, clung to Dan's arm. He guided her to the grave site, which was located in the most remote corner of the cemetery. It appeared that Carter Langly, for all his generosity in donating the plot, was intent on keeping Crawford a discreet distance from the departed cream of Hammin society, such as it was. It occurred to Dan that Crawford would have found an enormous amount of humor in the realization that his untimely death had brought with it ultimate acceptance on The Hill.

If anything, the mist seemed to be gaining density. It wasn't until they were within a hundred feet of the grave that Dan was able to make out the sum total of Crawford's cortege. There was Toby, Charlie, Father Handley from the Episcopal Church, and two grave diggers who were in the process of lowering Crawford's pine coffin into the earth.

The box hit bottom with a soft thud and the grave diggers pulled on their ropes to retrieve them from the hole, then faded noiselessly down the pathway. It was incredibly still. Any sound that might have emanated from outside the perimeter of the cemetery was smothered hopelessly by the dense air.

Toby looked down at the coffin and, with a sincerity that bordered on poignancy, said, "Well, Crawford, if it's any consolation, it's a hell of a rotten day for golf."

The father looked up aghast until he saw the expression on Toby's face. "Are you expecting anyone else?" he asked.

Toby looked around. "Tell you the truth, Father, I didn't expect this many."

"Then we can begin." It was a statement punctuated by the opening of The Book of Common Prayer. "I won't read the whole service. I'll just begin with what we normally say at the grave." His tone was at once both a request for permission and an apology.

"This is your department, Father," Toby said.

"Man, that is born of a woman, hath but a short time to live, and is full of misery. He cometh up, and is cut down, like a flower; he fleeth as it were a shadow, and never continueth in one stay."

The fog seemed to be lifting slightly and Dan let his gaze wander from the grave across the marble sentinels strung out in neat rows across the lush green grass. At first he thought it was only some kind of optical illusion. He saw small blotches of color bleeding through the mist—blue, red, yellow, brown. The colors were moving.

Toby picked up the quizzical look on Dan's face, then glanced in the same direction. He saw them, too.

"Thou knowest, Lord, the secrets of our hearts: shut not thy merciful ears to our prayer. . . ."

The fog seemed to thin momentarily.

People.

Ten . . . fifty . . . no a hundred people or more in raincoats. Many carried umbrellas.

Crawford had drawn a crowd after all. They stopped and stood a respectful distance away.

Very strange, Dan thought. Then he understood why. He was able to make out three of Toby's policemen manning a rope that had been strung across their path.

"He that raised up Jesus from the dead will also quicken our mortal bodies. . . ."

Tears trickled down Rita's cheeks and she dabbed at her eyes with a handkerchief.

The priest leaned over and picked up a silver trowel, scooped up some dirt, and then let it fall onto the coffin. "Unto Almighty God we commend the soul of our brother departed, and we commit his body to the ground; earth to earth; ashes to ashes, dust to dust. . . ."

Father Handley read on, but Dan no longer heard the words, just the cadence of the litany. He noticed that the phalanx of colorful raincoats and umbrellas had managed to press closer to the grave. What do they expect to see, he wondered. What in the hell draws people to something like this? Morbid fascination, he presumed.

"Amen."

"Amen," he heard himself say reflexively. It was over.

The priest seemed bent on making the fastest and most direct exit possible within the fringes of dignity. He nodded his good-byes and left with the undertaker in the hearse. As if by some prearranged cue, the grave diggers materialized again, shovels in hand.

Rita pulled her arm out of Dan's. "I'll take you home," he said.

"No, you go ahead with Toby and Charlie. My parents are buried here, you know. Anderson's, too," she added as an afterthought. "I haven't been to their graves since Easter. I'll be fine," she said, walking away.

The policemen dropped the restraining line and the crowd surged toward the grave for a closer look. They were not to be denied. Their only concession was to step aside so that Rita could pass unhindered.

"Will you look at those goddamn vultures?" Toby said with disgust. The question was addressed to both Charlie and Dan, but he did not expect them to answer. "We could have charged admission."

The three men made their way through the crowd and headed down the washed gravel path that led to the cemetery entrance. A couple of latecomers approached them and hurried past. "Did we miss it?" one asked.

"Yeah," Toby answered.

The couple showed their disappointment.

"But don't worry, they're going to dig him up and do it all over again in thirty minutes."

After a moment of shocked silence, the couple hurried away. Toby, Charlie, and Dan continued walking, their silence filled by the steady crunch of feet on gravel.

Toby stared off into the gray wall. "Somewhere out in that fog, there are about a half dozen reporters, maybe more by now, who are still looking for me. And when they find me, I'm going to have to say something about this goddamn hex business. And that presents one big problem. If I refuse to say anything, we'll never get rid of them. If I say too much, they'll blow everything all to-hell-and-gone out of proportion."

"I can't advise you on what to say," Dan said, "but I can tell you one thing: "If we don't find out who's behind this very soon, you're going to have two and maybe three more deaths on your hands."

"What are you talking about?"

"I'm talking about Carole and Anderson. And maybe Judy Simpson. I haven't seen her, so I don't know what shape she's in. But I'm telling you, we could very easily lose them to the hex."

"Lose them?" Charlie's emphasis asked for clarification.

"They're sick. *Very* sick," Dan said with a gravity that carried conviction. "More than that, they're scared. Literally scared to the brink of death."

The time had come, Dan felt, that both Toby and Charlie should understand the full implications of the hex. Briefly, he told them about his two years on the

Ivory Coast, about Tureau, about the power of induced suggestion. He explained reverse mental therapy and cited other examples of self-generated neurosis and psychosomatic illness.

"It is," he said at last by the way of summary, "mental poison. And it can kill with the same finality as any chemical poison."

Charlie regarded Dan suspiciously. "You know, Doctor, I had no idea you were so familiar with all of this. I'm a little surprised that you haven't said something before now."

"What I should or shouldn't have done is something to sort out later. The main thing now is to find out who's behind this."

"And we really aren't any closer to that than we were when we started." Charlie made a gesture of futility.

"Except," Dan said, "I still think the family angle makes sense. It would have to be someone who was terribly hurt by her death."

"That was Mr. North's feeling, too," said Charlie. "But so far I haven't been able to figure out even where to start looking. Of course, after what we learned the other night. . . ."

Toby cut him off, "What are you talking about?"

Dan and Charlie exchanged glances. "Well, I'm sure you'd find out sooner or later," Charlie said. "Apparently, Mr. North had an affair with this Cathy. Met her in New York."

"Anderson had an affair with her?" Toby's amazement was genuine. "Does Rita know?"

"No, I don't think so," Charlie said.

"Well, son of a bitch. I didn't think he had it in him. Sounds like this little girl was really spreading it around." Toby looked directly at Dan to see what kind of reaction his last statement would make.

"It seems that way, doesn't it," Dan said, showing a touch of disillusionment.

"At least this supports the revenge motive," Charlie added. "It all fits."

"Except for Carole," Toby put in. "Just doesn't seem to be a link there at all."

"And yet there is," Dan said solemnly.

Both Charlie and Toby snapped their heads in Dan's direction, their expressions asking for an explanation.

"It's me. I'm the link."

"What do you mean?" Toby demanded.

"I got a phone call last night. It was a woman's voice, although she tried to muffle it. She made it quite clear that I was to pay with Carole's life for what I'd done to Cathy."

"But you saved her life," Toby said.

"According to the woman, I also helped kill her. Each of us—Anderson, Crawford, Judy, Reeson, and I—we're all responsible for her death. Each of us gave her a push. Apparently, I'm not going to get a doll. Instead, I get to watch Carole die."

"What I want to know is, what the hell you're supposed to have done to her?" Toby was hotly defensive.

Dan shook his head. "I don't know. In fact, it really doesn't make any sense. In a way, she hurt *me*. She literally disappeared without so much as a word."

"I remember you telling me," Charlie said. "It was when you'd left Hammin to be with your father."

"So I don't know what I could have done. But whatever it was, Carole's suffering for it." Dan's face grew taut with grim resolve. "But I can tell you one thing —she's not going to die. I can promise you that."

Dan halted at the wrought-iron gates of the cemetery entrance. Some of the sightseers had turned back. The sight of them caused the three men to cross the street and head for a small park. Its mute cannon and white benches were obscured by the fog.

Toby eased himself down on the barrel of one of the cannons and then quickly stood up, realizing that he'd wet the seat of his pants. "Damn! That was stupid."

He made a futile swipe with his hand at the wet spot, then looked squarely at the two men.

"Look, I guess until now I've kind of assumed that this thing was going to somehow resolve itself. Obviously, I was wrong. That's not to say that I have just been sitting on my hands. . . ." His explanation sounded exactly like the defense it was intended to be, so he abandoned it. "Well, that doesn't matter now. We've got to act. Instead of just talking about this girl's family, we've got to track them down."

"Mr. North said he'd met Cathy Parks in New York," Charlie said defensively. "How do you expect me to find out anything in a city with millions of people?"

"You won't have to go that far," Dan said quietly. "I think at least one of them is in Hammin, maybe more."

"Why do you say that?" Toby asked.

"A hex is not something you can do by long distance. Especially one involving five people."

"Okay, so how do we locate them?" Toby put his foot up on the cannon and rested his elbow on his knee.

"For starters I suggest we draw up a list of the people who have moved into Hammin in the last six months. Concentrate on the renters. At least that gives us some place to begin."

"Done," Toby said. "I can get the real estate firms to help me out. But it'll take time. And then. . . ." Toby slid his foot off the cannon and kicked at its base. "You want to know the irony in all this?"

Dan nodded his head, inviting an explanation.

"Even if we do find who we're looking for, there's not all that much we can charge 'em with."

"What do you mean?" Charlie looked at him with disbelief. "Lives have been threatened."

"Yeah, and that's it. The only law that covers this kind of thing comes under the heading of *Threatening*.

And that a Class A Misdemeanor punishable by not more than a year in jail. And that's assuming we can prove that our dollmaker sent the pictures or made the phone calls."

"When we find out who's behind this," Dan said intently, "I'm interested in just one thing."

Toby eyed him cautiously. "What's that?"

"The dolls."

XX

Dan drove from the cemetery to the courthouse square, parked his car, then climbed the stairs to his office. Since mornings were devoted to making rounds in the hospital, he knew that no one would be there.

He went into his consultation room to stretch out on the sofa. He'd had little sleep. After last night's phone call from the unidentified woman, he'd wandered aimlessly around the perimeter of the lake until, exhausted, he dragged himself back to the trailer and lay down beside Carole. The burden of knowing that he was responsible for Carole's suffering had kept tugging him back to consciousness each time his body drifted into sleep.

Carole had awakened at eight and Dan thought she looked better. The rest and being there with him apparently had helped. He told her about Rita's call and suggested she wait for him at the trailer. Carole had smiled weakly, understanding his concern, feeling his love, and assured him that she was all right. For an instant Dan had considered telling her about the second phone call; it might relieve her to know that she was merely a pawn and he the victim. Then he had resisted, weighing the possible benefits against the potential harm to her present state of mind.

The clock on the wall over the sterile cabinet told him it was almost noon. He slipped a pillow from the sofa under his head, bringing him to a half sitting position. Then he began to concentrate on clearing his mind.

Got to try and think this through logically, he

thought. I wonder if Miizi had a system for locating witch doctors? If he did, it was omitted from my education.

Dan found himself going back over the death of the Frenchman, Tureau. The key to his death, to the ouanga, had been the constant reinforcement that had been supplied by the drums and more directly by his house servants. They had been the ones to ensure that he understood fully the meaning of the corpse in the jungle. They had been the ones to comment on his deteriorating condition and to grieve openly over his impending death.

Dan wondered, Is there a parallel here? It was reasonable to assume that the perpetrator might have enlisted the help of others. People who could get close to the victims. People who, by their proximity, could provide the reinforcement, could make sure that every physical change or discomfort would be assessed in terms of the hex. Some of the answers to the hex lay with the people closest to the victims.

Dan swung his legs to the floor and sat up. As he did, he berated himself for not having explored this possibility sooner. Especially for not forcing Toby and Charlie to take some action before this.

His thought process was abruptly interrupted by the phone. He stood up, crossed the room, and answered it.

"Dr. Frederickson." He paused. "Yes, Toby." Another pause. "What! When?" His voice leaped into the phone. "I'm on my way," he said and dashed from the office.

Dan took the stairs two at a time and Toby matched him stride for stride. As they reached the second landing, they heard a female voice screaming, "Up here! Up here!" Heads peered out from apartment doorways. A few of the curious had begun cautiously to make their way to the third floor. They flattened themselves against the wall as soon as they recognized Dan and Toby.

Dan saw a heavy-set woman standing outside the door, wringing her hands, her face flushed and full of dread.

"In there! In there!" she cried.

Dan recognized her as Emma Ferguson, the woman who'd stayed with Judy the night she'd found the picture.

Toby stopped at the door to hold out the people whose curiosity could only be satisfied with a firsthand look.

Dan glanced around the living room, then dashed into the bedroom. The light was on in the bathroom and he rushed to the door and looked in.

He blanched.

Judy Simpson lay in the bathtub. Her head was propped up on a towel. Water filled the tub to the brim.

It was blood-red. She'd slit her wrists.

"Oh, Jesus!" Toby blurted as he stepped into the bathroom.

On the side of the tub, a bloody razor blade in its hand, was Judy's doll. Like Judy, it was nude. Its wrists had been slit and its body was stained red with blood. Carefully, Dan picked it up. Long silver pins had been thrust through the gashes on the wrists. The eyes were closed. The mouth hung open, the face muscles relaxed like someone who had fallen placidly asleep while the life drained out.

"Look," Dan said as he turned the doll upside down. "They weren't very subtle, were they?" A large wedge between the doll's legs had been crudely hacked away.

Toby took the doll and placed it on a towel.

Dan bent over and felt the water. "Cold. I'd say she's been dead at least twelve hours." Then, for no particular reason other than that it would have to be done sometime, he pulled up the drain plug. A large bubble gurgled up and broke the surface, sending ripples of red water over the side.

It was the ultimate sadness, he thought. To die alone. Afraid. And by your own hand. There was no indication that she'd had second thoughts. No sign that she'd panicked or tried to save herself as she watched her blood mix with the water. She must have been at the very end, the absolute bottom of her will to live.

Dan's thoughts turned to Carole. He cringed as he contemplated the possibility that she might do the same. He'd have to watch her. Stay with her every minute. She could not be left alone.

"Put the shower curtain over her," Toby said. "I'll call somebody to take her away."

"Who found her?" Dan asked.

"That heavy-set dame—Ferguson—and the land-lady. The Ferguson woman said she was worried about her because she hadn't seen her in a couple of days. Rang her doorbell, tried her on the phone. And then went to the landlady and had her open the door. They came in and. . . ." Toby nodded toward the body.

A flashbulb popped.

"What in the . . . ?" Toby whirled around and con-fronted three of the reporters he had avoided so well . . . until now.

"Beautiful! Beautiful!" the man with the camera said as he took another shot.

"Look at that, will you!" Another reporter's voice underscored his unabashed fascination.

"Get the hell out of here!" Toby thundered

"Come on, Chief! This is a hell of a story. No way you can keep this thing under wraps."

"How about a statement? How do you assess this? What's behind this hex business? Have you got any suspects?"

More reporters shouldered their way into the bath-room, all of them firing questions. Another flashbulb went off. Toby just stood there and looked at them, dumbfounded. He'd never been accosted by this many reporters before.

Dan managed to push out of the bathroom, through the growing number of people in the living room, and make his way out to the hall. Above the din, he could hear Toby's shouts of "Out! Out!"

Dan hurried down the stairs, pushing past the stream of people who seemed to resent his movement against the natural flow. He walked quickly to his car, but it was completely blocked by a line of double-parked cars. The entire street was jammed.

Incredible how fast the word had spread. Flies descending on carrion. In their eyes he'd seen fright, fragments of terror, and macabre fascination. They feared death, yet could not resist its magnetism.

"Ghouls," he muttered. "I hate your guts," he heard himself saying. "I wish to hell I'd never come here!"

If anyone heard him, they were too concerned about seeing Judy Simpson to care.

Dan pushed his way through the mass and ran down the street toward the courthouse. He had only one thought in mind. He had to get to Carole.

Now!

xxi

Carole glanced at her watch as she paced back and forth in the living room of Dan's trailer. Eleven forty-five. She reached for the phone and called Hammin's only cab company. Within twenty minutes the driver had picked her up and she was on her way home.

As the taxi pulled into her driveway, she saw six well-dressed people standing on the front lawn staring at the house. They turned to look at the cab and she could see that they were not from Hammin. Even before she could pay the driver, the five men and one woman were peering in the cab windows. A man in a brown sport coat, with heavy black hair and horn-rimmed glasses to match, opened the door and offered his arm to assist her out.

"Are you Carole Peters?" he asked.

Carole nodded as her eyes fell on the pads of paper that suddenly started appearing in their hands.

Reporters.

"Can you tell us what effect the hex is having on you?" The question came from a particularly unctuous reporter whose forehead and nose were producing inordinate amounts of sweat.

Carole stepped out of the cab into another question. "Do you believe in hexes, Miss Peters?"

"I don't know," she answered tentatively, feeling a little overwhelmed. "I'm not sure."

"Who do you think is behind this? Is there someone who might want to threaten you or do you harm?" The reporters jockeyed for position as she started up the walk to her front door. Her only thought was to get away, to hide from these strangers who seemed to find some morbid delight in peppering her with questions.

The lone female reporter produced a cassette tape recorder and ran in front of Carole, turning around and walking backward so they were face to face.

"Miss Peters, Valerie Sturges from 'All News Radio.' I wonder if you could describe what you're feeling right now? What thoughts are going through your mind?"

Carole stopped and stared at the woman. Her plastic facade of warm sincerity was worn with the subtlety of too much rouge. The reporter held up her microphone in front of Carole's face like someone with a crucifix trying to ward off evil.

There was a screech of tires braking at the curb. A thin young man with only a fringe of brown hair around his head jumped out of the car and ran up the drive.

"The Simpson woman's committed suicide. Slashed both her wrists!" he shouted as he approached the group. "They just found her."

The female reporter turned sharply to Carole, again pushing the microphone into her face. "Can you give us your reaction to the suicide?"

Carole broke into tears and made a dash for her front door. She dug into her handbag for the key.

The young reporter who had brought the news of Judy's death took up a position in the bushes to Carole's right. "They say a doll was found in Judy Simpson's bathroom. Would you comment on that?"

Carole fumbled with the key. It didn't seem to fit. She frantically tried to wiggle it into the hole, then realized it was upside down.

"What are you going to do now?" one of the reporters asked.

The door still resisted and she shook the handle, pushing and pulling with childlike frustration. She was surrounded by hungry faces that pressed increasingly closer.

"It it true that all five victims share a common link?"

"How well did you know the others?"

"Have you received a doll?"

The door swung open and Carole bolted inside. "Leave me alone!" she screamed, and slammed the door.

She ran upstairs and stood by her window, tears streaming down her face. The reporters below had fallen back and taken up a position in the middle of the front yard. They were talking among themselves as though planning their next assault.

"I've got to find a car," Dan said as he ran down the street from Judy's apartment building into the square. Quickly he looked around for someone he recognized. "Got to get to Carole."

"Dan! What's going on?" The voice came from the open window of a blue Chevy that was about to turn down the street toward Judy's. It was Charlie.

Dan ran over to him. "Judy Simpson's dead. My car's blocked," he said, pointing to the snarl of traffic and people in front of the apartment house. "I've got to get out to my trailer, fast!"

"Get in," Charlie said, immediately rising to Dan's need. As Dan closed the door, Charlie swung out of Taylor Street and started around the courthouse. He ignored the three stoplights and sped through town out to route 421. Dan filled him in on the details of Judy's death and then expressed his fear that Carole might do the same.

Charlie turned off 421 onto Dan's road and pulled up next to the trailer, a cloud of dust following close behind. Dan leaped out of the car and ran inside. In a moment he reappeared at the door.

"She's not here!"

"Maybe she's gone home," Charlie said. "I'll run you over there."

"Let me call first."

Dan went back inside and dialed her number. One ring. Then a second. He made no effort to mask his rising panic. A third ring. A fourth.

"Hello?" Carole's voice was guarded.

"Are you all right?" Dan asked anxiously.

"Yes," she answered slowly. "But I've been getting calls from reporters and there are a bunch of them standing on my front lawn."

"Don't let them in. Stay where you are. I'll be right over." He started to hang up, then turned his back on Charlie, who had followed him inside. "Hey, I love you. Everything's going to be all right. Believe me."

Carole didn't answer. The phone clicked off.

"Goddamn reporters all over the place." Dan quickly dialed Toby and arranged for police protection. Then he ran back to Charlie's car.

The car spun around and roared away from the trailer, bouncing down the rutted dirt road back onto 421. As they pulled up in front of Carole's, Toby and two of his policemen had succeeded in backing the reporters off the lawn onto the sidewalk. Legally, that was about all they could do.

Carole peered out at the scene from a position far enough inside her living room to be obscured from view. She watched as Dan, Toby, and Charlie stood away from the reporters, talking among themselves. At first, Charlie talked while the other two listened. After several minutes she noticed that Dan was slowly shaking his head. Toby said something and held out his arms as if to ask, "What else are we going to do?" Dan said something. Toby interrupted him. Finally, Dan appeared to give in. Carole tried to read his expression as he turned and led the other two men up to the front door.

Why is he bringing them in here, she wondered.

What more would they want from her? Carole felt her stomach constrict and hot rivets of acid kicked up into her throat. She shuddered. Involuntarily, she wrapped her arms around herself as though trying to restrain the tremors.

Slowly, she walked across the room and opened the door. Dan came in first and gave her a light embrace, then led her over to the couch and sat down. Toby and Charlie followed him in and offered perfunctory greetings.

Carole searched their faces for some indication, some sign that would reveal what they had been talking about. She nodded toward two chairs opposite the couch and suggested Toby and Charlie sit down.

Dan heaved a sigh. "Charlie's got a plan that he and Toby think will expose whoever's behind this. They feel pretty confident that it will work. If it does, then we can put an end to all this. There's only one thing. It involves you, and I'm against that. But I agreed to at least let Charlie explain what he'd like to do so that we could get your opinion."

Carole looked at him blankly, holding the fearful expectancy just below surface.

"Before we get into that, there's something I think you ought to know." Dan paused.

What's he leading up to? She was screaming inside for an answer.

"All along," he began, "we've been trying to find the link. Based on what we've discovered, we're pretty sure it's Cathy Parks and that the motive is revenge. It appears that whoever's behind this feels that each of the other four was in some way responsible for the girl's suicide."

Carole turned away, hiding her face. She waited for the blow to come crashing down, shattering everything she cared about, hoped for, dreamed.

"There was only one problem," Dan continued in

a flat tone of voice. "We couldn't link you to Cathy until last night."

She had always felt sure it would come—sometime. But to have it come now, in front of Toby and Charlie, would mean that along with the pain there would be unmitigated humiliation.

"You see," she heard Dan saying, "it's me. I'm the link."

Carole whipped her head around and stared at Dan in gaping shock.

"And they're punishing me by trying to hurt the one person who means more to me than anyone else in the world."

Carole's face seemed to fall.

"I'm sorry, Carole. When I think of how you've had to suffer because of me, I, well. . . ." Dan couldn't seem to find the words.

At first it sounded like a cry of anguish as Carole turned away, her head rolling back, face up to the ceiling. The sound spiraled up in a crescendo of grief ending in short staccato bursts of hysterical laughter.

"You're wrong, Dan! You're wrong! They're not after you. It's me! I *know* it's me!" She was screaming in a high soprano pitch. "Because I know what I did to her! I know what I did!"

The three men looked at her in stunned silence.

"Don't you understand?" she shrieked, throwing out her arms toward Dan. "They know *exactly* what they're doing! They want me because of what *I* did to her!"

Dan grabbed her by the shoulders. "Carole, get a hold of yourself!"

"It's true! It's true!" she cried, pulling away. "I'm the reason she disappeared. I'm the reason you never saw Cathy Parks again!" Carole leaned forward until her head touched the cushions. Her sobs came in deep gulps.

"Carole!" Dan said, pulling her up. "You don't know what you're saying. You barely knew Cathy!"

"Oh, I knew her." The sobs gave way to bitterness. "I knew Cathy Parks better than you ever did. And I hated her. I hated her for having consumed you. For having mesmerized you. And I would have given anything to trade places with her. When she was around, I didn't exist. I was nothing more than another fixture in your office."

"That's not true," Dan protested.

"Oh, but it was, it was." Carole paused. She looked deep into Dan's blue eyes and shook her head slowly. "You can never know how much I wanted you. How my heart literally jumped into my throat those few times when you asked me to join you for lunch. My God! I was suffering like a schoolgirl over her first love. You didn't see it, but Cathy Parks did. She knew I was in love with you. She made sure that I knew she knew it.

"I'll admit, I was jealous of her. Jealous of her hold on you and jealous of those blue eyes and blond hair and big breasts. If God didn't want to make me beautiful, at least he could have given me big breasts," she added with a plaintive, self-deprecating laugh.

Dan started to protest, but she cut him off. "No, Dan. Let me say it all, now. This may be the end of everything between us, but I want you to hear the whole story."

Toby and Charlie remained frozen in their chairs, totally taken aback at what they were hearing.

"Maybe I started it. I know I wasn't all that friendly to her at first. And I'm sure I was short with her— maybe even rude. Mark it up to instant envy. But once she got started on me, she proved to be the master. She got an emotional high from taunting me. I remember one day she walked into the office with a tiny ampule of perfume; she flopped down on the couch to wait for you and started dabbing it on her front. 'Dan and I are going on a picnic,' she cooed, 'and I've just bought this new perfume. It's guaranteed to turn men

on, and I can't think of anyone more fun to test it on.'
And then you both left me there with visions of her
seducing you on a picnic blanket. You have no idea
how that hurt.

"Another time, she sat across the room staring at
me for several minutes without speaking. Then, very
casually and very sweetly, she said, 'It must be won-
derful working for Dan. I'm amazed that you're able
to keep your hands off him.' Then she hid her smirk
behind a magazine. There was nothing I could say,
no possible comeback other than doing something
violent—and I confess I was tempted.

"All that summer she kept it up. A comment here,
a dig there. 'He makes the most *complete* house calls,'
she'd say. Even after it was obvious that I was absolutely no competition, she kept it up."

"But I never heard any of that," Dan said. His tone
was not meant to challenge Carole, but to express his
innocence.

"Of course not. In front of you she treated me just
the opposite. I can still hear her one morning, 'Dan,
Carole is the most fabulous woman I've ever met. I
don't know what you'd do without her.' And you
agreed, gave me a pat on the head, and just about
said 'Nice nurse, here's a bone, now run and play.' I
hated you for being so blind, so absolutely blind to
the game she was playing. Finally, I made up my mind
to quit. To leave Hammin and go back to St. Louis."

"And you did," Dan added, "so how can you say
you were to blame——"

"Wait." Carole was now in control of her emotions.
"Now we come to Act Two—Carole Peters Strikes
Back. It was Tuesday after Labor Day. Your call
came into the office around noon. Your father was
dying and they didn't think he had much time. You'd
flown to New York. I remember I had been worried
about you all morning. You asked me to cancel your
appointments and notify the hospital. You gave me a

number where you could be reached and said, 'Be sure to tell Cathy Parks where I am. And have her call me.' There were other instructions—I've forgotten what.

"That afternoon Cathy called and I said you weren't in. She wanted to know where you were and just as I was about to tell her the second line began to ring. I put her on hold and took the call. It was somebody wanting to make an appointment. But the interruption gave me a moment to think. Suddenly, it was all so clear. The whole thing just laid itself out. But it was so unthinkable, I rejected the idea immediately. Then, all that hate welled up and I found myself asking, 'Why not?'

"I got Cathy back on the line and told her you'd left town for a couple of days, but that you'd written her a note and she could come by and pick it up. She said she would. Then I went into your office and wrote her a letter on your typewriter, the one with the *e*'s and *o*'s filled in. It was a very clinical letter. I explained that your association with her had been for the purpose of therapy and that it was now in danger of going beyond that. You felt it was time for her to stand on her own two feet, that it would be best if she didn't see you again because she might become overly dependent. Then I forged your signature.

"Just before she came in, I found myself having second thoughts. I was going to tell her that I'd made a mistake and give her your number. But with the first words out of her mouth, I decided to go through with it."

"Have you ever been made love to in the rain," Cathy asks, sweeping into the room. Carole looks up, her face flushes. "Oh, you really must, it's absolutely out of this world." Carole quickly hands her the letter and excuses herself, saying she has work to do. A self-

gratified smile creeps over Cathy's face as Carole ducks her head.

Cathy walks a few steps away and slips her finger under the envelope flap. Odd that he should write her a note, she thinks, but she immediately recognizes the type. She skims over the contents of the letter. The words explode in her face. She can not believe what she reads. She goes back over the letter—slowly at first—then her eyes race on to his signature.

Suddenly she spews forth a stream of invectives. "That dirty bastard! That rotten son of a bitch! So that's why he wouldn't make love to me last night. All this shit has been his idea of fucking therapy!"

Carole's eyes widen at the bitter words. For a moment she is confused. Before she can say anything, Cathy has slammed out of the office.

The afternoon passes like an eternity for Carole. The words and numbers in Dan's files all blur into an unreadable jumble through her tears. She realizes she has done a terrible thing, but doesn't know how to rectify it. Should she call Dan? Or should she call Cathy instead? In her indecision, she does nothing.

An hour before closing, Carole hears a door slam: Cathy has returned. Instead of the demure dress she wore earlier, Cathy has changed into a tight-fitting, sheer dress; the fabric shows her nipples prominently. She teeters on black patent leather spiked heels and the stench of alcohol is plain on her breath as she leans over the desk toward a horrified Carole. A suitcase, tattered and brown, stands by the door.

Guilt and fear race through Carole: Is she responsible for the sudden transformation of the blond, sweet Cathy into a drunken slattern? By taking Dan away, has she sent the young girl over the brink?

"I want you to give your doctor a message. Tell him that Cathy says he's an asshole and that I hope he rots in hell. And you can tell him something else," she says, pirouetting for Carole and giggling drunkenly. "Tell

*him that he missed seeing the real me. I'd have given
him a good time." She draws out the word "good" in
a nasty way and smiles. "And tell him he doesn't have
to worry, I won't be lonely. I just met a guy a little
while ago at the Hammin Inn and I know that he and
I are going to get it on real good. At least he won't go
limp on me like that bastard doctor of yours did."*

*Completely shocked and convinced that Cathy has
suffered some kind of mental relapse, Carole quickly
stands up, knocking over her chair. As she backs away,
Cathy laughs and turns to leave. She staggers a bit as
she retrieves her suitcase, then draws herself up proud-
ly. "He's all yours, honey. I was tired of playing
Goody Two-Shoes anyway." Her laughter follows her
out the door.*

Carole looked directly at Dan. "For days I was sick.
I thought I was responsible for her behavior, but I
didn't know what to do. I drove over to the house
where she rented a room, but the landlady said Cathy
had left for good with some bearded hippie type. I
didn't know what to do next and I couldn't face you.

"You returned the end of September and I told you
I was leaving. You asked me to reconsider, but, of
course, I couldn't. Not after Cathy. I left the next day.
So you see, my darling, you're wrong. You're not the
link. You did nothing to Cathy. It's me they want. It's
me," her voice trailed off. She was drained. There was
no emotion left. Slowly she stood up. "I'm very tired,"
she said, turning and walking toward the stairs.

Dan watched her climb the steps. He was immobile.

Toby and Charlie exchanged uncomfortable glances.
Toby pushed himself up out of the chair, his head
bowed as if to mask his embarrassment. "I guess we'll
be going," he mumbled and gestured for Charlie to
follow.

Dan did not look after them. It was hard for him to
believe that Carole had been talking about the same

Cathy Parks. But then, he had found it hard to believe her affair with Crawford or the fact that she'd been Anderson's mistress or that she'd run off with Reeson. It was as if she were several different people. Or maybe, and this seemed more logical, maybe I saw in her only what I wanted to see.

Now, too, he understood Carole's reluctance to fight. She was accepting the hex as her punishment. She must have known what it was all about almost from the moment she got the picture. Her decision to put off the wedding date, her growing estrangement, the steady withdrawal, it all fell into place.

Suddenly, Dan found himself confronting a profusion of questions. How should he react? How did he *want* to react? What should he be feeling? Should he forgive her? How could he not?

But more than anything, he found himself wondering what this admission—this confession—would do to them. Had it destroyed everything? Could they wall it away with time? Would Carole, in years to come, find herself wondering if he was secretly resentful of what she'd done? Wondering if he blamed her for Cathy's death?

Finally, Dan found himself with just one question —the most important one: How could he let Carole know—make her truly believe—that he loved her more than he could ever have loved Cathy Parks?

He went upstairs, opened the door, and saw her lying facedown on the bed. He said nothing, but climbed in beside her and held her very tight. He found it curious that he felt closer to her and more in love than he ever had before. A psychologist might be able to explain it, he thought, but I won't even try.

Yet, as he lay there wrapping her in his love, he could not help but wonder how much of her would remain for him to love a month from now—a year. He knew very well there would be no woman at all unless he found the dolls.

xxii

Within an hour the phone started to ring incessantly and the reporters periodically pushed on the doorbell, pleading for just one statement.

Dan called Toby and asked for him to bring his car over to Carole's. Then the three of them walked through the barrage of questions, got into the car, and quickly lost the reporters that tried to follow. After dropping off Toby, Dan and Carole silently drove out to his trailer.

Before he got out, Dan leaned over and with a determination that brooked no argument said, "We're finding a Justice of the Peace tomorrow."

Carole smiled weakly and nodded her acquiescence.

Dan unlocked the trailer door and stepped inside, groping for the light switch. As always after having been shut up all day, the trailer was steaming hot. He opened the windows and turned on the fan in the bedroom, then went into the kitchen alcove, filled two glasses with ice and club soda and squeezed lemon into them. He went outside and sank heavily into a deck chair next to Carole. It would take a good half hour for the residual heat of the day to be circulated out of the trailer.

Dan was tired to the marrow. The unbridled acceleration of the day had brought tragedy, revelation, and pain, but little discernible progress toward discovering *who*.

Dan's weariness blurred his mind and there was no coherence to his thoughts, no semblance of logic. He decided not to fight it and seized the opportunity to

think of nothing . . . to feel nothing . . . to fall torpid
into the momentary void. Then, from somewhere in
the outer reaches of his cerebral cortex, a word spun
out like a comet streaking across the sky.

Paradise!

*"You've never told me where you're from," he says.
"I rent a room over on Barker Place," she replies. He
rephrases his question. "I mean, where are you from
originally?"*

*Her eyes sparkle with silent laughter. "I'm from
Paradise."*

*Dan laughs and tells her that he's not in the least
bit surprised.*

*"Pennsylvania," she adds. "There really is such a
place."*

Dan's plane landed at the Philadelphia International
Airport at twelve fifteen. By twelve twenty he was in
front of the Avis counter, and ten minutes later he was
pulling out of the airport onto Interstate 95, heading
west. Just beyond Chester, Pennsylvania, he turned off
onto U.S. 322, headed north to the Baltimore Pike
—turned left through Painters Crossroads, Chadds
Ford, and the Brandywine Battlefield.

He'd told no one where he was going, not even
Carole. The decision to go had been triggered immediately with the recall of his conversation with Cathy.
At that moment, he had been convinced that he'd find
the answers that had eluded them so far. The next
morning, after he'd taken Carole home and as he drove
to the airport, he began to temper his expectations. He
faced the possibility that the trip might not net him
anything in the way of new information. But even if
that turned out to be the case, at least he would have
satisfied himself with the knowledge there was nothing
to be learned in Paradise.

Five or six miles beyond Kennet Square a large

green sign pointed the way to Pennsylvania 41 and Cochranville. The two-lane highway rolled gently with the countryside, which was dotted with farms and crops waiting for harvest.

Route 41 ended in the town of Gap, which straddled U.S. 30. A red light at the intersection gave Dan a chance to glance at his map. Paradise was just east of Lancaster. On the map, it appeared only as a small dot just beyond another dot identified as Kinzers. During his plane ride, Dan had pictured Paradise as a small town snuggled away in the hills of the Pennsylvania Dutch country against a backdrop that would give substance and credibility to its name. The illusion was immediately challenged as he turned onto U.S. 30, a busy, three-lane highway of commerce between Philadelphia and Lancaster. Trucks, vans, and cars pounded back and forth; endless rows of small commercial establishments, houses, and hundreds of signs made it abundantly clear that this was Pennsylvania Dutch country and Amish country and Menonite country. Like hucksters at a county fair, they screamed at passersby: *This is Dutch Country, Gifts. See the Amish Farm. Jesus Saves. Shoo-Fly Pies. Motel Vacancy. Mobile Homes for Sale. Eat Here. Stop There. Buy Here.* Visual pollution. It reminded Dan of the outskirts of Hammin.

No, it was not at all what he'd imagined.

Kinzers came . . . and apparently went, though there was nothing to mark its passing. He was nearing Paradise, a mile or more at the most. He noticed that many of the buildings were very old and pressed close to the edges of the highway, calling up a time when traffic consisted of wagons and coaches. Over the years the highway had steadily encroached on whatever frontal area the buildings might have had, giving the road a dominance that was never intended.

A school appeared on the right, identifying itself as the Paradise Township School. Was this Paradise? Dan had seen a sign welcoming travelers to Kinzers, but none so far had extended the same greeting to Paradise. He drove on, slower, searching through the plethora of signs. The nerve ends in his stomach gave birth to butterflies of anticipation.

Another spate of signs. *Paradise Motel. Paradise Restaurant. Paradise Whatnots. Paradise TV. Paradise Used Cars.*

Dan had arrived.

He began to look for what might be considered the "main" part of town, a central point where he could stop, park, and get his bearings. But as he drove on, it became more and more apparent that the town, for all intents and purposes, was strung out for about two miles and no more than a block deep on either side of the highway. Beyond the buildings, between a funeral parlor and a store selling authentic Amish handicrafts, he could glimpse flashes of open farmland.

Dan slowed down and pulled off to the side to gather his thoughts and decide on a course of action. Just ahead and across the highway an Amish farmer was waiting patiently with his horse and wagon for an opportunity to make the perilous crossing of U.S. 30. God, he thought. I wonder how many of them have died on this highway trying to make nineteenth-century peace with a twentieth-century tractor trailer? The farmer saw his chance, urged the horse across the three lanes, and made it safely into the refuge of a side road. Dan found himself feeling sorry for the farmer and those like him who, probably without consent, had been commercialized and advertised as players in a nonstop pageant for the benefit of tourists.

Dan waited for two trucks to pass—Jesus, they go through here at a heck of a pace, he thought—then pulled out and continued west. Giving way to impulse, he turned left onto a small road that led away from U.S. 30. Almost immediately, Paradise began to reflect its name. The rolling Pennsylvania hills were lush, farmhouses were neat white stucco, large white barns and silos had gleaming silver tops. Flower beds ringed the farmhouses and dotted the front yards, reflecting the Dutch influence. Black-and-white holstein cattle grazed peacefully in neatly laid-out pastures. If they could only roll up U.S. 30 and pack it away someplace, Dan mused, it would indeed be Paradise.

Two right turns headed him back toward the highway and he began to consider how he would go about getting some information on Cathy and her family. As he had driven up from Philadelphia, he had wondered if the people of Paradise might be reluctant to talk about a local family to a stranger. In anticipation of that possibility, he developed a short scenario which had him on a sales trip to Lancaster to call on Armstrong Cork. He would tell anyone who demanded an explanation of his inquiries that his wife had had a friend in New York some years ago by the name of Cathy Parks and they'd lost touch with her. When his wife heard that he was to be in Lancaster, she requested that he stop by Paradise and try to locate her, find out why they hadn't heard from her, and get an address.

Dan went over the story several times in his mind. It was just simple enough to be plausible and it was certainly the best he could come up with at the moment.

He pulled to a stop at the intersection of U.S. 30 and waited out a line of cars and trucks, then tromped on the accelerator and jumped onto the highway. He drove past some more stores, a row of brick houses, and a gas station. A gas station. He checked the rearview mirror, stepped on the brake, and turned in. It seemed as good a place as any to start. He drove his car through the pump island and stopped just beyond the service bays in front of the air pump, turned off the motor, got out, and quickly surveyed the situation.

An attendant was servicing a car that had followed him into the station. Two men were entering a small diner that was attached to and part of the station operation. Dan decided that the diner would be his first stop. As he walked past the service bays, a young man in garage overalls emerged, wiping his hands on an oil rag.

"Yes, sir, can I help you?" he asked with a genuine smile.

Dan was about to indicate his intention of going into the diner when he changed his mind and decided to put his question to the young man. "Yeah, I . . . ahhh, I'm looking for someone and I'm not really sure where to start." Immediately he felt the need to fall back on the crutch of the nonexistent wife. "The girl was a friend of my wife and she lived here four or five years ago before going to New York. We've lost track of her and my wife wanted me to try to locate her family. Of course, we don't know if they're still here."

The young man listened patiently and by the expression on his face, Dan realized that there had been no need to offer so detailed an explanation . . . especially since none had been asked for.

"What's the name?" the young man asked.

"Cathy Parks."

"Cathy Parks . . . Parks," the young man repeated as he quickly ran the name through his memory bank. He shook his head. "Parks doesn't ring a bell. But then I've lived here only three years. I'll tell you what you ought to do. Go see our tax collector. He knows everyone. His name's Lester Brennan. Been in Paradise all his life, I expect."

A perfect source, Dan thought. It would never have occurred to him, but of course the tax collector would know everyone. "Where can I find him?"

"He works at the lumber mill in the yard office. It's just down the road here about half a mile. You can't miss it. If the Parks family still live here, he'll know them."

Dan thanked the man, got back in his car, backed up, and pulled out of the station heading east. Within three minutes, he had found the lumber mill and the yard office. Inside, Dan saw a man in his mid-fifties leaning on the counter totaling some figures. He looked up at Dan, then glanced back down at his papers.

"G'afternoon," he said. "Be right with you."

Dan waited for him to finish, then said, "I'm looking for a Lester Brennan."

"Look no further," the man said, appearing to enjoy the fact that he was, indeed, Lester Brennan.

Once again, Dan found himself setting up his question with the fabricated story. As soon as Dan brought Cathy's name into the conversation, Lester Brennan started to nod.

"Oh, sure. I knew Cathy Parks, almost from the day she was born. Beautiful girl, absolutely beautiful. Had everything any woman could want and still wasn't satisfied." And then, parenthetically, he added, "Parks was her married name, you know."

Dan, of course, did not know. He prodded Lester to tell him more. It was hardly necessary, as the man proved to be loquacious to a fault and without the press of other customers felt no compunction to rush or skip over details.

By the time Dan left he understood more about *why* and had the answer to *who*.

xxiii

Dan's headlights caught the Hammin exit sign on the Interstate and he slowed down to make the turnoff. He glanced at the clock on his dash—just after midnight. Across from the exit ramp a soft flourescent glow illuminated two pay phones. Dan pulled up, got out, and dialed information. He requested a number, waited for the operator to find it, then repeated it back to her. He pressed down on the hook, let it go, inserted the dime, and dialed.

"Hello?" came a sleepy voice at the other end.

"Charlie, this is Dan Frederickson. Sorry to bother you so late, but I thought you ought to know, I've solved it. I know who our dollmaker is."

"You do? Who?" All the residue of sleep left his voice.

"Not on the phone," Dan replied. "You mind if I come over?"

"No, no, come ahead," Charlie said eagerly. "I'll put the coffee on."

Dan hung up and fished in his pocket for another dime. This time he called Toby. Briefly he told him what he'd discovered, then said, "I'll be with Charlie. Meet us there. But on your way, I want you to pick up a few things for me."

"Like what?" Toby asked.

"I'll need five gallons of kerosene, a couple of shopping bags full of sawdust, some ordinary garden lime, a butcher's knife or a small hand ax——"

Toby cut him off. "What in the hell do you need all this for?"

269

"I'm hoping I won't need them at all. In any event, I'll explain when I see you. Just trust me."

"Well," Toby said hesitantly, "it's going to take a little scrounging around."

"Do what you have to do, but please, get everything I've asked for. Believe me, they could be very important," Dan added emphatically. "Oh, I almost forgot, there's one other thing."

"What's that?"

"A live chicken."

Dan sat at one end of the white table in Charlie's kitchen. The appliances were vintage 1930s, just like the rest of the house. The cabinets were pale yellow, made even paler by the harshness of the bare bulb hanging on a cord from the overhead fixture. Charlie had put on a pair of faded pants and slipped into an armless white undershirt. His slippers scuffed across the floor as he brought over the coffee, poured it, and sat down across from Dan. Charlie's first question as Dan walked in the door had been, "Who?" but instead of answering, Dan asked to use the bathroom. When he came out, he insisted on starting with a summary of everything they knew.

Charlie set his cup down, folded his arms, resting his elbows on the table. His expression said that he'd been dangled long enough. "So much for the prologue, okay? You said you knew who our dollmaker is."

"I do."

"Well . . . ?"

"You, Charlie."

Charlie gawked and stiffened in his chair. "Me!" He gaffawed sharply. "What is this, some kind of put on?"

"Not at all," Dan said with cool certainty. "You see, I've been to Paradise."

Charlie started to blanch, but covered it quickly.

"I was there this afternoon and had a talk with a man by the name of Brennan. Lester Brennan. Do I have to say any more?" Dan expected him to protest and make an attempt to refute the accusation. He was even prepared for a show of violence, and pulled his legs back to either side of the chair while sliding his hands under the edge of the table so that he could throw it up as a defense.

Charlie's reaction was quite unexpected. He simply sighed a sigh of resignation and stared down at his coffee cup. After a moment, Dan thought he detected a slight smile on his lips. Charlie pushed back his chair and rose slowly. Got to be ready for anything, Dan warned himself. But Charlie showed no sign of even considering an aggressive response, no inclination to mount some sort of self-defense.

"I think I'd like something a little stronger," he said, crossing to the cabinet where he kept his liquor supply. His face seemed to hang heavier and the tone of his voice carried with it his full admission. There would be no denials. Charlie could not know exactly what Lester told Dan, but he could be sure that it was enough.

Lester Brennan had fully accepted Dan's story about trying to locate a friend of his wife's. Not for a moment had he had an inkling he might be incriminating Charlie. As Dan did his best to try and maintain a mostly passive expression, Brennan told him that Cathy had been the daughter of John and Marie Nesbit. Marie died when Cathy was six and her father asked his maiden sister, Hilda Nesbit, to come live with them and look after Cathy, which she did happily. Just before Cathy's sixteenth birthday, John Nesbit died of a stroke, leaving very little in the way of an estate to care for his daughter and sister. But according to Brennan, the Nesbits had a bachelor neighbor and family friend by the name of C. C. Parks, a man of substantial means. Parks quietly assumed a guardian role and made both Cathy and Hilda emotionally a part of the family he'd never had. Within two months after Nesbit's death, he had become the father figure.

That lasted three years. Then, just a month after her nineteenth birthday, Cathy agreed to become Mrs. Parks. According to Brennan, even though C.C. was eighteen years Cathy's senior, they seemed to be happy, living quietly in his large, rambling home well north of U.S. 30 in a valley setting that neither words nor pictures could adequately describe. Then one day, after two years, it was over. No one knew exactly the cause of the break-up, but that didn't dampen speculation.

"Then she left Paradise," Brennan told him, "and C.C. . . . well, he became somewhat of a recluse. Except for Hilda Nesbit, he hardly saw anybody. The divorce really tore him apart. 'Course, when you think about it, there was no way it was going to last. She probably should never have married him in the first place. I got a feeling she did it more because Hilda pushed her than anything else."

"Do you think he'd talk to me if I went up to see him?"

"Probably. But he's not there. According to what I've heard, he's been traveling for the last couple of years. Best thing for him. Got to bury the past, you know what I mean? Travel will do that for you, or so I'm told."

"The initials—C.C.—what do they stand for?" Dan asked.

Charles Cole Parks poured himself a large drink, then sat back down across from Dan. He took a large gulp and let it slide down slowly. "I'm glad you know," Charlie said, avoiding eye contact with Dan. "It gives me a chance to apologize. I was wrong about you, okay? You see, I thought you had written that letter to Cathy. I was really surprised to hear Carole Peters say *she'd* written it."

The answer had been so obvious, Dan thought, so

obvious that none of us were able to see it. Like a master magician, Charlie had used misdirection, forcing them to see only what he wanted them to see. As Anderson's personal investigator and the man they all were looking to for answers, he had guided them, pushed them, held up every piece of the puzzle, and showed them where it fit so that there would be no mistaking *why*.

He had been the one who first suggested that Cathy might be the link. He'd been the one to force Crawford deftly into the admission that he had been the father of Cathy's unborn child. He had been the one who set up the confrontation between Crawford and Judy Simpson. And, of course, Charlie had arranged for the medium to perform the second seance in his house, where he could control the illusion of the materialization. Dan recalled Charlie's remark after the seance as they stood on his porch: "There was no way she could have rigged anything without my knowing it." Of course not. He had literally—even tauntingly—implicated himself, yet Dan had failed to pick it up. Misdirection. The magician analogy held up well. And then there was the matter of the doll appearing in the back of Crawford's car after the accident. Who else but Charlie could have put it there? Begrudgingly, Dan conceded that Charlie had given a masterful performance, orchestrating the entire affair with great patience and cunning.

As Dan watched Charlie lift his glass again, he was suddenly aware of a curious air of calm in the room, a pause forced by a turning point. From here, they would take to their respective trenches and the confrontation would begin. It was, Dan knew, the *dénouement*. Once past, it would not come again. There were loose ends to be bound up.

"How did you find out?" Dan began. "I mean, you had to know about Crawford and Judy and the others before you came to Hammin. Did Cathy tell you?"

"No." He paused and looked up slowly, considering his answer. "I guess in a way I'd have to say she did. Not directly, of course. We never talked after she left me. Understand, it was not an angry parting, okay? It was, well, it was just an ending. I got a couple of postcards from her and Hilda got some letters—only one from Hammin. That was in August, when apparently you were seeing a lot of each other. Then there was nothing until a phone call in December. Hilda said she sounded very down, very depressed. That was the last we heard from her.

"It wasn't my intention to interfere with her life. But after almost six months and no word, Hilda and I decided to track her down. We really didn't know where to start until Hilda remembered that Cathy's last call had been collect. All we had to do was get out her telephone bill, which had both the city and the calling number. It was Reeson's place, upstate. Right afterward, we heard about Cathy's death.

"For a long time, I just couldn't accept it. None of it made sense to me; I made up my mind to find out what happened. It took me almost a year to piece it together. I got most of my answers out of Reeson, but it took eight months."

"Why so long?"

"Because I didn't want to rouse his suspicion. You see, I'd already made up my mind to avenge Cathy's death and I was afraid if he suspected that I had more than just a casual curiosity, he'd clam up or run off. So I let him think I was just some country hick looking for perversion, which was his main stock in trade. After a while, he began to think I was his personal money pump—but I found out what I wanted to know. I also got a chance to search his house, which turned up Cathy's things. Among them was the letter I thought you'd written." Charlie paused a moment and looked directly at Dan for the first time. "I guess you know Cathy loved you very much. When Hilda gave me her letter to read, I was. . . ." He stopped and started again. "Well, let me just say I would have given anything to have had her feel that way about me."

Charlie glanced down at his empty glass, then rose slowly and walked over to the cabinet, took out a bottle, and poured himself a refill. He looked back at Dan. "Can I get you something?"

Dan shook his head. "The materialization," Dan tossed the words out like a subject heading. "Some kind of optical effect, I presume?"

Charlie smiled thinly. "Straight from Hollywood with a not-inexpensive assist from Pauline Baoukas. You remember that night in my living room? We had the whole thing planned to include you and Carole Peters. But when she begged off, we had to make some last-minute changes in our program."

Which is why the image never spoke to me, Dan thought. For an instant he considered asking how they had achieved the effect, but immediately discarded the question as superfluous. Charlie's acquiescence to his questions might end at any minute, and there was one other thing he had to know. "Why the voodoo? Why the hex?"

"You answered that yourself the other day," Charlie said, leaning back against the counter. "The punishment can be pretty severe when you put poison in someone's coffee. But more than that, it seemed a kind of ironic justice. There's no law that could have punished them for driving Cathy to commit suicide. And while they might charge me with—what was it Mitchell said? Threatening?—there's no law that can punish me for their deaths."

"I take it you've had some experience with the hex."

"Where I come from in Pennsylvania, we're not strangers to it. It's part of the folklore, you might say.

In fact, my mother, rest her soul, was quite a practioner, though she never used it to hurt anyone."

"One more thing I don't understand," Dan persisted. "Why did Reeson come to Hammin?"

A smile grew over Charlie's face. "Let's say I coaxed him here for 'treatment,' and not so incidentally, I wanted his death to have an effect on the others. I must say, it was most accommodating of him to die that night at the carnival. That was really a piece of luck."

"I presume you had help?"

"Help?"

"People working with you, other than Hilda."

Charlie nodded.

"Who?"

Charlie shook a condescending finger at Dan. "I don't think it would be in their best interests for me to tell you their names."

"Well," Dan said, pushing back from the table, "I guess that about does it."

"Except for one thing, Doctor," Charlie said intently. "I'm not sure you truly appreciate *why* I've done all this, okay? You more than anyone—I'd like to have you understand. I think it best I tell you now, because I'm sure that after tonight, we'll not have an occasion to talk like this again."

Dan nodded his concurrence, but said nothing.

"I am not a handsome man, Doctor, as you can plainly see." Charlie permitted himself a deprecatory chuckle. "Women have never been attracted to me, and I can appreciate that. Yet, I unfortunately have the same desires . . . I'm slave to the same emotions and needs as anyone else. You can imagine, then, how I felt when Cathy agreed to marry me. To say that I was happy would be an understatement. But at the same time, I was terrified. Terrified that I might wake up and find it all to be a cruel joke. Even after we were married, I lived in fear that I'd come home one evening and find she'd left me. I'm not sure that I can really explain myself except that my love for her was completely out of balance. Often I'd find myself staring at her to the point of making myself ridiculous in her eyes."

Charlie lowered his head. "I sound foolish, don't I? Well, I was. I was also overprotective and blindly jealous at the least provocation. Every time I saw her talking to another man, I was sure she was arranging a rendezvous." He took a long drink of the scotch.

"I became an embarrassment for her. She was ashamed to be seen with me." Quickly, in her defense, he added, "But I really can't blame her. She was so young. She had a right to expect so much more from a husband than I could give her. I remember the look in her eyes when she told me she wanted a divorce. It was fear. Fear that I might try to stop her. But I knew I couldn't. I didn't even ask her to reconsider. I just said, 'Whatever you want, then that's what I want.'"

She averts her eyes so she won't have to look into his big, sad face. "Believe me, I never wanted to hurt you, Charlie. You've done an awful lot for Hilda and me, and I really appreciate it. But if I stayed here much longer, I'd just dry up and die. I want to live, I want to do things and experience the world while I'm still young enough to enjoy it. I want to find me, whoever I am. And I can't do it here with you."

He looks at her from a deep well of hurt. He tries to hide the pain that tears his insides. Since the day she asked for the divorce and moved back in with Hilda, Charlie has tried to prepare himself for this moment. It is an impossible task.

"Write me occasionally," he says in a choked voice.

"No," she replies. "Let this be the end of it. We both need to build new lives and the best way to do that is to make a clean break with the past."

"Please," he begs, "at least a card now and then.

You may need a friend sometime. At least let me be that."

"I'll think about it," she says abstractly.

A disembodied voice over the loudspeaker announces her bus. Charlie has offered to drive her to New York or to take her to the Metroliner in Philadelphia. She has refused, permitting him only to drive her the few miles to Lancaster and the bus station. It is hardly a setting for remembered good-byes.

Cathy leaves Charlie to give Hilda a hug and to say good-bye.

The bus dispatcher waits impatiently. Cathy walks toward the open door without looking back. Charlie stands alongside the bus hoping to see her face in the window, but she purposely takes a seat on the opposite side.

The door closes. The engine whines up to an ir- ritating level. The bus moves out and with it all that has ever mattered, or will matter, to Charles Cole Parks.

Charlie turned his back on Dan as he reached over the sink to a wall rack and ripped off a paper towel to blow his nose. "She was not a strong person, Doctor. She thought she was, but she wasn't. She was really very dependent, she needed people. And that made her vulnerable to bastards like North and Spencer and Reeson. They saw she was weak and took advantage of her. They changed her. They're the ones that destroyed her," he said, his voice rising. "Cathy would never have done the things they said she did. Never!" he added emphatically. "Underneath it all . . . underneath it . . . she was . . . she was. . . ." He did not finish, but simply braced himself against the sink and stared into the black emptiness outside the kitchen window. "I've never stopped loving her, Doctor," he said at length.

Dan looked at the frumpish, balding man, the flesh circling his girth hanging round and full over his belt.

Charlie, Dan said to himself, you've made her more in death than she could ever have been in life. The Cathy you remember never existed except in the memory you've fabricated for her. But Dan could never tell him that. No one could.

"It's finished," Dan said quietly. "You've had your revenge. They've all paid more dearly than they had any obligation to. Now it's time to end it."

Charlie did not look up, but shook his head firmly. "I can't."

"Why not?" Dan shot back. "Three people are dead and two others will never be the same."

Again Charlie shook his head resolutely.

Dan decided to try another tack. "Do you think Cathy would have wanted this? Are these deaths a monument to your love for her? No one's asking you to forgive them. Just stop the hex. Break it."

There was a short knock on the kitchen door, followed by Toby, who did not wait to be let in.

Charlie glanced at Toby, then at Dan. "Does he know?"

"He knows," Dan replied.

"So you admit it?" Toby confirmed, sounding more than a little surprised.

Charlie said nothing.

Dan stood up and took a step toward Charlie. "I want the dolls. I want the hex broken."

"I don't know what you're talking about," Charlie said, turning away.

Obviously, Charlie had decided there was nothing to be gained by incriminating himself in front of Toby.

Toby looked at Dan. "Can you prove he's our doll-maker?"

"I can prove it," Dan said convincingly. "But right now that's not important. I want the dolls," he repeated, still staring at Charlie.

Charlie turned back to the two men with a tense

expression on his face. "I can't help you. Now I think you should both leave."

Dan started for the door, stopped, and wheeled around sharply, looking Charlie in the eyes. "I grieve for Cathy. And I think you know that. I understand how you must have felt about her. But to sustain her memory and your love for her on hate and death. . . ." Dan stopped and turned to Toby. "Did you get everything?"

Toby's expression registered his disbelief over the shopping list. "Yeah, it's all there. In my trunk."

"Charlie," Dan warned with intense confidence, "understand one thing. I will do what I have to do in order to get those dolls." Dan paused to be sure that Charlie had grasped the implied meaning, and then repeated himself. *"I will do what I have to do."*

Toby looked at Dan with concern. "What are you talking about?"

"Toby," Dan said, "you are about to witness an exhibition of jungle magic. Very powerful jungle magic, I might add."

Dan smiled when Charlie's expression changed slightly to one of quizzical concern.

"Is that what all that stuff I got is for?" Toby asked.

Dan nodded, but did not take his eyes off Charlie. "I was afraid Charlie might not want to give up the dolls, so on the way back this afternoon, I stopped at a little store just outside of Paradise. It's a kind of souvenir shop that specializes in hex-related items. I bought a doll—one that I think looks a lot like Charlie. Then, when I first got here—remember, Charlie, I asked to use your bathroom? I found some hair in your brush and took the liberty of borrowing one of your dirty undershirts." Dan gestured to the bulge in his pocket. "As my friends on the Ivory Coast would say, 'It has been soaked in your essential juices.' "

Toby stared at Dan incredulously.

"I'm going to kill you, Charlie, slowly and more

painfully than anything you'd ever imagine, unless you give me the dolls." Dan was grim, but his intensity was controlled.

Charlie looked at him skeptically.

Dan read it. "Have no doubt that I will, Charlie. The magic I learned in Africa is more horrible than you could possibly know. I'll have the dolls, Charlie, or I'll have your life."

Toby continued to gape.

"Come on, Toby," Dan said, leading him to the door. "By the way, Charlie, you might want to watch this from your front window. I think you'll find it—" he paused and let a cold grin crack his stern glare "—educational."

Dan walked down the drive, Toby close behind, to where they had parked their cars. The night was brilliantly awash in moonlight.

"Dan!" Toby said, grabbing him by the arm. "What are you going to do? I'll lock you up before I let you do anything you'll regret."

Dan shook him off. "This is the only way. You'll have to trust me! I've got to make him give up those dolls, or Carole and Anderson haven't got a chance."

Toby nodded reluctantly. "Okay, what do you want me to do?"

Dan opened the trunk of Toby's car. "Just help me carry this stuff into the front yard." Dan picked up the five-gallon can of kerosene and the small cage holding the chicken and led the way to a spot directly in front of Charlie's house. Toby followed with the two bags of sawdust, the lime, and the butcher's knife.

"Put it all there," Dan said as he hurried back to his own car. He opened the passenger side door and removed a long box about ten inches wide and two feet in length and carried it back to where Toby stood waiting.

"You want to tell me how this is supposed to work?"

"It's complicated," Dan said by way of dismissing the question.

"Well, at least tell me how the dolls are going to save Carole and North."

For a brief moment, Dan considered telling Toby about the unbaptism ceremony that he would perform for Carole and Anderson, but immediately thought better of it. "Later," he said in a voice that asked for trust. "I'll explain it all later. Now I think it best that you just go sit in your car. This is going to take a while."

Toby looked as if he were about to say something, then turned around and walked back to his car.

Dan looked up at the white frame house, luminescent in the moonlight. The large triple-sash living-room window was directly in front of him. Inside, it was dark, but Dan could make out Charlie's sleeveless white undershirt in the middle of the room. Dan paused and took a deep breath. He knew that what he was about to do would be psychologically debilitating. It would rip at his emotional guts. Yet, it would work. He knew in the end it would work.

Dan picked up the bag of lime, tore a small hole in one end, and began to form a five-foot triangle on Charlie's lawn, the vortex pointing directly toward the house. Once he'd made the outline, he filled in the center with the remaining lime so that the triangle glowed brilliantly against the dark grass. That done, he picked up the sawdust and carefully made a neat circle, about ten feet in diameter, around the triangle. Then he began to soak the sawdust in kerosene. He traversed the circle four times before the kerosene ran out. He tossed the can as far from the circle as he could, then stepped inside and dropped a match into the sawdust. Immediately, orange flames leaped up a foot or more and began to dart left and right around the circle until they reunited on the far side, forming a ring of fire that sent ominous fingers of color slashing against the night.

Dan placed the chicken cage to the left of the triangle and laid the butcher knife on top. He put the other box on the right side and stepped into the triangle. Here goes, he thought, dropping to his knees. He reached over for the box on his right and took off the top, very deliberately, very purposely, so that Charlie, peering at him from the living room, would miss nothing. Dan held up the doll. It was not as detailed as the ones Charlie had created, but that made no difference. It was only the intent that mattered. The body was about two feet long, with well-formed hands. The hands had been important to Dan and one of the reasons he had selected this particular doll. Its face was painted on some type of composition material that had been molded to look like a man. Its brown hair protruded through many tiny holes drilled in its head.

Slowly, Dan stripped away the pants and jacket that had come with the doll. He reached into his pocket and pulled out the undershirt he had taken from Charlie, wrapped it around the doll, and laid it in the center of the triangle. From the other pocket, Dan extracted a wad of toilet paper which he opened, revealing Charlie's hair. Carefully, he entwined the hairs with those of the doll.

Dan rocked back on his haunches, looked at the doll, and quickly stole a glance at the house to be sure he had not lost his audience. Charlie was still there.

Everything was ready.

Dan reached over and pulled the chicken cage closer. The bird squawked in protest. Quickly, he reached in and grabbed it. The chicken continued to squawk, flapping its wings desperately. Dan picked up the butcher knife with his free hand and in one quick, sure motion, cut off its head. The body shook and twisted; blood poured from the severed neck.

Dan held the twitching chicken over the doll, covering it with blood, while he shouted out the words of the ritual:

"I baptize thee in the name of the devil, the demon horde, and the powers of darkness! I baptize thee Charles Cole Parks!"

With the last remaining drops of blood, he drew an upside-down cross against the white lime, then threw the limp chicken out of the fiery circle into the surrounding darkness. Then he began the incantations—strange sounds and words that Dan recalled from the baptism of Tureau's human effigy. On and on he went, the same words over and over. Time slowed down and stood still as the three men formed a fixed tableau: a stupefied Toby Mitchell, hiding in his patrol car; the unmoving figure of Charlie Cole, standing silently by a window; a frenzied Dan Frederickson, no longer the town's respected family doctor.

Sweat poured down Dan's face; his voice had become increasingly intense and strident as he built to a crescendo. His whole being was concentrated on the chanting, his ears filled with the sound of his voice and his heavy breathing, so that he did not realize that another sound mingled with his words. It was the odd sound of a piped tune like dancing wind. . . . Then, suddenly, Dan stopped and looked directly at the house.

Inside, Charlie had watched the grisly ceremony from the very beginning. Several times, he tried to pull himself from the window, to avert his eyes from the spectacle on the front lawn. But he found he could not. He was transfixed, unable to move. The circle of flames and the sing-song incantations were hypnotizing. More and more, he felt his being drawn into the circle. He could sense the presence of himself within the doll. He could feel its arms and legs, feel the cloth of the undershirt around his body. Slowly, he realized that his life was in the doll . . . pulled there, seduced, sucked into it by some means which he could not hope to fathom.

Then, suddenly, Dan stopped. His hands reached for the box in which the doll had come. Slowly, Dan withdrew two long silver needles. They glistened and danced in the reflected firelight.

Charlie's heart beat faster; his breath came in short gasps. His whole being was there, lying on top of the white lime triangle, looking up at the man looming dark and large above him. He saw Dan place one silver needle in each hand, then slowly raise them over his head. Charlie was looking at Dan through the eyes of the doll. Terror tore at his insides. The hands and needles were poised . . . waiting . . . alive. Then, in one violent thrust, they started down and pierced the outstretched hands of the doll.

In that millisecond, that fraction of a moment, Charlie felt the cold steel penetrate. He cried out with pain and stared at the blood that gushed up from the punctures in the palms of his hands. And then, the fear that has lived in the deepest recesses of man since the dawn of time fled screaming out of the mind of Charles Cole Parks.

XXIV

The next day, an exchange took place between Dr. Dan Frederickson and a very drawn, very depleted Charles Cole Parks. After giving Dan a large cardboard box, Charlie went back to his house, cleared out his possessions, and disappeared. His house soon displayed a prominent For Rent sign. Charlie's departure was followed by that of Hilda Nesbit, once the housekeeper for Mr. and Mrs. Anderson North, and also of Emma Ferguson, once a concerned neighbor of Judy Simpson. Crawford Spencer's girlfriend, Natalie Tate, had already left town before his funeral. Some time later, after the Hammin Inn had been safely sold, Skeet Fischer quietly moved on.

Carrying the cardboard box, Dan Frederickson went directly to the hospital where, rumor has it, a curious and barbaric ceremony was conducted behind closed doors. The participants were Dan, Carole Peters, and Anderson North.

Two weeks later to the day, Anderson, still badly scarred and with a walking cast on one leg, but otherwise in good condition, was released from the hospital and taken home. At approximately that same hour, on the outskirts of Hammin, near a small lake, a farmer watched from the distance as Dan and Carole Frederickson hooked up his trailer to a car. Arms entwined, they turned toward town for a last look, then revved up the engine. The wheels spun and car and trailer bounded forward, down the rutted road; they turned north on state route 421 and left Hammin forever.

Neither they nor the farmer noticed that the dust, swirled by the spinning wheels, was still dancing in the air, dancing to a tune played by the wind over hollow reeds. . . .